Priscilla's

George A. Birmingham

Alpha Editions

This edition published in 2024

ISBN 9789362514516

Design and Setting By
Alpha Editions
www.alphaedis.com
Email - info@alphaedis.com

Contents

CHAPTER I

The summer term ended in a blaze of glory for Frank Mannix. It was a generally accepted opinion in the school that his brilliant catch in the long field—a catch which disposed of the Uppingham captain—had been the decisive factor in winning the most important of matches. And the victory was particularly gratifying, for Haileybury had been defeated for five years previously. There was no doubt at all that the sixty not out made by Mannix in the first innings rendered victory possible in the "cock house" match, and that his performance as a bowler, first change, in the second innings, secured the coveted trophy, a silver cup, for Edmonstone House. These feats were duly recorded by Mr. Dupré, the house master, in a neat speech which he made at a feast given in the classroom to celebrate the glory of the house. When the plates of the eleven were finally cleared of cherry tart and tumblers were refilled with the most innocuous claret cup, Mr. Dupré rose to his feet.

He chronicled the virtues and successes of the hero of the hour. The catch in the Uppingham match was touched on—a dangerous bat that Uppingham captain. The sixty not out in the house match had been rewarded with a presentation bat bearing a silver shield on the back of it. No boy in the house, so Mr. Dupré said, grudged the sixpence which had been stopped from his pocket money to pay for the bat. Then, passing to graver matters, Mr. Dupré spoke warmly of the tone of the house, that indefinable quality which in the eyes of a faithful schoolmaster is more precious than rubies. It was Mannix, prefect and member of the lower sixth, who more than any one else deserved credit for the fact that Edmonstone stood second to no house in the school in the matter of tone. The listening eleven, and the other prefects who, though not members of the victorious eleven, had been invited to the feast, cheered vigorously. They understood what tone meant though Mr. Dupré did not define it. They knew that it was mainly owing to the determined attitude of Mannix that young Latimer, who collected beetles and kept tame white mice, had been induced to wash himself properly and to use a clothes brush on the legs of his trousers. Latimer's appearance in the old days before Mannix took him in hand had lowered the tone of the house. Mannix' own appearance—though Mr. Dupré did not mention this—added the weight of example to his precepts. His taste in ties was acknowledged. No member of the school eleven knotted a crimson sash round his waist with more admired precision. Nor was the success of the hero confined to the playing fields and the dormitory. Mr. Dupré noted the fact that Mannix had added other laurels to the crown of the house's glory by winning the head master's prize for Greek iambics.

Mr. Dupré sat down. Mannix himself, blushing but pleasurably conscious that his honours were deserved, rose to his feet. As President of the Literary Society and a debater of formidable quality, he was well able to make a speech. He chose instead to sing a song. It was one, so he informed his audience, which Mr. Dupré had composed specially for the occasion. The tune indeed was old. Every one would recognise it at once and join in the chorus. The words, and he, Frank Mannix, hoped they would dwell in the memory of those who sang them, were Mr. Dupré's own. The eleven, the prefects and Mr. Dupré himself joined with uproarious tunefulness in a chorus which went tolerably trippingly to the air of "Here's to the Maiden of Bashful Fifteen."

"Here's to the House, Edmonstone House.

Floreat semper Edmonstone House."

Mannix trolled the words out in a clear tenor voice. One after another of the eleven, even Fenton, the slow bowler who had no ear for music, picked them up. The noise flowed through the doors and windows of the classroom. It reached the distant dormitory and stimulated small boys in pyjamas to thrills of envious excitement It was Mannix again, Mannix at his greatest and best, who half an hour later stood up in his place. With an air of authority which became him well, he raised his hand and stilled the babbling voices of the enthusiastic eleven. Then, pitching on a note which brought the tune well within the compass of even Fenton's growling bass, he began the school songs,

"Adsis musa canentibus

Laeta voce canentibus

Longos clara per annos

Haileyburia floreat."

House feeling, local patriotism to the tune of "The Maiden of Bashful Fifteen," was well enough. Behind it, deep in the swelling heart of Mannix, lay a wider thing, a kind of imperialism, a devotion to the school itself. Far across the dim quadrangle rang the words "Haileyburia Floreat." It was Mannix's greatest moment.

Three days later the school broke up. Excited farewells were said by boys eagerly pressing into the brakes which bore them to the Hertford station. Mannix, one of the earliest to depart, went off from the midst of a group of admirers. It was understood by his friends that he was to spend the summer fishing in the west of Ireland—salmon fishing. There would be grouse shooting too. Mannix had mentioned casually a salmon rod and a new gun. Happy Mannix!

The west of Ireland is a remote region, wild no doubt, half barbarous perhaps. Even Mr. Dupré, who knew almost all things knowable, admitted, as he shook hands with his favorite pupil, that he knew the west of Ireland only by repute. But Mannix might be relied on to sustain in those far regions the honour of the school. Small boys, born hero-worshippers, gathered in groups to await the brakes which should carry them to less splendid summer sports, and spoke to each other in confidence of the salmon which Mannix would catch and the multitude of grouse which would fall before the explosions of his gun.

CHAPTER II

Edward Mannix, Esq., M. P., father of the fortunate Frank, holds the office of Parliamentary Under-Secretary of the War Office, a position of great importance at all times, but particularly so under the circumstances under which Mannix held it. His chief, Lord Tolerton, Secretary of State for War, was incapacitated by the possession of a marquisate from sitting in the House of Commons. It was the duty, the very onerous duty, of Mr. Edward Mannix to explain to the representatives of the people who did not agree with him in politics that the army, under Lord Torrington's administration, was adequately armed and intelligently drilled. The strain overwhelmed him, and his doctor ordered him to take mud baths at Schlangenbad. Mrs. Mannix behaved as a good wife should under such circumstances. She lifted every care, not directly connected with the army, from her husband's mind. The beginning of Frank's holidays synchronised with the close of the parliamentary session. She arranged that Frank should spend the holidays with Sir Lucius Lentaigne in Rosnacree. She had every right to demand that her son should be allowed to catch the salmon and shoot the grouse of Sir Lucius. Lady Lentaigne, who died young, was Mrs. Mannix's sister. Sir Lucius was therefore Frank's uncle. Edward Mannix, M. P., worried by Lord Torrington and threatened by his doctor, acquiesced in the arrangement. He ordered a fishing rod and a gun for Frank. He sent the boy a ten-pound note and then departed, pleasantly fussed over by his wife, to seek new vigour in the mud of Germany.

Frank Mannix, seventeen years old, prefect and hero, stretched himself with calm satisfaction in a corner of a smoking carriage in the Irish night mail. Above him on the rack were his gun-case, his fishing-rod, neatly tied into its waterproof cover, and a brown kit-bag. He smoked a nice Egyptian cigarette, puffing out from time to time large fragrant clouds from mouth and nostrils. His fingers, the fingers of the hand which was not occupied with the cigarette, occasionally caressed his upper lip. A fine down could be distinctly felt there. In a good light it could even be seen. Since the middle of the Easter term he had found it necessary to shave his chin and desirable to stimulate the growth upon his upper lip with occasional applications of brilliantine. He was thoroughly satisfied with the brown tweed suit which he wore, a pleasant change of attire after the black coats and grey trousers enjoined by the school authorities. He liked the look of a Burberry gabardine which lay beside him on the seat. There was a suggestion of sport about it; yet it in no way transgressed the line of good taste. Frank Mannix was aware that his ties had set a lofty standard to the school. He felt sure that his instinctive good taste had not deserted him in choosing the brown suit and the gabardine.

Of his boots he was a little doubtful. Their brown was aggressive; but that, so the gentleman in Harrod's Stores who sold them had assured him, would pass away in time. Aggressiveness of colour is inevitable in new brown boots.

At Rugby he lit a second cigarette and commented on the warmth of the night to an elderly gentleman who entered the carriage from the corridor. The elderly gentleman was uncommunicative and merely growled in reply. Mannix offered him a match. The gentleman growled again and lit his cigar from his own matchbox. Mannix arrived at the conclusion that he must be, for some reason, in a bad temper. He watched him for a while and then decided further that he was, if not an actual "bounder," at all events "bad form." The elderly gentleman had a red, blotched face, a thick neck, and swollen hands, with hair on the backs of them. He wore a shabby coat, creased under the arms, and trousers which bagged badly at the knees. Mannix, had the elderly gentleman happened to be a small boy in Edmonstone House, would have felt it his duty to impart to him something of the indefinable quality of tone.

Shortly before reaching Crewe, the old gentleman having smoked three cigars with fierce vigour, left the carriage. Mannix, feeling disinclined for more tobacco, went to sleep. At Holyhead he was wakened from a deep and dreamless slumber. A porter took his kit-bag and wanted to relieve him also of the gun-case, the fishing-rod, and the gabardine. But Mannix, even in his condition of half awakened giddiness clung to these. He followed the porter across a stretch of wooden pier, got involved in a crowd of other passengers at the steamer's gangway, and was hustled by the elderly gentleman who had smoked the three cigars. He still seemed to be in a bad temper. After hustling Mannix, he swore, pushed a porter aside and forced his way across the gangway. Mannix, now almost completely awake, resented this behaviour very much and decided that the elderly gentleman was not in any real sense of the word a gentleman, but simply a cad.

Indignation, though a passion of a harassing nature, does not actually prevent sleep in a man of seventeen years of age who is in good general health. Mannix coiled himself up on one of the sofas which line the corridors of the Irish mail steamers. He was dimly conscious of seeing the old gentleman who had hustled him trip over the gun case which lay at the side of the sofa. Then he fell asleep. He was wakened—it seemed to him rather less than five minutes later—by a steward who told him that the steamer was rapidly approaching Kingstown Pier. He got up and sought for means to wash. It is impossible for a self-respecting man who has been brought up at an English public school to begin the day in good humour unless he is able to wash himself thoroughly. But the designer of the steamers of this particular line did not properly appreciate the fact. He provided a meagre supply of basins for the passengers, many of whom, in consequence, land at Kingstown Pier in irritable moods, Frank Mannix was one of them.

The elderly gentleman, who appeared less than ever a gentleman at five o'clock in the morning, was another. Mannix retained, in spite of his sleepiness and his sensation of grime, a slight amount of self-control. He was moderately grateful to an obsequious sailor who relieved him of his kit bag. He carried, as he had the night before, his own gun-case and fishing-rod. The elderly gentleman, who carried nothing, had no self-control whatever. He swore at the overburdened sailor who took his things ashore for him. Mannix proceeded in his turn to cross the gangway and was unceremoniously pushed from behind by the elderly gentleman. He protested with frigid politeness.

"Don't dawdle, boy, don't dawdle," said the elderly gentleman.

"Don't hustle," said Mannix. "This isn't a football scrimmage."

In order to say this effectively he stopped in the middle of the gangway and turned round.

"Damn it all," said the elderly gentleman, "go on and don't try to be insolent."

Mannix was a prefect. He had, moreover, disposed of the captain of the Uppingham eleven by a brilliant catch in the long field at a critical moment of an important match. He had been praised in public by no less a person than Mr. Dupré for his excellent influence on the tone of Edmonstone House. He was not prepared to be sworn at and insulted by a red-faced man with hairy hands at five o'clock in the morning. He flushed hotly and replied, "Damn it all, sir, don't be an infernal cad." The elderly gentleman pushed him again, this time with some violence. Mannix stumbled, got his fishing-rod entangled in the rail of the gangway, swung half round and then fell sideways on the pier. The fishing-rod, plainly broken in pieces, remained in his hand. The gun-case bumped along the pier and was picked up by a porter. Mannix was extremely angry. A tall lady, apparently connected with the offensive red-faced gentleman, observed in perfectly audible tones that schoolboys ought not to be allowed to travel without some one in charge of them. Mannix's anger rose to boiling point at this addition of calculated insult to deliberate injury. He struggled to his feet, intending then and there to speak some plain truths to his assailant. He was immediately aware of a pain in his ankle. A pain so sharp as to make walking quite impossible. The sailor who carried his bag sympathised with him and helped him into the train. He felt the injured ankle carefully and came to the conclusion that it was sprained.

Between Kingstown and Dublin Mannix arranged plans for handing over his assailant to the police. That seemed to him the most dignified form of revenge open to him. He was fully determined to take it. Unfortunately his train carried him, slowly indeed, but inexorably, to the station from which another train, the one in which he was to travel westwards to Rosnacree, took its departure. The elderly gentleman and the lady with the insolent manner, whose destination was Dublin itself, had left Kingstown in a different train. Mannix saw no more of them and so was unable to get them handcuffed.

Two porters helped him along the platform at Broadstone Station and settled him in a corner of the breakfast carriage of the westward going mail. A very sympathetic attendant offered to find out whether there was a doctor in the train. It turned out that there was not. The sympathetic attendant, with the help of a young ticket-collector in a neat uniform offered to do the best he could for his ankle. The cook joined them, leaving a quantity of bacon hissing in his pan. He was a man of some surgical knowledge.

"It's hot water," he said, "that's best for the like of that."

"It could be," said the ticket-collector, "that it's broke on him."

"Cold water," said Mannix firmly.

"With a sup of whiskey in it," said the attendant

"If it's broke," said the ticket-collector, "and you go putting whiskey and water on it it's likely that the young gentleman will be lame for life."

"Maybe now," said the cook derisively, "you'd be in favour of soda water with the squeeze of a lemon in it."

"I would not," said the ticket-collector, "but a drop of sweet oil the way the joint would be kept supple."

"Get a jug of cold water," said Mannix, "and something that will do for a bandage."

The attendant, with a glance at the cook, compromised the matter. He brought a basin full of lukewarm water and a table napkin. The cook wrapped the soaked napkin round the ankle. The ticket-collector tied it in its place with a piece of string. The attendant coaxed the sock over the bulky bandage. The new brown boot could by no means be persuaded to go on. It was packed by the attendant in the kit bag.

"It's my opinion," said the ticket-collector, "that you'd get damages out of the steamboat company if you was to process them."

Mannix did not want to attack the steamboat company. He felt vindictive, but his anger was all di-rected against the man who had injured him.

"There was a fellow I knew one time," said the ticket-collector, "that got £200 out of this company, and he wasn't as bad as you nor near it."

"I remember that well," said the attendant "It was his elbow he dislocated, and him getting out at the wrong side of the carriage."

"He'd have got more," said the ticket-collector. "He'd have got £500 instead of £200 if so be he'd have gone into the court, but that's what he couldn't do, by reason of the fact that he happened to be travelling without a ticket when the accident came on him."

He gazed thoughtfully out of the window as he spoke.

"It might have been that," said the attendant, "which was the cause of his getting out at the wrong side of the carriage."

"He tried it," said the ticket-collector, still looking straight in front of him, "because he hadn't a ticket."

No one spoke for a minute. The story of the fraudulent traveller who secured £200 in damages was an affecting one. At length the cook broke the silence.

"The young gentleman here," he said, "has his ticket right enough surely."

"He may have," said the ticket-collector.

"I have," said Mannix, fumbling in his pocket "Here it is."

"I'm obliged to you," said the ticket-collector. "It was it I wanted to see."

"Then why didn't you ask me for it?" said Mannix.

"He wouldn't do the like," said the attendant, "and you with maybe a broken leg."

"I would not," said the ticket-collector. "It would be a queer thing for me to be bothering you about a ticket, and me just after tying a bit of cord round as nasty a leg as ever I seen."

"But when you wanted to see the ticket—" said Mannix.

"I drew down the subject of tickets," said the collector, "the way you'd offer me a look at yours, if so be you had one, but as for asking you for it and you in pain, it's what I wouldn't do."

There are travellers, cantankerous people, who complain that Irish railway officials are not civil. Perhaps English porters and guards may excel them in the plausible lip service which anticipates a tip. But in the Irishman there is a natural delicacy of feeling which expresses itself in lofty kinds of courtesy. An Englishman, compelled by a sense of duty to see the ticket of a passenger, would have asked for it with callous bluntness. The Irishman, knowing that his victim was in pain, approached the subject of tickets obliquely, hinting by means of an anecdote of great interest, that people have from time to time been known to defraud railway companies.

CHAPTER III

Rosnacree House, the home of Sir Lucius Lentaigne and his ancestors since the Revocation of the Edict of Nantes brought the family to Ireland in search of religious freedom, stands high on a wooded slope above the southern shore of a great bay. From the dining-room windows, so carefully have vistas been cut through the trees, there is a broad prospect of sea and shore. For eight miles the bay stretches north to the range of hills which bound it. For five or six miles westward its waters are dotted over with islands. There are, the people say, three hundred and sixty-five of them, so that a fisher-man with a taste for exploration, could such a one be found, might land on a different island every day for a whole year. Long promontories, some of them to be reckoned with the three hundred and sixty-five islands when the tide is high, run far out from the mainland. Narrow channels, winding bewilderingly, eat their way for miles among the sea-saturate fields of the eastward lying plain. The people, dwelling with pardonable pride upon the peculiarities of their coast line, say that any one who walked from the north to the south side of the bay, keeping resolutely along the high-tide mark, would travel altogether 200 miles. He would reach after his way-faring a spot which, measured on the map, would be just eight miles distant from the point of his departure. Sir Lucius, who loved his home, while he sometimes affects to despise it, says that he believes this estimate of the extent of the sea's meanderings to be approximately correct, but adds that he has never yet met any one with courage enough to attempt the walk. You do, in fact, come suddenly on salt-water channels in the midst of fields at long distances from the sea, and find cockles on stretches of mud where you might expect frog spawn or black slugs. Therefore, it is quite likely that the high-tide line would really, if it were stretched out straight, reach right across Ireland and far out into St. George's Channel.

In Rosnacree House, along with Sir Lucius, lives Juliet Lentaigne, his maiden sister, elderly, intellectual, dominating, the competent mistress of a sufficient staff of servants. She lived there in her girlhood. She returned to live there after the death of Lady Lentaigne. Priscilla, Sir Lucius' only child, comes to Rosnacree House for such holidays as are granted by a famous Dublin school. She was sent to the school at the age of eleven because she rebelled against her aunt. Having reached the age of fifteen she rebels more effectively, whenever the coming of holidays affords opportunity.

Being a young woman of energy, determination and skill in rebellion, she made an assault upon her Aunt Juliet's authority on the very first morning of her summer holidays. She began at breakfast time.

"Father," she said, "I may go to meet Cousin Frank at the train, mayn't I?"

"Certainly," said Sir Lucius.

It was right that some one should meet Frank Mannix on his arrival. Sir Lucius did not want to do so himself. A youth of seventeen is a troublesome guest, difficult to deal with. He is neither man enough to associate on quite equal terms with grown men nor boy enough to be turned loose to play according to his own devices. Sir Lucius did not look forward to the task of entertaining his nephew. He was pleased that Priscilla should take some part, even a small part, of the business off his hands.

Priscilla glanced triumphantly at her aunt.

"There is no possible objection," said Miss Lentaigne, "to your meeting your cousin at the train, but if you are to do so you cannot spend the morning in your boat."

Priscilla thought she could.

"I'm only going as far as Delginish to bathe," she said. "I'll be back in lots of time."

"Be sure you are," said Sir Lucius.

"After being out in the boat," said Miss Lentaigne, "you will be both dirty and untidy, certainly not fit to meet your cousin at the train."

Priscilla, who had a good deal of experience of boats, knew that her aunt's fears were well founded. But she had not yet reached the age at which a girl thinks it desirable to be clean, tidy and well dressed when she goes to meet a strange cousin. She treated Miss Lentaigne's opposition as beneath contempt.

"I must bathe," she said, "It's the first day of the hols."

"Holidays," said Miss Lentaigne.

"Sylvia Courtney," said Priscilla, "who won the prize for English literature at school calls them 'hols.'"

"That," said Sir Lucius, "settles it. The authority of any one who wins a first prize in English literature——"

"And besides," said Priscilla, "she said it, hols that is, to Miss Pettigrew when she was asking when they began. *She* didn't object."

Miss Lentaigne poured out her second cup of tea in silence. Against Miss Pettigrew's tacit approval of the word there was no arguing. Miss Pettigrew, the head of a great educational establishment, does more than win, she awards prizes in English literature.

Priscilla, released from the tedium of the breakfast table, sped down the long avenue on her bicycle. Across the handle bars was tied a bundle, her towel and scarlet bathing dress. From the back of the saddle, wobbling perilously, hung a much larger bundle, a new lug sail, the fruit of hours and hours of toilsome needlework on the wet days of the Christmas "hols."

From the gate at the end of the avenue the road runs straight and steep into the village. At the lower end of the village is the harbour, with its long, dilapidated quay. This is the centre of the village life. Here are, occasionally, small coasting steamers laden with coal or flour, and heavy brigantines or topsail schooners which have felt their way from distant English ports round a wildly inhospitable stretch of coast. Here, almost always, are the bluff-bowed hookers from the outer islands, seeking cargoes of flour and yellow Indian meal, bringing in exchange fish, dried or fresh, and sometimes turf for winter fuel. Here are smaller boats from nearer islands which have come in on the morning tide carrying men and women bent on marketing, which will spread brown sails in the evening and bear their passengers home again. Here at her red buoy lies Sir Lucius' smartly varnished pleasure boat, the *Tortoise*, reckoned "giddy" in spite of her name by staid, cautious island folk; but able, with her centre board and high peaked gunter lug to sail round and round any other boat in the bay. Here, brilliantly green, lies Priscilla's boat, the *Blue Wanderer*, a name appropriate two years ago when she was blue, less appropriate last year, when Peter Walsh made a mistake in buying paint, and grieved Priscilla greatly by turning out the *Blue Wanderer* a sober grey. This year, though the name still sticks to her, it is less suitable still, for Priscilla, buying the paint herself at Easter time, ordained that the *Blue Wanderer* should be green.

Above the quay, at the far side of the fair green, stands Brannigan's shop, a convenient and catholic establishment. To the left of the door as you enter, is the shop of a publican, equipped with a bar and a sheltering partition for modest drinkers. To the right, if you turn that way, is a counter at which you can buy anything, from galvanised iron rowlocks to biscuits and jam. On the low window sills of both windows sit rows of men who for the most part earn an honest living by watching the tide go in and out and by making comments on the boats which approach or leave the quay. It is difficult to find out who pays them for doing these things, but it is plain that some one does, for they are not men of funded property, and yet they live, live comfortably, drink, smoke, eat occasionally and are sufficiently clothed. Of only one among them can it be said with certainty that he is in receipt of regular pay from anybody. Peter Walsh earns five shillings a week by watching over the *Tortoise* and the *Blue Wanderer*.

Priscilla leaped off her bicycle at the door of Bran-nigan's shop. The men on the window sills took no notice of her. They were absorbed in watching the operation of warping round the head of a small steamer which lay far down the quay. The captain had run out a hawser and made the end of it fast to a buoy at the far side of the fair-way. A donkey-engine on the steamer's deck was clanking vigorously, hauling in the hawser, swinging the head of the steamer round, a slow but deeply interesting manoeuvre. "Peter Walsh," said Priscilla, "is that you?" "It is, Miss," said Peter, "and it's proud and pleased I am to see you home again." "Is the *Blue Wanderer* ready for me?" "She is, Miss. The minute you like to step into her she's there for you. There's a new pair of rowlocks and I've a nice bit of rope for a halyard for the little lug. Is it it you have tied on the bicycle?"

"It is," said Priscilla, "and it's a good sail, half as big again as the old one."

"I'd be glad now," said Peter, "if you'd make that same halyard fast to the cleat on the windward side any time you might be using the sail."

"Do you think I'm a fool, Peter?"

"I do not, Miss; but sure you know as well as I do that the mast that's in her isn't over and above strong, and I wouldn't like anything would happen."

"There's no wind any way."

"There is not; but I wouldn't say but there might be at the turn of the tide."

"Haul her up to the slip," said Priscilla. "I'll be back again long before the tide turns."

The steamer swung slowly round. The rattle of her donkey-engine was plainly audible. The warp made fast to the buoy dipped into the water, strained taut dripping, and then dipped again. Suddenly the captain on the bridge shouted. The engine stopped abruptly. The warp sagged deep into the water. A small boat with one man in her appeared close under the steamer's bows, went foul of the warp and lay heavily listed while one of her oars fell into the water and drifted away.

"That's a nice sort of fool to be out in a boat by himself," said Priscilla.

"He was damn near having to swim for it," said Peter, as the boat righted herself and slipped over the warp.

"Who is he?"

"I don't rightly know who he is," said Peter, "but he paid four pounds for the use of Flanagan's old boat for a fortnight, so I'm thinking he has very little sense."

"He has none," said Priscilla. "Look at him now."

The man, deprived of one of his oars, was pushing his way along the steamer's side towards the quay. The captain was swearing heartily at him from the bridge.

"Anyhow," said Priscilla, "I haven't time to stay here and see him drown, though of course it would be interesting. I'm going to bathe and I have to get back again in time to meet the train."

Peter Walsh laid the *Blue Wanderer* alongside the slip. He laced the new lug to its yard, made fast the tack and hoisted it, gazing critically at it as it rose. Then he stepped out of the boat. Priscilla flung her bathing-dress and towel on board and took her seat in the stern.

"You'll find the tiller under the floor board, Miss. With the little air of wind there is from the south you'll slip down to Delginish easy enough if it's there you're thinking of going."

"Shove her head round now, Peter, and give her a push off. I'll get way on her when I'm out a bit from the slip."

The sail flapped, bellied, flapped again, finally swung over to starboard. Priscilla settled herself in the stern with the sheet in her hand.

"The tide's under you, Miss," said Peter Walsh, "You'll slip out easy enough."

The *Blue Wanderer*, urged by the faint southerly breeze, slid along. The water was scarcely rippled by the wind but the tide ran strongly. One buoy after another was passed. A large black boat lay alongside the quay, loaded heavily with gravel. The owner leaned over his gunwale and greeted Priscilla. She replied with friendly familiarity.

"How are you, Kinsella? How's Jimmy and the baby? I expect the baby's grown a lot."

"You're looking fine yourself, Miss," said Joseph Antony Kinsella. "The baby and the rest of them is doing grand, thanks be to God."

The *Blue Wanderer* slipped past. She reached one and then another of the perches which mark the channel into the harbour. The breeze freshened slightly. Little wavelets formed under the *Blue Wandere's* bow and curled outwards from her sides, spreading slowly and then fading away in her wake. Priscilla drew a biscuit from her pocket and munched it contentedly.

- 14 -

Right ahead of her lay the little island of Delginish with a sharply shelving gravel shore. On the northern side of it stood two warning red perches. There were rocks inside them, rocks which were covered at full tide and half tide, but pushed up their brown sea-weedy backs when the tide was low. Priscilla put down her tiller, hauled on her sheet and slipped in through a narrow passage. She rounded the eastern corner of the island and ran her boat ashore in a little bay. She lowered the sail, slipped off her shoes and stockings and pushed the boat out. A few yards from the shore, she dropped her anchor and waited till the boat swung shorewards again to the length of her anchor rope. Then, with her bathing-dress in her hand she waded to the land. The tide was falling. Priscilla had been caught more than once by an ebbing tide with a boat left high and dry. It was not an easy matter to push the Blue Wanderer down a stretch of stony beach. Precautions had to be taken to keep her afloat.

A few minutes later, a brilliant scarlet figure, she was wading out again, knee deep, waist deep. Then with a joyful plunge she swam forward through the sun-warmed water. She came abreast of the corner of her bay, the eastern point of Delginish, turned on her back and splashed deliciously, sending columns of glistening foam high into the air. Standing upright with outspread hands and head thrown back, she trod water, gazing straight up into the sky. She lay motionless on her back, totally immersed save for eyes, nostrils and mouth. A noise of oars roused her. She rolled over, swam a stroke or two, and saw Flanagan's old boat come swiftly down the channel. The stranger, who had courted disaster by fouling the steamer's warp, tugged unskilfully at his oars. He headed for the island. Priscilla shouted to him.

"Keep out," she said. "You're going straight for the rocks."

The young man in the boat turned round and stared at her.

"Pull your right oar," said Priscilla.

The young man pulled both oars hard, missed the water with his right and fell backwards to the bottom of the boat. His two feet stuck up ridiculously. Priscilla laughed. The boat, swept forward by the tide, grounded softly on the sea wrack which covered the rocks.

"There you are, now," said Priscilla. "Why didn't you do what I told you?"

The young man struggled to his feet, seized an oar and began to push violently.

"That's no use," said Priscilla, swimming close under the rocks. "You'll have to hop out or you'll be stuck there till the tide rises, and that won't be till swell on in the afternoon."

The young man eyed the water doubtfully. Then he spoke for the first time.

"Is it very deep?" he said.

"Where you are," said Priscilla, "it's quite shallow, but if you step over the edge of the rock there's six foot of water and more."

The young man sat down and began to unlace his boots.

"If you wait to do that," said Priscilla, "you'll be high and dry altogether. Never mind your boots. Hop out and shove."

He stepped cautiously over the side of his boat, seized his gunwale and shoved. The boat slipped off the rock, stern first. The young man staggered, loosed his hold on her and then stood gaping helplessly, ankle deep in water perched on a very slippery rock, while the boat slipped away from him, stemming the tide as long as the impulse of his push lasted.

"What shall I do now?" he asked.

"Stand where you are," said Priscilla. "She'll drift down to you again. I'll give her a shove so that she'll come right up to you."

She swam after the boat and laid a hand on her gunwale. Then, kicking and splashing, guided her back to the young man on the rock. He climbed on board.

"Where do you suppose you're going?" asked Priscilla.

"To an island," said the young man.

"If one island is the same to you as another," said Priscilla, "and you haven't any particular one in your mind, I'd advise you to stop at this one."

"But I have."

"Which one?"

The young man looked at her suspiciously and then took his oars.

"I hope your island is quite near," said Priscilla, "For if it isn't you're not likely to get there. Were you ever in a boat before?"

The young man pulled a few strokes and got his boat into the channel beyond the red perches.

"I think," said Priscilla, "that you might say 'thank you,' Only for me you'd have been left stranded on that rock till the tide rose again and floated you off somewhere between four and five o'clock this afternoon."

"Thank you," said the young man, "thank you very much indeed."

"But where are you going?"

The question seemed to frighten him. He began to row with desperate energy. In a few minutes he was far down the channel. Priscilla watched him. Then she swam to her bay, pushed the *Blue Wanderer* a little further from the shore and landed.

The island of Delginish is a pleasant spot on a warm day. Above its gravel beach rises a slope of coarse short grass, woven through with wild thyme and yellow crowtoe. Sea-pinks cluster on the fringe of grass and delicate groups of fairy-flax are bright-blue in stony places. Red centaury and yellow bed-straw and white bladder campion flourish. Tiny wild roses, clinging to the ground, fleck the green with spots of vivid white. The sun reaches every yard of the shadeless surface of the island. Here and there grey rocks peep up, climbed over, mellowed by olive green stonecrops. Priscilla, glowing from her bath, lay full stretch among the flowers, drawing deep breaths of scented air and gazing at the sky. But nothing was further from her mind than soulful sentimentalising over the beauties of nature. She was puzzling about the young man who had left her, endeavoring to arrive at some theory of who he was and what he could be doing in Rosnacree. After awhile she turned over on her side, fumbled in her pocket and drew out two more biscuits in crumbly fragments. She munched them contentedly.

At eleven o'clock she raised herself slowly on one elbow and looked round. The tide had nearly reached its lowest, and the Blue Wanderer lay half in, half out of the water; her stern perched high, her bow with the useless anchor rope depending from it, dipped deep. Priscilla realised that she had no time to lose. She put her shoulder to the stern of the boat and pushed, springing on board as the boat floated. The Blue Wanderer, even with her new lug sail, does not work well to windward. It is possible by very careful steering to make a little by tacking if the breeze is good and the tide is running favourably. With a light wind and in the slack water of the ebb the most that can be done is not to go to leeward. Priscilla, with the necessity of meeting a train present in her mind, unstepped the mast and took her oars. In twenty minutes she was alongside the slip where Peter Walsh stood waiting for her.

"I was talking to Joseph Anthony Kinsella," he said, "since you were out—him that lives beyond in Inishbawn."

"Were you?" said Priscilla. "I saw him in his boat as I was going out, with a big load of gravel on board. He says the baby's all right."

"It may be," said Peter. "Any way, he said nothing to the contrary when he was with me. It wasn't the baby we were speaking of. Will you mind yourself now, Miss. That slip is terribly slippery at low tide on account of the green weed that does be growing on it. Take care but you might fall."

The warning came a little too late. Priscilla stepped from the boat and immediately fell forward on her hands and knees. When she rose there was a large, damp green patch on the front of her dress.

"Will you look at that, now?" said Peter. "Didn't I tell you to go easy? Are you hurted, Miss?"

"If it wasn't the new baby you were talking about," said Priscilla, "what was it?"

"Joseph Anthony Kinsella is just after telling me that he's seen that young fellow that has Flanagan's old boat out beyond among the islands."

"Which island? I asked him, but he wouldn't tell me."

"Joseph Anthony didn't rightly know, but it's his belief that he's on Ilaunglos, or Ardilaun, or one of them to the north of Carrowbee."

"He can't be living there, then. There isn't a house on any of those islands."

"Joseph Anthony was saying that he might maybe have a tent with him and be sleeping in it the same as the tinkers would. I've heard of the like."

"Did he see the tent?"

"He did not; but there could be a tent without his seeing it. What I seen myself was the things the young fellow bought in Brannigan's and put into Flanagan's old boat. He had a can of paraffin oil with a cork drove into the neck of it, and he'd two loaves of bread done up in brown paper, and he'd a couple of tins that might be meat of one kind or another, and along with them he had a pound of tea and maybe two of sugar. I misdoubted when I saw him carrying them down the quay, but it was some kind of a picnic he was out for. Them kind of fellows has very little sense."

"I expect," said Priscilla, "that he'll be drowned before long, and then they'll find some papers on his body that'll tell us who he is. I must be off now, Peter, or I'll be late for the train."

"You're time enough, Miss. Sure them trains is never punctual."

"They are not," said Priscilla, "except on the days when you happen to be late for them. Then they make a point of being up to the minute just to score off you."

CHAPTER IV

The train, as Priscilla prophesied, was strictly punctual. It was drawn up at the platform when she leaped off her bicycle in front of the station. As she passed through the gate she came face to face with Frank Mannix supported by the station master and the guard.

"Hullo!" she said. "You're my cousin Frank, I suppose. You look rather sick."

Frank gazed at her.

"Are you Priscilla?" he asked.

He had formed no very definite mental picture of his cousin beforehand. Little girls of fifteen years of age are not creatures of great interest to prefects who have made remarkable catches in the long field and look forward to establishing their manhood among the salmon and the grouse. So far as he had thought of Priscilla at all he had placed her in the background, a trim, unobtrusive maiden, who came down to dessert after dinner and was kept under proper control at other times by a governess. It shocked him a little to see a girl in a tousled blue cotton frock, with a green stain on the front of it, with a tangle of damp fair hair hanging round her head in shining strings, with unabashed fearless eyes which looked at him with a certain shrewd merriment.

"You look wobbly," said Priscilla. "Can't you walk by yourself?"

"I've met with an accident," said Frank.

"That's all right. I was afraid just at first that you might be the sort that collapsed altogether after being seasick. Some people do, you know, and they're never much good for anything. I'm glad you're not one of them. Accidents are different of course. Nobody can ever be quite sure of not meeting an accident."

She glanced at the stain on the front of her dress as she spoke. It was the result of an accident.

"I've sprained my ankle," said Frank.

"It's my belief," said the guard, "that the young gentleman's leg is broke on him. That's what the ticket-collector was after telling me at the junction any way."

"Would you like me to cut off your sock?" said Priscilla. "The station-master's wife would lend me a pair of scissors. She's sure to have a pair. Almost everybody has."

"No, I wouldn't," said Frank.

There had been trouble enough in getting the sock on over the damp table napkin. He had no wish to have it taken off again unnecessarily.

"All right," said Priscilla, "I won't if you'd rather not of course; but it's the proper thing to do for a sprained ankle. Sylvia Courtney told me so and she attended a course of Ambulance lectures last term and learnt all about first aid on the battle-field. I wanted to go to those lectures frightfully, but Aunt Juliet wouldn't let me. Rather rot I thought it at the time, but I saw afterwards that she couldn't possibly on account of her principles."

Frank, following Priscilla's rapid thought with difficulty, supposed that Ambulance lectures, dealing necessarily with the human body, might be considered by some people slightly unsuitable for young girls, and that Aunt Juliet was a lady who set a high value on propriety. Priscilla offered a different explanation.

"Christian Science," she said. "That's Aunt Juliet's latest. There's always something. Can you sit on a car?"

"Oh yes," said Frank. "If I was once up I could sit well enough."

"Let you make your mind easy about getting up," said the station-master. "We'll have you on the side of the car in two twos."

They hoisted him up, Priscilla giving advice and directions while they did so. Then she took her bicycle from a porter who held it for her.

"The donkey-trap will bring your luggage," she said. "It will be all right."

She turned to the coachman.

"Drive easy now, James," she said, "and mind you don't let the cob shy when you come to the new drain that they're digging outside the court house. There's nothing worse for a broken bone than a sudden jar. That's another thing that was in the Ambulance lectures."

The car started. Priscilla rode alongside, keeping within speaking distance of Frank.

"But my ankle's not broken," he said.

"It may be. Anyhow I expect a jar is just as bad for a sprain. Very likely the lecturer said so and Sylvia Courtney forgot to tell me. Pretty rotten luck this, for you, Cousin Frank, on account of the fishing. You can't possibly fish and the river's in splendid order. Father said so yesterday. But perhaps Aunt Juliet will be able to cure you. She thinks she can cure anything."

"I shall be all right," said Frank, "when I can rest my leg a bit—I don't think it's really bad I daresay at the end of a week——"

"If Aunt Juliet cures you at all she'll do it quicker than that. She had Father out of bed the day after he got influenza last Easter hols. He very nearly died afterwards on account of having to travel up to Dublin to go to a nursing home when his temperature was 400 and something, but Aunt Juliet said he was perfectly well all the time; so she may be able to fix up that ankle of yours."

They have, so it is understood, tried experiments in vegetarianism at Haileybury; but Christian Science is not yet part of the regular curriculum even on the modern side. Frank Mannix had only the vaguest idea of what Miss Lentaigne's beliefs were. He knew nothing at all about her methods. Priscilla's account of them was not very encouraging.

"All I want," he said, "is simply to rest my ankle."

"Do you think," said Priscilla, "that you could sit in a boat? That's mine, the green one beside the slip. If you turn your head you'll see her. But perhaps it hurts you to turn your head. If it does you'd better not try. The boat will be there all the same even if you don't see her."

They were passing the quay while she spoke, and Priscilla, who was a little behind at the moment, pointed to the *Blue Wanderer*. Frank discovered one of the disadvantages of an Irish car. The view of the passengers, even if each one is alone on his side, is confined almost entirely to objects on one side of the road. Only by twisting his neck in a most uncomfortable way can any one see what lies directly behind him. Frank made the effort and was unimpressed by the appearance of the *Blue Wanderer*. She was exceedingly unlike the shining outriggers in which he had sometimes rowed on the upper reaches of the Thames during earlier summer holidays.

"I expect," said Priscilla, "that the salt water will be jolly good for your ankle, in reality, though Aunt Juliet will say it wont. She's bound to say that, of course, on account of her principles. All the same it may. Peter Walsh was telling me the other day that it's perfectly splendid for rheumatism. I shouldn't wonder a bit if sprained ankles and rheumatism are much the same sort of thing, only with different names. But of course we can't go this afternoon. Aunt Juliet will demand to have first shy at you. If she fails we may manage to sneak off to-morrow morning. But perhaps you don't care for boats, Cousin Frank."

"I like boats very much."

He spoke in a slightly patronising tone, as an elderly gentleman might confess to a fondness for chocolates in order to please a small nephew. He felt it necessary to make it quite clear to Priscilla that he had not come to Rosnacree to be her playmate and companion. He had come to fish salmon in company with her father and such other grown men as might from time to time present themselves. Nursery games in stumpy green boats were not consonant with his dignity. He did not want to hurt Priscilla's feelings, but he was anxious that she should understand his position. She seemed unimpressed.

"That's all right," she said. "I'll row you. You can sit in the stern and let your legs dangle over in the water. I've often done that when Peter Walsh has been rowing. It's quite a jolly thing to do."

It was a thing which Frank Mannix was quite determined not to do. The suggestion that he should behave in such a way struck him as "cheeky" in a very high degree. A lower schoolboy in Edmondstone House, if he had ventured to speak in such a way, would have been beaten with a fives bat. But Priscilla was a girl and, as Frank understood, girls are not beaten. He answered her with kindly condescension.

"Perhaps we'll be able to manage it some day," he said, "before I leave."

They arrived at Rosnacree House and Frank was helped up the steps by the butler and the coachman. Sir Lucius expressed the greatest regret when he heard of his nephew's accident.

"It's too bad," he said, "too bad, and the river in such fine condition after a fortnight's rain. I was looking forward to seeing you get into your first salmon. But cheer up, Frank, I daresay it won't turn out to be very tedious. We'll have you hobbling along in a week or a fortnight. We've a good while before us yet. I'll get up O'Hara this afternoon, our local practitioner. Not a bad fellow at all, though he drinks a bit. Still he'll know what to do with a sprained ankle. Oh! by the way perhaps——"

Sir Lucius' sentence ended abruptly. His sister entered the room. She greeted Frank and inquired whether he had enjoyed his journey. The story of the accident was told to her. It was evident at once that she took a keen interest in the sprained ankle. Priscilla, describing the scene afterwards to Rose, the under housemaid, said that Miss Lentaigne's eyes gleamed and sparkled with joy. Every one in the household had for many weeks carefully refrained from illness or disability of any kind. If Miss Lentaigne's eyes really did sparkle they expressed a perfectly natural delight. There is nothing more trying than to possess a power of healing and to find no opportunity for exercising it.

"Perhaps," she said, "Frank and I may have a little talk together after luncheon."

Sir Lucius was a man of hospitable instincts with high old-fashioned ideas of the courtesy due by a host to his guest. He did not think it quite fair to subject Frank to a course of Christian Science. But he was also very much afraid of his sister, whom he recognised as his intellectual superior. He cleared his throat and made a nervous protest on Frank's behalf.

"I'm not sure, Juliet," he said, "I'm really not at all sure that your theory quite applies to sprains, especially ankles."

Miss Lentaigne smiled very gently. Her face expressed a tolerant patience with the crude ideas entertained by her brother.

"Of course," Sir Lucius went on, "there's a great deal in your idea. I've always said so. In the case of any internal disease, nerves you know, and that kind of thing where there's nothing actually visible, I'm sure it works out admirably, quite admirably, but with a sprained ankle! Come now, Juliet, there's the swelling you know. You can't deny the swelling. Hang it all, you can measure the swelling with a tape. Is your ankle much swelled, Frank?"

"A good deal. But it's not worth making a fuss about. It'll be all right."

Miss Lentaigne smiled again. In her opinion it was all right already. There was not really any swelling, although Frank, in his ignorance, might honestly think there was. She hoped, after luncheon, to convince him of these pleasant truths.

Sir Lucius was a coward at heart. He was exceedingly sorry for his nephew, but he made no further effort to save him from the ministrations of Miss Lentaigne. Nor did he venture to mention the name of O'Hara, the excellent, though occasionally inebriate, local practitioner. Frank, as yet unaware of the full beauty of the scientific Christian method of dealing with illness, was very polite to Miss Lentaigne during luncheon. He talked to her about Parliament and its doings as a subject likely to interest her, assuming the air of a man who knows the inner secrets of the Cabinet. He did, in fact, know a good deal about the habits and manners of our legislators, having picked up details of an interesting kind from his father. Miss Lentaigne was greatly delighted with him. So was Priscilla, who winked three times at her father when neither Frank nor her aunt was looking at her. Sir Lucius was uneasy. He feared that his nephew was likely to turn out a prig, a kind of boy which he held in particular abhorrence.

When luncheon was over he said that he intended to take his rod and go up the river for the afternoon. He invited Priscilla to go with him and carry his landing net. Frank, preceded by Miss Lentaigne, was conducted by the butler to a hammock chair agreeably placed under the shade of a lime tree on the lawn. When Sir Lucius and Priscilla, laden with fishing gear, passed him, he was still making himself politely agreeable to Miss Lentaigne. Priscilla winked at him. He returned the salutation with a stare which was intended to convince her that winking was a particularly vicious kind of bad form. Miss Lentaigne, as Priscilla noticed, sat with two treatises on Christian Science in her hand.

Priscilla, returning without her father at half past six o'clock, found Frank sitting alone under the lime tree. He was in a singularly chastened mood and inclined to be companionable and friendly, even with a girl of no more than fifteen years old.

"I say, Priscilla," he said, "is that old aunt of yours quite mad?"

There was something in the way he expressed himself which delighted Priscilla. He had reverted to the phraseology of an undignified schoolboy of the lower fifth. The veneer of grown manhood, even the polish of a prefect, had, as it were, peeled off him during the afternoon.

"Not at all," said Priscilla. "She's frightfully clever, what's called intellectual. You know the sort of thing. How's your ankle?"

"She says it isn't sprained. But, blow it all, it's swelled the size of the calf of your leg."

He did not mean Priscilla's leg particularly; but with a slight lift of an already short skirt she surveyed her own calf curiously. She wanted to know exactly how thick Frank's injured ankle was.

"Then she didn't cure it?"

"Cure it!" said Frank, "I should think not. She simply kept on telling me I only thought it was sprained. I never heard such rot talked in all my life. How do you stand it at all?"

"That's nothing," said Priscilla. "We're quite glad she's taken to Christian Science; though she did nearly kill poor father. Before that she was all for teetotallity—that's not quite the right word, but you know the thing I mean, drinking nothing but lemonade, either homemade or the kind that fizzes. I didn't mind that a bit for I like lemonade, both sorts, but father simply hated it. He told me he'd rather go up to that nursing home in Dublin every time he feels ill than live through another six months on lemonade. Before that she was frightfully keen on a thing called uric acid. Do you know what that is, Cousin Frank?" "No," he said, "I don't. How did it take her?" "She wouldn't give us anything to eat," said Priscilla, "except queer sort of mashes which she said were made of nuts and biscuits and things. I got quite thin and as weak as a cat." "I wonder you stuck it out." "Oh, it didn't last long. None of them do, you know. That's our great consolation; though we rather hope the Christian Science will on account of its doing us no particular harm. She doesn't mind what we eat or drink, which is a great comfort. She can't you know, according to her principles, because when there's no such thing as being sick it can't matter how much whipped cream or anything of that sort you eat just before you go to bed at night. She didn't like it a bit when I got up on Christmas night and foraged out nearly a quarter of a cold plum pudding. She was just going up to bed and she caught me. She wanted awfully to stop me eating it, but she couldn't without giving the whole show away, so I ate it before her very eyes. That's the beauty of Christian Science." "But I say, Priscilla, weren't you sick?" "Not a bit. When Father heard about it next morning he said he thought there must be something in Aunt Juliet's theory after all. He has stuck to that ever since, though he says it doesn't apply to influenza. She had a great idea about fresh air one time, and got up a carpenter to take the window frames, windows and all, clean out of my room. I used to have to borrow hairpins from Rose—she's the under housemaid and a great friend of mine—so as to fasten the bedclothes on to the mattress. Otherwise they blew away during the night, while I was asleep. That was one of the worst times we ever had, though I don't think Father minded it so much. He used to go out and smoke in the harness room. But I hated it worse than anything except the uric acid. You never knew where your clothes would be in the morning if it was the least stormy, and my hair used to blow into soup and tea and things, which made it frightfully sticky."

"Do you think," said Frank, "that she'll leave me alone now? Or will she want to have another go at me to-morrow?"

"Sure to," said Priscilla, "unless you give in that your ankle is quite well."

"But I can't walk."

"That won't matter in the least. She'll say you can. Aunt Juliet is tremendously determined. Poor Rose—I told you she is the under housemaid, didn't I? She is any way. Poor Rose once got a swelled face on account of a tooth that she wouldn't have out. Aunt Juliet kept at her, reading little bits out of books and kind of praying, in passages and pantries and places, wherever she met Rose. That went on for more than a week. Then Rose got Dr. O'Hara to haul the tooth and the swelling went down. Aunt Juliet said it was Christian Science cured her. And of course it may have been. You never can tell really what it is that cures people."

"I wonder," said Frank, "if I could manage to get down to the boat to-morrow. You said something about a boat, didn't you, Priscilla? Is it far?"

"I'll work that all right for you. As it just happens, luckily enough there's an old bath-chair in a corner of the hay-loft. I came across it last hols when I was looking for a bicycle pump I lost. I was rather disappointed at the time, not thinking that the old chair would be any use, whereas I wanted the pump. Now it turns out to be exactly what we want, which shows that well directed labour is never really wasted. The front-wheel is a bit groggy, but I daresay it'll hold all right as far as the quay. I'll go round after dinner to-night and fish it out. I can wheel you quite easily, for it's all down hill."

Frank had not intended when he left England to go about the country in a bath-chair with a groggy front-wheel. For a moment he hesitated. A wild fear struck him of what the Uppingham captain—that dangerous bat whose innings his brilliant catch had cut short—might say and think if he saw the vehicle. But the Uppingham captain was not likely to be in Rosnacree. Christian Science was a more threatening danger. He pictured to himself the stare of amazement on the countenance of Mr. Dupré and the sniggering face of young Latimer who collected beetles and hated washing. But Mr. Dupré, Latimer and the members of the house eleven, were, no doubt, far off.

Miss Lentaigne was very near at hand. He accepted Priscilla's offer.

"Right," she said. "I'll settle the chair, if I have to tie it together with my hair ribbon. It's nice to think of that old chair coming in useful in the end. It must have been in the loft for ages and ages. Sylvia Courtney told me that her mother says anything will come in useful if you only keep it long enough; but I don't know whether that's true. I don't think it can be, quite, for I tried it once with a used up exercise-book and it didn't seem to be the slightest good even after years and years, though it got most frightfully tattered. Still it may be true. You never can tell about things of that sort, and Sylvia Courtney says her mother is extremely wise; so she may be quite right.

"Christian Science," said Frank bitterly, "wouldn't be of any use if you kept it for centuries. What's the use of saying a thing isn't swelled when it is?"

CHAPTER V

A night's rest restored self-respect to Frank Mannix. He felt when his clothes were brought to him in the morning by a respectful footman that he had to some extent sacrificed his dignity in his confidential talk with Priscilla the day before. He had committed himself to the bath-chair and the boating expedition, and he had too high a sense of personal honour to back out of an engagement definitely made. But he determined to keep Priscilla at a distance. He would go with her, would to some extent join in her childish sports; but it must be on the distinct understanding that he did so as a grown man who condescends to play games with an amusing child. With this idea in his mind he dressed himself very carefully in a suit a cricket flannels. The garments were in themselves suitable for boating as he understood the sport. They were also likely, he thought, to impress Priscilla. The white flannel coat, bound round its edges with crimson silk, was at Haileybury part of a uniform set apart for the sole use of members of the first eleven who had actually got their colours. The crimson sash round his waist was a badge of the same high office. Small boys, who played cricket on the house pitches in the Little Side ground, bowed in awed humility before a member of the first eleven when he appeared before them in all his glory and felt elated if they were allowed to walk across the quadrangle with any one who wore the sacred vestments. Frank had little doubt that Priscilla, who was to be his companion for the day would realise the greatness of her privileges.

But Priscilla seemed curiously unimpressed. She met him in the breakfast room before either Sir Lucius or Miss Lentaigne came down.

"Great Scot! Cousin Frank," she said, "you are a howler!"

Frank drew himself up; but realised even as he did so that he must make some reply to Priscilla. It was impossible to pretend not to know that she was speaking about his clothes.

"An old suit of flannels," he said with elaborate carelessness. "I hope you didn't expect me to be grand."

"I never saw anything grander in my life," said Priscilla. "I thought Sylvia Courtney's summer Sunday hat was swankey; but it's simply not in it with your coat. I suppose that belt thing is real silk."

"School colours," said Frank.

"Oh! Ours are blue and dark yellow. I have them on a hockey blouse."

The bath-chair turned out to be rather more dilapidated and disreputable than Frank expected. The front-wheel—bound to its place with string, not hair ribbon—seemed very likely indeed to come off. He eyed it doubtfully.

"If you're afraid," said Priscilla, "that it will dirty your beautiful white trousers, I'll give it a rub-over with my pocket-handcher. But I don't think that'll be much use really. You'll be filthy from head to foot in any case before we get home."

Frank, limping with as much dignity as possible, sat down in the chair. He got out his cigarette case and asked Priscilla not to start until he had lit his cigarette.

"You don't object to the smell, I hope," he said politely.

"Not a bit. I'd smoke myself only I don't like it. I tried once—Sylvia Courtney was shocked. That's rather the sort she is—but it seemed to me to have a nasty taste. You're sure you like it, Cousin Frank? Don't do it simply because you think you ought."

Priscilla pushed the bath-chair from behind. Frank guided the shaky front wheel by means of a long handle. They went down the avenue at an extremely rapid pace, Priscilla moving in a kind of jaunty canter. When they reached the gate Frank's cigarette had gone out. There was a pause while he lit it again. Then he asked Priscilla to go a little less quickly. He wished his approach to the public street of the village to be as little grotesque as possible.

"By the way," said Priscilla, "have you any money?"

"Certainly. How much do you want?"

"That depends. I have eightpence, which ought to be enough unless you want something very expensive to drink."

"Why should we take anything to drink? We said at breakfast that we'd be back for luncheon."

"We won't," said Priscilla, "nor we won't for tea. Lucky if we are for dinner."

"But Miss Lentaigne said she'd expect us. If we stay out she won't like it."

"Let her dis.," said Priscilla. "Now what do you want to drink? I always have lemon flavoured soda. It's less sticky than regular lemonade. Stone ginger beer is better than either, of course, but Brannigan doesn't keep it, I can't imagine why not."

"If we're going to stay out," said Frank, "I'll have beer, lager for choice."

"Right. Lager is twopence. Lemon flavoured soda twopence if we bring back the bottles. That will leave fourpence for biscuits which ought to be enough."

Fourpence worth of biscuits seemed to Frank an insufficient supply of food for two people who are to be on the sea for the whole day. He saw, besides, an opportunity of asserting once for all his position of superiority. He made up his mind to tip Priscilla. He fumbled in his pocket for a coin.

"You get quite a lot of biscuits for fourpence," said Priscilla, "if you go in for plain arrowroot. Of course they're rather dull, but then you get very few of the better sorts. Take macaroons, for instance. They're nearly a halfpenny each in Brannigan's. Sheer robbery, I call it."

Frank, determined to do the thing handsomely if he did it at all, passed half a crown to Priscilla over the back of the bath chair.

"My dear child," he said, "buy macaroons by all means if you like them. Buy as many as you want."

Priscilla received the half-crown without any appearance of shame.

"If you're prepared to lash out money in that way," she said, "we may as well have a tongue. Brannigan has small ones at one and sixpence. Brawn of course is cheaper, but then if you have brawn you want a tin-opener. The tongues are in glass jars which you can break with a stone or a rowlock. The lids are supposed to come off quite easily if you jab a knife through them, but they don't really. All that happens is a sort of fizz of air and the lid sticks on as tight as ever. Things hardly ever do what they're supposed to according to science, which makes me think that science is rather rot, though, of course, it may have its uses only that I don't know them."

Priscilla wheeled the bath-chair for some distance along the road without speaking. Then she asked another question.

"Which would you rather have, the tongue or a tin of Californian peaches. They're one and sixpence too, so we can't have both, for it would be a pity to miss the chance of one and fourpence worth of macaroons. I don't remember ever having so many at one time before. Though of course they're not really so many when there are two of us to eat them."

"I'll give you another one and sixpence," said Frank, "and then you'll be able to get the peaches too if you want them. I rather bar those tinned fruits myself. They have no flavour."

On Saturday evenings, when prefects and all self-respecting members of the upper and middle schools have tea in their studies, Frank was accustomed to eat tinned lobsters and sometimes tinned salmon, but he knew that superiority to such forms of food was one of the marks of a grown man. He hoped, by speaking slightingly of the Californian peaches, to impress Priscilla with the idea that he was a sort of uncle of hers. The luncheon was involving him in considerable expense, but he did not grudge the money if it produced the effect he desired. Unfortunately it did not.

"Well have a gorgeous bust," said Priscilla. "I shouldn't wonder if Brannigan got some kind of fit when we spend all that in his shop at once. He's not accustomed to millionaires."

Frank, not being able to find a shilling and a sixpence in his pocket, handed over another half crown. Priscilla promised to give him his change. She stopped the bath-chair at the door of Brannigan's shop. The men of leisure who sat on the window sills stared curiously at Frank. Young gentlemen dressed in white flannels and wheeled in bath-chairs are rare in Rosnacree. Frank felt embarrassed and annoyed.

"Excuse me half a mo.," said Priscilla. "I'll just speak a word to Peter Walsh and then do the shopping. Peter, you're to get the sails on the *Tortoise* at once."

She spoke with such decisive authority that Peter Walsh felt quite certain that she had no right to give the order.

"Is it the *Tortoise*, Miss?"

"Didn't I say the *Tortoise*. Go and get the sails at once."

"I don't know," said Peter, "whether would your da be pleased with me if I sent you out in the *Tortoise*. Sure you know——"

"Mr. Mannix and I," said Priscilla, "are going out for the day in the *Tortoise*."

Peter Walsh took a long look at Frank. He was apparently far from satisfied with the result of his inspection.

"Of course if the young gentleman in the perambulator is going with you, Miss—the *Tortoise* is a giddy kind of a boat, your honour, and without you'd be used to her or the like of her—but sure if you're satisfied—but what it is, the master gave orders that Miss Priscilla wasn't to go out in the *Tortoise* without either himself or me would be along with her."

Frank was painfully aware that he was not used to the *Tortoise* or to any boat the least like her. He had never in his life been to sea in a sailing boat for the management of which he was in any way responsible. He was, in fact, entirely ignorant of the art of boat sailing. But the men who sat on the window sills of Brannigan's shop, battered sea dogs every one of them, had their eyes fixed on him. It would be deeply humiliating to have to own up before them that he knew nothing about boats. Sir Lucius's order applied, very properly, to Priscilla who was a child. Peter Walsh looked as if he thought that Frank also ought to be treated as a child. This was intolerable. The day seemed very calm. It was difficult to think that there could be any real risk in going out in the __Tortoise__. Priscilla nudged him sharply with her elbow. Frank yielded to temptation.

"Miss Lentaigne," he said, "will be quite safe with me."

He spoke with lordly self-confidence, calculated, he thought, to impress the impudent loafers on the window sills and to reduce Peter Walsh to prompt submission. Having spoken he felt unreasonably angry with Priscilla who was grinning.

Peter Walsh ambled down to the quay. He climbed over the dredger, which was lying alongside, and dropped from her into a small water-logged punt. In this he ferried himself out to the *Tortoise*. Priscilla bounded into Brannigan's shop. The sea dogs on the window sills eyed Frank and shook their heads. It was painfully evident that his self-confident tone had not imposed on them.

"There's not much wind any way," said one of them, "and what there is will be dropping with the ebb."

"It'll work round to the west with the flood," said another. "With the weather we're having now it'll follow the sun."

Priscilla came out of the shop laden with parcels which she placed one by one on Frank's lap.

"Beer and lemonade," she said. "The beast was out of lemon flavoured soda, so I had to get lemonade instead, but your lager's all right. You don't mind drinking out of the bottle, do you, Cousin Frank? You can have the bailing tin of course, if you like, but it's rather salty. Macaroons and cocoanut creams. They turned out to be the same price, so I thought I might as well get a mixture. The cocoanut creams are lighter, so one gets more of them for the money. Tongue. I told him not to put paper on the tongue. I always think brown paper is rather a nuisance in a boat. It gets so soppy when it's the least wet. There's no use having more of it than we can help. Peaches. He hadn't any of the small one and sixpenny tins, so I had to spend your other shilling to make up the half-crown for the big one. I hope you don't mind. We shall be able to finish it all right I expect. Oh, bother! I forgot that the peaches require a tin-opener. Have you a knife? If you have we may be able to manage by hammering it along through the lid of the tin with a rowlock."

Frank had a knife, but he set some value on it He did not want to have it reduced to the condition of a coarse toothed saw by being hammered through a tin with a rowlock. He hesitated.

"All right," said Priscilla, "if you'd rather not have it used I'll go and try to stick Brannigan for the loan of a tin-opener. He may not care for lending it, because things like tin-openers generally drop overboard and then of course he wouldn't get it back. But he'll hardly be able to refuse it I offer to deposit the safety pin in my tie as a hostage. It looks exactly as if it is gold, and, if it was, would be worth far more than any tin-opener."

She went into the shop again. It was nearly ten minutes before she came out. Frank was seriously annoyed by a number of small children who crowded round the bath-chair and made remarks about his appearance. He tried to buy them off with macaroons, but the plan failed, as a similar one did in the case of the Anglo-Saxon king and the Danes. The children, like the Norse pirates, returned almost immediately in increased numbers. Then Priscilla appeared.

"I thought I should have had a frightful rag with Brannigan over the tin-opener," she said, "but he was quite nice about it. He said he'd lend it with pleasure and didn't care whether I left him the safety pin or not. The only trouble was that he couldn't find one. He said that he had a gross of them somewhere, but he didn't know where they'd been put. In the end it was Mrs. Brannigan who found them in an old biscuit tin under some oilskins. That's what delayed me."

Peter Walsh was hoisting a sail, a gunter lug, on the *Tortoise*. He paused in his work now and then to cast a glance ashore at Frank. Priscilla wheeled the bath-chair down to the slip and hailed Peter.

"Hurry up now," she said, "and get the foresail on her. Don't keep us here all day."

Peter pulled on the foresail halyards with some appearance of vigour. He slipped the mooring rope and ran the *Tortoise* alongside the slip, towing the water logged punt behind her.

"Joseph Antony Kinsella," said Peter, "was in this morning on the flood tide and he was telling me he came across that young fellow again near Illaunglos."

"Was he talking to him?" said Priscilla.

"He was not beyond passing the time of day or the like of that for Joseph Antony had a load of gravel and he couldn't be wasting his time. But the young fellow was in Flanagan's old boat and it was Joseph Antony's opinion that he was trying to learn himself how to row her."

"He'd need to. But if that's all that passed between them I don't see that we're much further on towards knowing what that man is doing here."

"Joseph Antony did say," said Peter, "that the young gentleman was as simple and innocent as a child and one that wouldn't be likely to be doing any harm."

"You can't be sure of that."

"You cannot, Miss. There's a terrible lot of fellows going round the country these times, sent out by the government that would be glad enough to be interfering with the people and maybe taking the land away from them. You'd never know who might be at such work and who mightn't, but Joseph Antony did say that the fellow in Flanagan's old boat hadn't the look of it. He's too innocent like."

"Hop you out now, Peter," said Priscilla, "and help Mr. Mannix down into the boat. He has a sprained ankle and can't walk by himself. Be careful of him!"

The task of getting Frank into the *Tortoise* was not an easy one for the slip was nearly as slimy as when Priscilla fell on it the day before. Peter, with his arm round Frank's waist, proceeded very cautiously.

"Settle him down on the starboard side of the centre-board case," said Priscilla. "We'll carry the boom to port on the run out."

"You will," said Peter, "for the wind's in the east, but you'll have to jibe her at the stone perch if you're going down the channel."

"I'm not going down the channel. I mean to stand across to Rossmore and then go into the bay beyond." Priscilla stepped into the boat and took the tiller.

"Did I hear you say, Miss, that you're thinking of going on to Inishbawn?"

"You did not hear me say anything about Inishbawn; but I may go there all the same if I've time. I want to see the Kinsellas' new baby."

"If you'll take my advice, Miss," said Peter, "you'll not go next nor nigh Inishbawn."

"And why not?"

"Joseph Antony Kinsella was telling me this morning that it's alive with rats, such rats nobody ever seen. They have the island pretty near eat away."

"Talk sense," said Priscilla.

"They came out on the tide swimming," said Peter, "like as it might be a shoal of mackerel, and you think there'd be no end to them climbing up over the stones and eating all before them."

"Shove her bow round, Peter; and keep that rat story of yours for the young man in Flanagan's boat. He'll believe it if he's as innocent as you say."

Peter shoved out the *Tortoise*. The wind caught the sail. Priscilla paid out the main sheet and let the boom swing forward. Peter shouted a last warning from the slip.

"Joseph Antony was telling me," he said, "that they're terrible fierce, worser than any rats ever he seen."

The *Tortoise* slipped along and was soon beyond the reach of his voice. She passed the heavy hookers at the quay side, left buoy after buoy behind her, bobbed cheerfully through a tide race at the stone perch, and stood out, the wind right behind her, for Rossmore Head.

CHAPTER VI

Rosnacree Bay is a broad stretch of water, but those who go down to it in boats are singularly at the mercy of the tides. Save for certain channels the water everywhere is shallow. At some remote period, it seems, the ocean broke in and submerged a tract of low land between the mountains which bound the north and south shores of the bay. What once were round hillocks rising from boggy pasture land are now islands, sloping eastwards to the water as they once sloped eastwards to green fields, but torn and chafed into steep bluffs where the sea beats on their western sides.

But the ocean's conquest is incomplete. Its empire is disputed still. The very violence of the assault has checked its advance by piling up a mighty breakwater of boulders right across the mouth of the bay. Gathered upon sullenly firm based rocks these great round stones roll and roar and crash when the full force of the Atlantic billows comes foaming against them. They save the islands east of them. There are gaps in the breakwater, and the sea rushes through these, but it is tamed of its ferocity, humiliated from the grandeur of its strength so that it wanders, puzzled, bewildered, through the waterways among the islands. The land asserts itself. Things which belong to the land approach with contemptuous familiarity the very verges of their mighty foe. On the edges of the water the islanders build their hayricks, redolent of rural life, and set up their stacks of brown turf. Geese and ducks, whose natural play places are muddy pools and inland streams, swim through the salt water in the sheltered bays below the cottages. Pigs, driven down to the shore to root among the rotting seaweed, splash knee deep in the sea. At the time of high spring tides, in March and at the end of September, the water flows in oily curves or splashes muddily against the very thresholds of the cottages. It penetrates the brine-soaked soil and wells turn brackish. It wanders far inland through winding straits. The wayfarer, stepping across what seems to be a ditch at the end of a field far from the sea wonders to hear brown wrack crackle under his feet.

A few hours later the land asserts itself again. The sea draws back sullenly at first. Soon its retreat becomes a very flight. The narrow ways between the islands, calm an hour before, are like swift rivers. Through the cleft gaps in the breakwater of boulders the sea goes back from its adventurous wanderings to the ocean outside; but not as in other places, where a deep felt homing impulse draws tired water to the voluminous mother bosom of the Atlantic. Here, even on the calmest days, steep wavelets curl and break over each other, like fugitives driven to desperate flight by some maddening fear, prepared, so great is the terror behind them, to trample on their own comrades in the race for security. One after another all over the bay the wrack-clad backs of rocks appear. Long swathes of brown slimy weed, tugging at submerged roots, lie writhing on the surface of the ebbing streams. The islands grow larger. Confused heaps of round boulders appear under their western bluffs. Cormorants perch in flocks on shining stones, stretching out their narrow wings, peering through tiny black eyes at the withdrawal of the sea. On the eastern shores of every island, stretches of pebble-strewn mud widen rapidly. The boats below the cottages lie dejected, mutely re-reproachful of the anchors which have held them back from following the departed waters. Soft green banks appear here and there, broaden, join one another, until whole stretches of the bay, miles of it, show this pale sea grass instead of water. Only the few deep channels remain, with their foolish stranded buoys and their high useless perches, to witness to the fact that at evening time the sea will claim its own again.

Very wonderful are the changes of the bay. The southwest wind sweeps rain over it in slanting drifts. The islands show dimly grey amid a welter of grey water, breaking angrily in short, petulant seas, which buffet boats confusedly and put the helmsmen's skill to a high test. Or chilly, curling mists wrap islands and promontories from sight. Terns, circling somewhere up above, cry to each other shrilly. Gulls flit suddenly into sight and out of sight again, uttering sorrowful wails. Now and again cormorants, low flying with a rushing noise, break the oily surface of the water with every swift downward flapping of their wings. Then the boatman needs something more than skill, must rely upon an inborn instinct for locality if he is not to find himself embayed and aground in some strange land-locked corner far from his home. Or, in the splendid summer days the islands seem poised a foot or two above the glistening water. The white terns hover and plunge, re-emerge amid the joyful callings of their fellows, each with some tiny silver fish to feed to the yellow chicks which gape to them from the short, coarse grass among the rocks. Curlews call to each other from island to island, and high answering calls come from the sea-saturated fields of the mainland. Small broad billed guillemots and puffins float at ease upon the water, swelling with obvious pride as they display the flocks of little ones which swim with infantile solemnity around them. Gulls cluster and splash noisily over shoals of fry. Then boats drift lazily along; piled high perhaps with brown turf, store of winter fuel for some home; or bearing stolid cattle from the cropped pasturage of one island to the untouched grass of another; or, paddled, noisily, carry a crowd of boys and girls home from school, mightily enriched no doubt with knowledge only to be obtained when the water is calm enough for children's sea-going in the summer days.

On such days all the drama of the flowing and ebbing tides may be watched with ever increasing wonder and delight. The sea is caught by the islands and goes whirling down the channels. It is turned backwards by some stray spit of land and set beating against some other current of the same tide which has taken a different way and reached the same point in strong opposite flow. The little glistening wavelets leap to meet each other, like lovers reunited whose mouths are hungry for the pressure of glad greetings. There are places where the water eddies round and round, where smooth eager lips, rising from the whirlpools, seem as if they reached up for something to kiss, and are sucked down again into the depths with voiceless passion. Foot by foot the water gains on the rocks beside the channels, on the fringes of the boulders, on the stony shores, and covers the stretches of mud:

The moving waters at their priestlike task

Of pale ablution round earth's human shore.

But they do not escape without defilement. On the surface of the tide, when it ebbs from the mudbanks, there gathers an iridescent slime. Tiny particles of floating sand catch and reflect the light. Fragments of dead weed, black or brown, are borne along. The tide has stolen across the beaches below the cottages and carried away the garbage cast there. It has passed where a little while before the cattle strayed, and passing has been stained. Here is no breaking of clear green waves against black defiant rocks, no tumultuous pitched battle between the ocean, inspired by the supreme passion of the tide, and the sullen resistance of unyielding cliffs. Instead a dubious sea wanders in and out amid scenes which the experience of many centuries has not made familiar to it.

It was into this shining bay that the *Tortoise* sped, her white sails bellied with the pleasant wind. Priscilla exulted, with flushed cheeks and sparkling eyes.

Frank, yielding a little to the fascination of the sailing, was yet ill at ease. His conscience troubled him, the acutely sensitive conscience of a prefect who had been responsible for the tone of Edmondstone House. He feared that he had done wrong in going with Priscilla in the *Tortoise*, wrong of a particularly flagrant kind. He thought of himself as a man of responsibility placed in the position of trust. Had he been guilty of a breach of trust? It seemed remotely unlikely, so cheerful and sparkling was the sea, that any accident could possibly occur. But with what feelings could he face a broken and reproachful father should anything happen and Priscilla be drowned? The blame would justly rest on him. The fault would be entirely his.

"Priscilla," he said, "I wish we hadn't come. I ought not to have come when Uncle Lucius has forbidden you to use this boat."

"Oh," said Priscilla, "don't you fret. Father doesn't really mind a bit. He only pretends to, has to, you know, on account of Aunt Juliet He knows jolly well that I can sail the *Tortoise*, any one could."

Frank could not; but Priscilla's tone comforted him a little. Yet his conscience was ill at ease.

"But Miss Lentaigne," he said, "your Aunt Juliet——"

"She'll object, all right, of course," said Priscilla. "If she knew where we are this minute she'd be dead, cock sure that we'd be drowned. She'd probably spend the afternoon planning out nice warm ways of wrapping up our clammy corpses when she got them back. But she doesn't know, so that's all right."

"She will know, this evening. We shall have to tell her."

On one point Frank was entirely decided. Priscilla should neither lure nor drive him into any kind of deceit about the expedition. But Priscilla had no such intention.

"We'll tell her right enough," she said, "when we get home. She'll be pretty mad, of course, inwardly; but she can't *say* much on account of her principles."

"I don't see what her principles have to do with it."

"Don't you? Then you must be rather stupid. Can't you see that if you haven't really got a sprained ankle, but only believe you have, and wouldn't have it if you believed you hadn't, then we shouldn't really be drowned, supposing we were drowned, I mean, which, of course, we're not going to be—if we believed we weren't drowned? And Aunt Juliet, with her principles, would be bound to believe we weren't, even if we were. We've only got to put it to her that way and she won't have a ghost of a grievance left. It's the simplest form of Christian Science. But in any case, whatever silliness Aunt Juliet may indulge in, we were simply bound to have the *Tortoise* today. It's a matter of duty. I don't see how you can get around that, Cousin Frank, no matter how you argue."

Frank did not want to get behind his duty. He had been brought up with a very high regard for the word. If it had been clearly shown him that it was his duty to take an ocean voyage in the *Tortoise*, with Priscilla as leader of the expedition, he would have bidden a long farewell to his friends and gone forth cheerfully. But he did not see that this particular sail, which seemed, indeed, little better than a humiliating, though agreeable, act of truancy, could possibly be sheltered under the name of duty. Priscilla enlightened him.

"I daresay you don't know," she said, "that there is a German spy at the present moment making a chart of this bay. We are hunting him."

There is something intensely stimulating to every healthy mind in the idea of hunting a spy. No prefect in the world, no master even, not Mr. Dupré himself, not the remote divine head-master in the calm Elysium of his garden, could have escaped a thrill at the mention of such a sport. Frank was conscious of a sudden relapse from the serenity of the grown man's common sense. For an instant he became a normal schoolboy.

"Rot!" he said. "What spy?"

"It's not rot," said Priscilla. "You've read 'The Riddle of the Sands,' I suppose. You must have. Well, that's exactly what he's at, mapping out mud-banks and things so as to be able to run a masked flotilla of torpedo boats in and out when the time comes. There was one of the same lot caught the other day sketching a fortification in Lough Swilly. Father read it to me out of a newspaper."

Frank had seen a report of that capture. German spies have of late, been appearing with disquieting frequency. They are met with in the most unlikely places. Frank was a little shaken in his scepticism.

"What makes you say there's a German spy?" he said

"I saw him. So did Peter Walsh. So did Joseph Antony Kinsella. You heard Peter Walsh talking about him this morning. I saw him yesterday. I was bathing at the time and he ran his boat on a rock off the point of Delginish. If it hadn't been for me he'd have been there still, only drowned, of course, for his boat floated away from him. I wish now that I'd left him there, but, of course, I didn't know at the time that he was a spy. That idea only came to me afterwards. I say, Cousin Frank, wouldn't it be absolutely spiffing if it turned out that he really was?"

It was impossible for any one to deny that such a thing would be spiffing in the very highest possible degree.

"If he is," said Priscilla, "and I don't see any reason why he shouldn't—anyhow it's jolly good sport to pretend—and if he is, it's our plain duty to hunt him down at any risk. Sylvia Courtney says that Wordsworth's 'Ode to Duty' is quite the most thrillingly impressive poem in the whole 'Golden Treasury' so you won't want to go back on it."

Frank's prize had been won for Greek Iambics, not for English literature. He was not in a position to discuss the value of Wordsworth's "Ode to Duty" as a guide to conduct in ordinary life.

"My plan," said Priscilla, "is to begin at the south of the bay and work across to the north, investigating every island until we light on the one where he is. That's the reason I had to take the *Tortoise*. The *Blue Wanderer* wouldn't have done it for us. She won't go to windward. But the *Tortoise* is a racing boat. Father bought her cheap at Kingstown because she never won any races, which is the reason why he called her the *Tortoise*. But she can sail faster than Flanagan's old boat, anyhow. And that's the one which the spy has got."

Frank was not inclined to discuss the appropriateness of the *Tortoise's* new name. He was just beginning to recover from the feeling of bewildered annoyance induced by the sudden introduction of Wordsworth's poem into the conversation.

"But what makes you say he's a spy?" he said. "I know there are spies, and I saw about the capture of that one in Lough Swilly. But why should this man be one?"

"I don't say he is," said Priscilla. "All I say is that until we've hunted him down we can't possibly be sure that he isn't. You never can be sure about anything until you've actually tried it. And, anyway, what else can he be? You can't deny that there's some mystery about him. Remember what Peter Walsh said about his looking as innocent as a child. That's the way spies always look. Besides, I don't think his clothes really belonged to him. I could see that at a glance. He had a pair of white flannel trousers with creases down the fronts of the legs, quite as swagger as yours, if not swaggerer, and a white sweater. He didn't look a bit comfortable in them, not as if they were the kind of clothes he was accustomed to wear. That's Rossmore head on the left there, Cousin Frank. He's not there. I didn't expect he would be, and he isn't. I don't expect he's in that bay to the southwest of it either. But we'll just run in a bit and make sure."

The breeze had freshened a little, and the *Tortoise* made good way through the calm water. Frank began to feel some little trust in Priscilla. She handled the boat with an air of confidence which was reassuring. His conscience was troubling him less than it did. There is nothing in the world equal to sailing as a means of quieting anxious consciences. A man may be suffering mental agonies from the recollection of some cruel and cold-blooded murder which he happens to have committed. On land his life would be a burden to him. But let him go down to the sea in a small white sailed ship, and in forty-eight hours or less, he will have ceased to feel any remorse for his victim. This may be the reason why all Protestant nations are maritime powers. Having denied themselves the orthodox anaesthetic of the confessional, these peoples have been obliged to take to the sea as a means of preventing their consciences from harrying them. Driven forth across the waves by the clamorous importunity of the voice within, they, of very necessity, acquire a certain skill in the management of boats, a skill which sooner or later leads to the burdensome possession of a navy and so to maritime importance. It is interesting to see how this curious law works out in quite modern times.

The Italian navy is now considerable, but it has only become so since the people were driven to the sea as a consequence of the anti-clerical feeling which led them to desert the confessional. It is quite possible that the Portuguese, having in their new Republic developed a strong antipathy to sacraments and so laid up for themselves a future of spiritual disquiet, may see their ancient maritime glories revived, and in seeking relief beyond the mouth of the Tagus from the gnawings of their consciences, may give birth to some reincarnation of Vasco da Gama or Prince Henry, the Navigator.

"I don't think," said Priscilla, looking round her searchingly, "that he's anywhere in this bay. How's your ankle?"

"It's quite comfortable," said Frank.

"I asked," said Priscilla, "because in order to get out of the bay I shall have to jibe, and that means that you've got to hop across the centreboard case."

Frank had not the least idea of what happens when a small boat jibes. He intended to ask for information, but was not given any opportunity. The boom, which had hitherto behaved with dignity and self-possession, suddenly swung across the boat with such swiftness that he had no time to duck his head to avoid it. His straw hat, struck on the brim, was swept over the side of the boat. He found himself thrown down against the gunwale, while a quantity of cold water poured over his legs. He grasped the centreboard case, the nearest stable thing at hand, and pulled himself up again into the middle of the boat. Priscilla, a good deal tangled in a writhing rope, was struggling past the tiller to the windward side.

"What's happened?" asked Frank.

"Jibed all standing," said Priscilla. "I didn't mean to, of course. I must have been sailing her by the lee. But it's all right. We didn't ship more than a bucketful. I say, I'm rather sorry about your hat; but that's a rotten kind of hat in a boat anyway. Would you mind getting up to windward? I've got to luff her a bit and she'll heel over."

"Is it gone?"

"What? Oh, the hat. Yes, quite. We couldn't get it without jibing again."

"Don't let us do that," said Frank, "if we can help it.

"I won't. But do get up to windward. That is to say if your ankle's not too bad. I must luff a bit or we'll go ashore. The water's getting very shallow."

Frank scrambled over the centreboard case and bumped down on the floor boards on the windward side of the boat Priscilla pushed over the tiller and began to haul vigorously on the main sheet. The *Tortoise* swept round, heeled over and rushed through the water on a broad reach. The wind, so it seemed to Frank, began to blow much harder than before. He clung to the weather stay and watched the bubbling water tear past within an inch or two of the lower gunwale. A sudden spasm of extreme nervousness seized him. He looked anxiously at Priscilla. She seemed to be entirely calm and self-possessed. His self-respect reasserted itself. He remembered that she was merely a girl. He set his teeth and determined to show no sign of fear. Gradually the exhilaration of the motion, the coolness of the breeze through his hair, the dancing, impulsive rush of the boat, and the shining white of the sail in front of him conquered his qualms. He began to enjoy himself as he had never in his life enjoyed himself before.

"I say, Priscilla," he said, "this is fine."

"Topping," said Priscilla.

The feel of the cricket ball caught clean in the centre of the bat, sent in one clear flight to square leg across the boundary line, is glorious. Frank knew the exultation of such moments. The dash across the goal line from a swiftly taken pass is a thing to live for. Frank, as a fast three-quarter back, knew that too. But this tearing of a heeling boat through bubbling green water became to him, when he got over the first terror of it, a delirious joy.

"That's Inishminna ahead of us to windward," said Priscilla. "Flanagan lives there, who hired him the old boat. He might be there, but he isn't. I can see the whole slope of the island. We'll slip under the lee of the end of it past Illaunglos. It's a likely enough island."

Frank suddenly remembered that they were in pursuit of a German spy. The remainder of his scepticism forsook him. Amid such surroundings, with the singing of the wind and the gurgling swish of the flying boat in his ears, any adventure seemed possible. The prosaic limitations of ordinary life dropped off from him. Only it seemed a pity to find the spy, since finding him would stop their sailing.

"I say, Priscilla," he said. "Don't let us bother about the old spy. Let's go on sailing."

"Just hunker down a bit," said Priscilla, "and look under the foot of the sail. I can't see to leeward. Is there anything like a tent on that island?"

Frank curled himself into a cramped and difficult attitude. He peered under the sail and made his report.

"There's nothing there," he said, "except three bullocks. But I can only see two sides of the island."

"We'll open the north side in a minute," said Priscilla. "He can't be at the west end of it, for it is all bluff and boulders. If he isn't on the north shore he's not there at all.

Frank twisted himself again into the bottom of the boat, and peeped under the sail. The north shore of Illaunglos held no tent.

"Good," said Priscilla. "Well stand on. The next island is Inishark. He may be there. There's a well on it, and he'd naturally want to camp somewhere within reach of water."

Frank, still curled up beside the centreboard case, gazed under the sail at Inishark. The boat, swaying and dipping in a still freshening breeze, sped on.

"Is there any large white stone on the ridge of the island?" he asked.

"No," said Priscilla. "There isn't a white stone of any size in the whole bay. It's most likely a sheep."

"It's not a sheep. Nobody ever saw a sheep with a back that went up into a point. I believe it's the top of a tent. Steer for it, Priscilla."

Frank was aglow with excitement. The sailing intoxicated him. The sight of the triangular apex of the tent put himself beside himself.

"Turn the boat, Priscilla. Go down to the island."

Priscilla was cooler.

"We'll hold on a minute," she said, "and make sure. There's no use running all that way down to leeward until we're certain. We'd only have to beat up again."

"It is a tent," said Frank. "I can see now. There are two tents."

Priscilla caught his excitement She knelt on the floor boards, crooked her elbow over the tiller, leaned over the side of the boat and stared under the sail at the island.

"That's him," she said. "Now, Cousin Frank, we'll have to jibe again to get down there. Do you think you can be a bit nippier in getting over the centreboard than you were last time. It's blowing harder, and it won't do to upset. You very nearly had us over before."

Frank was too excited to notice that she now put the whole blame of the sudden violence of the last jibe on him. Thinking over the matter afterwards, he remembered that she had apologised at the time for her own bad steering. Now she wanted to hold his awkwardness responsible for what might have been a disaster.

"All right," he said, "All right I'll do whatever you tell me."

"I won't risk it," said Priscilla. "You'd mean to do all right, but you wouldn't when the time came. That ankle of yours, you know. After all, it's just as easy to run her up into the wind and stay her."

"There's a man at the door of one of the tents looking at us through a pair of glasses," said Frank.

"Let him," said Priscilla.

She was hauling in the main sheet as the boat swept up into the wind.

"Now, Cousin Frank, ready about. You must slack off the jib sheet and haul down the other. That thin rope at your hand. Yes, that's it."

The meaning of this new manoeuvre was dim and uncertain to Frank. He grasped the rope indicated to him and then heard a noise as if some one at the bottom of the sea, an angry mermaid perhaps, was striking the keel of the boat hard with a hammer.

"She's touching," said Priscilla. "Up centreboard, quick."

Frank gazed at her in pained bewilderment. He had not the least idea of what she wanted him to do. The knocking at the boat's bottom became more frequent and violent. Priscilla gave the main sheet a turn round a cleat and stretched forward, holding the tiller with her left hand. She grasped a rope, one out of a tangled web of wet ropes, and tugged. The knocking ceased. The boat swept up into the wind. There was a sudden arrest of movement, a violent list over, a dart forward, a soft crunching sound, and then a dead stop.

"Bother," said Priscilla, "we're aground."

She sprang overboard at once, stood knee deep in the water, and tugged at the stern of the boat The centreboard, when she dropped its rope, fell to the bottom of its case, caught in the mud under the boat, and anchored her immovably. Priscilla tugged in vain.

"It's no good," she said at last, "and the tide's ebbing. We're here for hours and hours. I hope you didn't hurt your ankle, Cousin Frank, during that fray."

CHAPTER VII

"That fellow is still looking at us through his glasses," said Frank.

"Can't help it," said Priscilla, "If it amuses him he can go on looking at us for the next four hours."

She gathered her dripping skirt round her and stepped into the boat

"Sylvia Courtney," she said, "told me last term that her favorite poem in English literature, is 'Gray's Elegy' on account of it's being so full of calm. Sometimes I think that Sylvia Courtney is rather a beast."

"She must be a rotter," said Frank, "if she said that."

"All the same, there's no use our fretting ourselves into a fuss. We can't get out of this unless we had the wings of a dove, so we may as well take the sails off the boat."

She climbed across Frank, loosed the halyard and brought the lug down into the boat with a sudden run. Frank was buried in the folds of it. After some struggling he got his head out and breathed freely.

"I say, Priscilla," he said, "why didn't you tell me you were going to do that?"

Priscilla was gathering the foresail in her arms.

"I thought you knew," she said.

"I didn't know the beastly thing was going to come down on my head."

"That fellow on the island," said Priscilla, "is getting down his tents and seems to be in a mighty hurry. He's got a woman helping him. Do you think she could be a female spy? There are such things. They carry secret ciphers sewn into their stays and other things of that kind."

"I don't believe they're spies at all," said Frank, who was feeling dishevelled and uncomfortable after his struggle with the sail.

"Anyhow they seem pretty keen on getting away from Inishark. Just look at them."

There was no doubt that the people on the island were doing their best to strike their camp as quickly as possible. In their hurry they stumbled over guy ropes, got the fly sheet of one of their tents badly tangled round a packing case, and made the matter worse by trying to free it without proper consideration.

"Let them fuss," said Priscilla. "We can't help it if they do get away. If your ankle isn't too bad we might as well have lunch. You grub out the food when I get off my shoes and stockings, I'm a bit damp about the legs."

Frank felt under the thwart through which the mast was stepped and drew out one by one the parcel of macaroons, the tongue, the tin of peaches and the bottles. Priscilla wrung out her stockings over the stern of the boat and then hung them on the gunwale to dry. She propped her shoes up against the stern where they would get as much breeze as possible.

"I wish," said Frank, "that we'd thought of getting some bread."

"Why? Don't you like macaroons?"

"I like them all right, but they don't go very well with tongue."

"We'll begin with the tongue, then, and keep the macaroons till afterwards. Hand it over."

She took a rowlock and shattered the jar which held the tongue. She succeeded in throwing some of the broken glass overboard. A good deal more of it stuck in the tongue.

"What I generally do," she said, "when I'm out in the *Blue Wanderer* by myself and happen to have a tongue, which isn't often on account of their being so beastly expensive—but whenever I have I simply bite bits off it as I happen to want them. But I know that's not polite. If you prefer it, Cousin Frank, you can gouge out a chunk or two with your knife before I gnaw it."

This seemed to Frank a good suggestion. He got out his knife.

"Sylvia Courtney is always frightfully polite," said Priscilla.

Frank hesitated. The recollection of Sylvia Courtney's appreciation of Wordsworth's "Ode to Duty" and her fondness for "Gray's Elegy" for the sake of its calm came to him. He would not be classed with her. He put his knife back into his pocket and bit a small bit off the tongue. Then he leaned over the side of the boat and spat out a good deal of broken glass. He also spat out some blood.

"That seems to be rather a glassy bit you've got," said Priscilla. "Are you cut?"

"A little," said Frank, "but it doesn't matter."

Priscilla bit off a large mouthful and handed the tongue back to Frank. Her cheeks bulged a good deal, but she chewed without any appearance of discomfort. Frank had read in books about "the call of the wild." He now, for the first time, felt the lust for savage life. He took the tongue, tore off a fragment with his teeth, and discovered as he ate it, that he was exceedingly hungry.

"Your lemonade bottle," he said, a few minutes later, "has one of those glass stoppers in it instead of a cork. How shall I open it?"

"Shank of a rowlock," said Priscilla. "Those spies on the island have got their tents down at last. They're packing up now."

Frank opened the lemonade bottle and then glanced at the island. The female spy was packing a holdall. Her companion was staggering down the beach towards the place where Flanagan's old boat lay high and dry on her side. He carried the packing case on his shoulder. Priscilla, tilting her head back, drank the lemonade from its bottle in large gulps. Then she opened the parcel of biscuits and munched a macaroon contentedly.

"It's dashed annoying," said Frank, "having to sit here and watch them escape, just as we had them cornered too."

The inside of his lip hurt him a good deal while he ate. He wanted to grumble about something; but the fear of being compared to Sylvia Courtney kept him silent about the broken glass. Priscilla took another macaroon.

"We were doing Wordsworth's 'Excursion' last term," she said, "in English literature, and there's a long tract of it called 'Despondency Corrected.' I wish I had it here now. It's just what would do you good."

Frank nibbled a biscuit with his eyes on the island. The man was carrying down a bundle of rugs to the boat. The woman followed him with one of the tents. Then they went back together to their camping ground and collected a number of small objects which were scattered about. Frank became desperate.

"Priscilla," he said, "don't you think you could wade across to that island. There's only about an inch and a half of water round the boat now. I'd do it myself if it wasn't for this infernal ankle. I simply can't walk."

"I could," said Priscilla, "and what's more, I would, only that there's a deep channel between us and them. If I'd jibed that time instead of trying to stay her I should have kept in the channel and not run on to this bank. I knew it was here all right, but I forgot it just at the moment. That's the worst of moments. They simply make one forget things, however hard one tries not to. I daresay you've noticed that."

Frank had as a matter of fact noticed this peculiarity of moments very often. It had turned up in the course of his experience both on cricket and football fields. But it seemed to him that the consequences of being entrapped by it were much more serious in sailing boats than elsewhere. He was so far from blaming Priscilla for the plight of the *Tortoise* that he felt very grateful to her for not blaming him. His moment had come when she gave him the order about the centreboard. Then not only memory, but all power of coherent thought had deserted him.

"Let's have at the Californian peaches," said Priscilla. "But we'd better eat a bit slower now that the first pangs of hunger are allayed. If we hurry up too much we'll have no food left soon and we have absolutely nothing else to do except to eat until five o'clock this afternoon. We can't expect to get off before that."

The spies packed their belongings into Flanagan's old boat and then set to work to push her down to the sea. Frank, with the point of the opener driven through the top of the peach tin, paused to watch them. They shoved and pulled vainly. The boat remained where she was. Frank began to hope that they, too, might have to wait for the rising tide. They sat down on a large stone and consulted together. Then they took everything out of the boat and tried pushing and pulling her again. Her weight was still too great for them. They moved her forward in short jerks, but each time they moved her the keel at her stern buried itself deeper in the soft mud. They sat down, evidently somewhat exhausted, and had another consultation. Then the man got the oars and laid them out as rollers. He lifted the boat's stern on to the first of them.

"I thought," said Priscilla, "that they'd hit on that dodge sooner or later. Now they'll get on a bit. Go on scalping the peach tin, Cousin Frank."

The peaches had been cut in half by the kindly Californian who preserved them and a half peach fits, with a little squeezing, into any mouth of ordinary size. Priscilla and Frank fished them out with their fingers and ate them. Some juice, but considering the circumstances very little, dripped down the front of Frank's white flannel coat, the glorious crimson bound coat of the first eleven. He did not care in the least. He had lapsed hopelessly. No urchin in the lower school, brewing cocoa over a form room fire, ladling out condensed milk with the blade of a penknife, would have been more dead to the decencies of life than this degenerate hero of the lower sixth.

"They're getting the boat down," said Priscilla, swallowing a lump of peach. "Do you think that you could throw stones far enough to hit them when they get out into the channel? I'd grub up the stones for you. We might frighten them back that way."

Frank had won second prize in the sports at the end of the Easter term for throwing the cricket ball. He looked across the stretch of water and judged the distance carefully.

"No," he said, regretfully, "I couldn't."

"That's a pity," said Priscilla, "for I can't, either. I never could shy worth tuppence. Curious, isn't it? Hardly any girls can."

The spies had got old Flanagan's boat down to the water's edge. They went back to the place where she had lain first. By a series of laborious portages they got all their goods down to the beach and packed them into the boat.

"They're off now," said Frank, regretfully.

"I wouldn't be too sure," said Priscilla. "That fellow's an extraordinary ass with a boat."

Her optimism was well founded. By shoving hard the spies ran their boat into the water. The lady spy stopped at the brink. The man, with reckless indifference to wet feet, followed the boat, still shoving. It happens that the shore of the north side of Inishark shelves very rapidly into the deep channel. The boat floated suddenly, and urged by the violence of the last shove, slid rapidly from the shore. The man grasped at her. His fingers slid along the gunwale. He plunged forward knee-deep, snatched at the retreating bow, missed it, stumbled and fell headlong into the water. The boat floated free and swung into the channel on the tide.

Priscilla leaped up excitedly.

"Now they're done," she said. "They're far worse stuck than we are."

"Oh, do look at him," said Frank, "Did you ever see anything so funny?"

The man staggered to his feet and floundered towards the shore, squeezing the salt water from his eyes with his knuckles.

"Of course, I'm sorry for the poor beast in a way," said Priscilla, "but I can't help feeling that it jolly well serves him right. Oh, look at them now!"

She laughed convulsively. The scene was sufficiently ridiculous. The spy stood dripping forlornly, on the shore. The lady dabbed at various parts of his clothing with her pocket-handkerchief. Flanagan's old boat, now fairly in mid-channel, bobbed cheerfully along on the ebbing tide.

"I'd give a lot this minute," said Priscilla, "for a pair of glasses. I can't think why I was such a fool as not to take father's when we were starting."

"I can see well enough," said Frank. "What I'd like would be to be able to hear what he's saying."

"I don't take any interest in bad language, and in any case I don't believe he's capable of it. He looked to me like the kind of man who wouldn't say anything much worse than 'Dear me.'"

"Wouldn't he? Look at him now. If he isn't cursing I'll eat my hat."

The spy had shaken himself free of his companion's pocket handkerchief. He was waving his arms violently and shouting so loudly that his voice reached the *Tortoise* against the wind.

"I suppose," said Priscilla, "that that's his way of trying to get dry without catching a chill. Horrid ass, isn't he? It'd be far better for him to run. What's the good of yelling? I expect in reality it's simply temper."

But Priscilla underestimated the intelligence of the spy. It appeared very soon that he was not merely giving expression to emotion, but had a purpose in his performance. The lady, too, began to shout, shrilly. She waved her damp pocket handkerchief round and round her head. Priscilla and Frank turned and saw that another boat, a small black boat, with a very dilapidated lug sail, had appeared round the corner of the next island, and was making towards Inishark.

"Bother," said Priscilla, "that man, whoever he is, will bring them back their boat."

The steersman in the lug-sailed boat altered his course slightly and reached down towards the derelict. As he neared her he dropped his sail and got out oars.

"That's young Kinsella," said Priscilla. "I know him by the red sleeve his mother sewed into that gray shirt of his. No one else has a shirt the least like it. He's a soft-hearted sort of boy who'd do a good turn to any one. He's sure to take their boat back to them."

"He has a lady with him," said Frank.

"He has. I can't see who she is; but it doesn't look like his mother. Can't be, in fact, for she has a baby to mind. I collared a lot of flannel out of a box in Aunt Juliet's room last 'hols' and gave it to her for the baby. It's a bit of what I gave her that was made into a sleeve for Jimmy's shirt. I wonder now who it is he has got with him?"

Jimmy Kinsella overtook the drifting boat, took her painter, and began to tow her towards Inishark.

"That lady," said Priscilla, "is a black stranger to me. Who can she possibly be?"

Jimmy Kinsella rowed hard, and in about ten minutes ran his own boat aground on Inishark. He disembarked, dragged at the painter of Flanagan's boat and handed her over to the lady on the island. A long conversation followed. The whole party, Jimmy Kinsella, his lady, the dripping spy, and the original lady with the damp pocket handkerchief, consulted together eagerly. Then they took the hold-all out of Flanagan's boat. There was another conversation, and it became plain that the two ladies were expostulating with the dripping gentleman. Jimmy Kinsella stood a little apart and gazed placidly at the two boats. Then the hold-all was unpacked and a number of garments laid out on the beach. They were sorted out and a bundle of them handed to the spy. He walked straight up the slope of the island and disappeared over the crest of the hill.

"Gone to change his clothes," said Priscilla.

The two ladies repacked the hold-all. Jimmy Kinsella stowed it in the bow of Flanagan's boat. Then the lady of the island got it out again, unpacked it once more, and took something out of it.

"Clean pocket-handkerchief, I expect," said Priscilla.

The guess was evidently a good one, for she spread the wet handkerchief on a stone. Her companion reappeared over the crest of the island, clad in another pair of white trousers and another sweater. He carried his wet garments at arm's length. Jimmy Kinsella went to meet him. They talked together as they walked down to the boats. Then the two ladies kissed each other warmly. Priscilla watched the performance with a sneer.

"Awful rot, that kind of thing," she said.

"All women do it," said Frank.

Here at last he was unquestionably Priscilla's superior. Never, to his recollection, had he kissed any one except his mother, and he was generally content to allow her to kiss him.

"I don't; Sylvia Courtney tried it on with me when we were saying good-bye at the end of last term, but I jolly soon choked her off. Can't think where the pleasure is supposed to come in."

Jimmy Kinsella placed the spy lady in the stern of Flanagan's boat and handed in her companion. He arranged the oars and the rowlocks and then, standing ankle deep in the water, shoved her off. The spy took his oars and pulled away. Priscilla and Frank watched the boat until she disappeared.

"Pretty rough luck on us," said Priscilla, "Jimmy Kinsella turning up just at that moment. I wonder if that woman is a man in disguise. She might be, you know. They sometimes are."

"Couldn't possibly. No man would have been such a fool as to go trying to dry anybody with a pocket handkerchief. Only a woman——"

"If it comes to that," said Priscilla, "no woman would have been such a fool as to let that boat go the way he did. Girls aren't the only asses in the world, Cousin Frank."

"Besides," said Frank, "she evidently took a lot of trouble to persuade him to change his clothes. That looks as if——"

"It does, rather. I daresay she's his aunt. It's just the kind of thing Aunt Juliet would have done before she took to Christian Science. Now, of course, it would be against her principles. Let's have another Californian peach to fill in the time."

Frank handed the tin to her and afterwards helped himself.

"Have you drunk all your beer, Cousin Frank?"

"No. Want some?"

"I was only thinking," said Priscilla, "that perhaps you'd better not. I've just recollected King John."

"What about him?"

"It was peaches and beer that finished him off, after he'd got stuck in crossing the Wash. That's rather the sort of position we're in now, and I shouldn't like anything to happen to you."

Frank, by way of demonstrating his courage, took a long draught of lager beer, then he looked across at Inishark. Priscilla's eyes followed his. For a minute or two they gazed in silence.

Jimmy Kinsella's boat still lay on the shore. Jimmy Kinsella's lady had taken off her shoes and stockings and rolled up the sleeves of her blouse. Her skirt was kilted high and folded over a broad band which kept it well above her knees. Jimmy Kinsella himself, who was modest as well as chivalrous, sat on a stone with his back to her and gazed at the slope of the island. The lady waded about in the shallow water. Now and then she plunged her arms in and appeared to fish something up from the bottom. Priscilla and Frank looked at each other in amazement.

"I wonder what on earth's she's doing," said Priscilla. "Can she possibly be taking soundings?"

"No," said Frank. "Soundings aren't taken that way. You do it with a line and a lead from the deck of a ship."

"All the same," said Priscilla, "she's in league with the other spies. You saw the way they kissed each other."

"She may," said Frank, "be taking specimens of the sea bottom. That's a very important thing, I believe."

"It is, frightfully; but that's not the way it's done. There was a curious old johnny last term who gave us a lecture on hydrography—that's what he called it—and he said you gather up small bits of the bottom by putting tallow on the end of a lump of lead. I expect he knew what he was talking about, but, of course, he may not. You never can tell about those scientific lecturers. They keep on contradicting each other so."

"If she's not doing that, what is she doing?"

"She may possibly be trying to cure her rheumatism," said Priscilla. "They generally bathe for that; but she may not feel bad enough to go to such extremes. She looks rather fat. Fat people do have rheumatism, don't they?"

"No, gout."

"More or less the same thing," said Priscilla. "Of course, if that's what she's at, she's not a spy, and we oughtn't to go on treating her as if she was. I don't think it's right to suspect people of really bad crimes unless one knows. Do you, Cousin Frank?"

"Of course not. All the same, the way she's going on is rather queer. She's just put something that she picked up into that tin box she has slung across her back. That doesn't look to me as if she had gout."

"If only Jimmy Kinsella would turn this way," said Priscilla, "I'd wave at him and make him come over here. It's perfectly maddening being stuck like this when such a lot of exciting things are going on. What time is it?"

"A little after two."

"It's low water then," said Priscilla. "From this on the tide will be coming in again."

The *Tortoise* lay on the top of a grey bank from which the water had entirely receded. Between her and the channel, now a tangle of floating weed, lay a broad stretch of mud, dotted over with large stones and patches of gravel. The wind, which had been veering round to the south since twelve o'clock, had almost entirely died away. The sun shone very warmly.

The *Tortoise*, lying sadly on her side, afforded no shelter at all. Both the beer and the lemonade were finished.

Priscilla drank some peach juice from the tin.

CHAPTER VIII

After wading about for a little more than half an hour, Jimmy Kineslla's lady went ashore. She rolled down the sleeves of her blouse and let her skirt fall about her ankles, but she did not put on her shoes and stockings. Jimmy Kinsella was summoned from his stone and launched his boat.

"I daresay," said Priscilla, "that she thinks her rheumatism ought to be cured by now. That is to say, of course, if she really has rheumatism, and isn't a nefarious spy. I rather like that word nefarious. Don't you? I stuck it into an English comp. the other day and spelt it quite right, but it came back to me with a blue pencil mark under it. Sylvia Courtney said that I hadn't used it in quite the ordinary sense. She thinks she knows, and very likely she does, though not quite as much as she imagines. Nobody can know everything; which is rather a comfort when it comes to algebra. I loath algebra and always did. Any right-minded person would, I think."

"It looks to me," said Frank, "as if they were coming over here."

Jimmy Kinsella was heading his boat straight for the bank on which the *Tortoise* lay. In a few minutes she grounded on the edge of it. The lady stepped out and paddled across the mud towards the *Tortoise*. Seen at close quarters she was, without doubt, fat, and had a round good-humoured face. Her eyes sparkled pleasantly behind a pair of gold rimmed pince-nez.

"She is coming over to us," said Priscilla. "The thing is for you to keep her in play and unravel her mystery, while I slip off and put a few straight questions to Jimmy Kinsella. Be as polite as you possibly can so as to disarm suspicion."

Priscilla began the course of diplomatic politeness herself.

"We're delighted to see you," she said. "My name is Priscilla Lentaigne, and my cousin is Frank Mannix. We're out for a picnic."

"My name," said the lady, "is Rutherford, Martha Rutherford. I'm out after sponges."

"Sponges!" said Frank.

Priscilla winked at him. The statement about the sponges was obviously untrue. There is no sponge fishery in Rosnacree Bay. There never has been. Miss Rutherford, so to speak, intercepted Priscilla's wink.

"By sponges," she said, "I mean——"

"Won't you sit down?" said Priscilla.

She picked her stockings from the gunwale of the boat, leaving a clear space beside Miss Rutherford.

"Bother!" she said, "the dye out of the purple clocks has run. That's the worst of purple clocks. I half suspected it would at the time, but Sylvia Courtney insisted on my buying them. She said they looked chic. Would you care for anything to eat, Miss Rutherford?"

"I'm nearly starved. That's why I came over here. I thought you might have some food."

"We've lots," said Priscilla. "Frank will give it to you. I'll just step across and speak to Jimmy Kinsella. I want to hear about the baby."

"I'm afraid," said Miss Rutherford, when Priscilla left them, "that your cousin doesn't believe me about the sponges."

Frank felt deeply ashamed of Priscilla's behaviour. The prefect in him reasserted itself now that he was in the presence of a grown-up lady. He felt it necessary to apologise.

"She's very young," he said, "and I'm afraid she's rather foolish. Little girls of that age——"

He intended to say something of a paternal kind, something which would give Miss Rutherford the impression that he had kindly undertaken the care of Priscilla during the day in order to oblige those ordinarily responsible for her. A curious smile, which began to form at the corners of Miss Rutherford's lips and a sudden twinkling of her eyes, stopped him abruptly.

"I hope you'll excuse my not standing up," he said, "I've sprained my ankle."

"I'd like to get in and sit beside you if I may," said Miss Rutherford. "Now for the food."

"There's some cold tongue," said Frank.

"Capital. I love cold tongue."

"But—I'm afraid—" He fished it out from beneath the thwart, "—it may be rather grubby."

"I don't mind that a bit."

"And—the fact is my cousin—it's only fair to tell you—she bit it pretty nearly all over and——" Frank hesitated. He was an honourable boy. Even at the cost of losing Miss Rutherford's respect he would not refrain from telling the truth, "And I bit it too," he blurted out.

"Then I suppose I may," said Miss Rutherford. "I should like to more than anything. I so seldom get the chance."

She bit and munched heartily; bit again, and smiled at Frank. He began to feel more at his ease.

"There are some biscuits," he said. "The macaroons are finished, I'm afraid. But there are some cocoanut creams. I'm afraid they're rather too sweet to go well with tongue."

"In the state of starvation I'm in," she said, "marmalade would go with pea soup. Cocoanut creams and tongue will be simply delicious. Have you anything to drink?"

"Only the juice of the tinned peaches."

"Peach juice," said Miss Rutherford, "is nectar. Do I drink it out of the tin or must I pour it into the palm of my hand and lap?"

"Any way you like," said Frank. "I believe there's a bailer somewhere if you prefer it."

"I prefer the tin, if it doesn't shock you."

"Oh," said Frank, "nothing shocks me."

This was very nearly true. It had not been true a week before; but a day on the sea with Priscilla had done a great deal for Frank. Miss Rutherford threw her head back, tilted the peach tin, and quaffed a satisfying draught.

"I'm afraid," she said, "that you were just as sceptical as your cousin was about my sponges."

"I was rather surprised."

"Naturally. You were thinking of bath sponges and naked Indians plunging over the side of their boats with large stones in their hands to sink them. But I'm not after bath sponges. I'm doing the zoophytes for the natural history survey of this district."

"Oh," said Frank vaguely.

"They brought me over from the British Museum because I'm supposed to know something about the zoophytes. I ought to, for I don't know anything else."

"It must be most interesting."

"Last week I did the fresh water lakes and got some very good results. Professor Wilder and his wife are doing rotifers. They're stopping——"

"In tents?" said Frank with interest.

"Tents! No. In quite the sweetest cottage you ever saw. I sleep on a sofa in the porch. What put tents into your head?"

"Then it wasn't Professor Wilder and his wife whose boat you rescued just now?"

"Oh, dear no. I don't know who those people are at all. I never saw them before. Miss Benson is doing the lichens, and Mr. Farringdon the moths. They're the only other members of our party here at present, and I'm the only one out on the bay."

Frank was conscious of a sense of relief. It would have been a disappointment to him if the German spies had turned out to be harmless botanists or entomologists.

Jimmy Kinsella was sitting in front of his boat gazing placidly at the sea when Priscilla tapped him on the shoulder.

"What are you doing here, Jimmy?" she said.

"Is that yourself, Miss?" said Jimmy, eyeing her quietly.

"It is. And the only other person present is you. Now we've got that settled."

Jimmy Kinsella grinned.

"I thought it was the *Tortoise* when I saw her; but I said to myself 'There's strangers on board of her, for Miss Priscilla would know better than to run her aground on the bank when the tide would be leaving her.'"

"You haven't told me yet," said Priscilla, "what you're doing here."

"I'm out along with the lady beyond."

"I could see that much for myself. What's she doing?"

"Without she'd be trying the salt water for the good of her health, I don't know what she's doing."

"I thought at first that it might be that," said Priscilla. "Has she any sponges with her?"

"Not that I seen, Miss. But sure none of them would take a sponge with them into the sea. They get plenty of it without that."

"I just thought she hadn't."

"If I was to be put on my oath," said Jimmy slowly, "and was to be asked what I thought of her——"

"That's just what I am asking you."

"I'd say she was a high up lady; may be one of them ones that does be waiting on the Queen, or the wife of the Lord Lieutenant or such."

"What makes you say that?"

"The skin of her."

Jimmy's eyes which had been fixed on the remote horizon focussed themselves slowly for nearer objects. His glance settled finally on Priscilla's bare feet.

"Ah!" she said, "when she took off her shoes and stockings?"

"Saving your presence, Miss, the legs of her doesn't look as if she was accustomed to going about that way."

"And that's all you know about her?"

"Herself and a gentleman that was along with her settled with my da yesterday for the use of the boat, the way I'd row her anywhere she'd a fancy to go."

"That was the gentleman who has Flanagan's old boat, I suppose?"

"It was not then, but a different gentleman altogether."

"Then you can leave him out," said Priscilla, "and tell me all you know about the other couple, the ones who lost their boat."

"Them ones," said Jimmy, "has no sense, no more than a baby would have. Did you hear what they're after paying Flanagan for that old boat of his?"

"Four pounds a week."

"You'd think," said Jimmy, "that when they'd no more care for their money than to be throwing it away that way they'd be able to afford to pay for a roof over their heads and not to be sleeping on the bare ground with no more than a cotton rag to shelter them. It was last Friday they came in to Inishbawn looking mighty near as if they'd had enough of it. 'Is there any objection,' says he, 'to our camping on this island?' 'We'll pay you,' says the lady, 'anything in reason for the use of the land.' My da was terrible sorry for them, for he could see well that they weren't ones that was used to hardship; but he told them that it would be better for them not."

"On account of the rats?"

"Rats! What rats?"

"The rats that have the island very nearly eaten," said Priscilla.

"Sorra the rat ever I saw on Inishbawn, only one that came out in the boat one day along with a sack of yellow meal my da was bringing home from the quay; and I killed it myself with the slap of a loy."

"I just thought Peter Walsh was telling me a lie about the rats," said Priscilla. "But if it wasn't rats will you tell me why your father wouldn't let them camp on Inishbawn?"

"He said it would be better for them not," said Jimmy, "on account of there being fever on it, for fear they might catch it and maybe die."

"What fever?"

"I don't rightly know the name of it; but sure my ma is covered thick with yellow spots the size of a sixpence or bigger; and the young lads is worse. The cries of them at night would make you turn round on your bed pitying them."

"Do you expect me to believe all that?" said Priscilla.

"Three times my da was in for the doctor," said Jimmy, "and the third time he fetched out a powerful fine bottle that he bought in Brannigan's, but it was no more use to them than water. Is it likely now that he'd allow a strange lady and a gentleman to come to the island, and them not knowing? He wouldn't do it for a hundred pounds."

"If you're going on talking that kind of way there's not much use my asking you any more questions. But I'd like very much to know where those camping people are now."

"I shouldn't wonder," said Jimmy, "but they're drowned. The planks of that old boat of Flanagan's is opened so as you could see the daylight in between every one of them, and it would take a man with a can to be bailing the whole time you'd be going anywhere in her; let alone that the gentleman——"

"I know what the gentleman is in a boat," said Priscilla.

"And herself is no better. It was only this morning my ma was saying to me that it's wonderful the little sense them ones has."

"I thought," said Priscilla, "that your mother was out all over yellow spots. What does she know about them?"

Jimmy Kinsella grinned sheepishly.

"Believe you me, Miss," he said, "if it was only yourself that was in it——"

"There'd be neither rats nor fever on the island, I suppose."

Jimmy looked towards the *Tortoise* and let his eyes rest with an inquiring expression on Frank Mannix.

"That gentleman's ankle is sprained," said Priscilla, "so whatever it is that you have on your island, you needn't be afraid of him."

"That might be," said Jimmy.

"You can tell your father from me," said Priscilla, "that the next time I'm out this way I'll land on Inish-bawn and see for myself what it is that has you all telling lies."

"Any time you come, Miss, you'll be welcome. It's a poor place we have, surely, but it would be a queer thing if we wouldn't give you the best of what might be going. But I don't know how it is. There's a powerful lot of strangers knocking around, people that might be decent or might not."

His eyes were still fixed on Frank Mannix when Priscilla left him.

The tide was flowing strongly and the water began to cover the lower parts of the bank. Priscilla measured with her eye the distance between the *Tortoise* and the sea. She calculated that she might get off in about an hour.

When she reached the *Tortoise* she found Frank pressing the last half peach on their guest.

"Miss Rutherford," said Priscilla, "have you landed on Inishbawn, that island to the west of you, behind the corner of Illaunglos?"

"No," she said. "I wanted to, but the boy who's rowing me strongly advised me not to."

"Rats?" Said Priscilla, "or fever?"

Miss Rutherford seemed puzzled by the inquiry.

"What I mean," said Priscilla, "is this: did he give you any reason for not landing on the island?"

"As well as I recollect," said Miss Rutherford, "he said something to the effect that it wasn't a suitable island for ladies. I didn't take much notice of what he said, for it didn't matter to me where I landed. One of the islands is the same thing as another. In fact Inishbawn, if that's its name, doesn't look a very good place for sponges."

"Oh, you still stick to those sponges?" said Priscilla.

"Miss Rutherford," said Frank, "is collecting zoophytes for the British Museum."

"Investigating and tabulating," said Miss Rutherford, "for the Royal Dublin Society's Natural History Survey."

"I took up elementary science last term," said Priscilla, "but we didn't do about those things of yours. I daresay we'll get on to them next year. If we do I'll write to you for the names of some of the rarer kinds and score off Miss Pennycolt with them. She's the science teacher, and she thinks she knows a lot. It'll do her good to be made to look small over a sponge that she's never seen before, or even heard of."

"I'll send them to you," said Miss Rutherford. "I take the greatest delight in scoring off science teachers everywhere. I was taught science myself at one time and I know exactly what it's like."

Jimmy Kinsella sat on a stone with his back to the party in the *Tortoise*. An instinct for good manners is the natural inheritance of all Irishmen. The peasant has it as surely as the peer, generally indeed more surely, for the peer, having mixed more with men of other nations, loses something of his natural delicacy of feeling. When, as in the case of young Kinsella, the Irishman has much to do with the sea his courtesy reaches a high degree of refinement. As the advancing tide crept inch by inch over the mudbank Jimmy Kinsella was forced back towards the *Tortoise*. He moved from stone to stone, dragging his boat after him as the water floated her. Never once did he look round or make any attempt to attract the attention of Miss Rutherford. He would no doubt have retreated uncomplaining to the highest point of the bank and sat there till the water reached his waist, clinging to the painter of the boat, rather than disturb the conversation of the lady whom he had taken under his care. But his courtesy was put to no such extreme test. He made a move at last which brought him within a few feet of the *Tortoise*. A mere patch of sea-soaked mud remained uncovered. The water, advancing from the far side of the bank, already lapped against the bows of the *Tortoise*. Miss Rutherford woke up to the fact that the time for catching sponges was past.

"I'm afraid," she said, "that I ought to be getting home. I can't tell you how much obliged to you I am for feeding me. I believe I should have fainted if it hadn't been for that tongue."

"It was a pleasure to us," said Priscilla. "We'd eaten all we could before you came."

"I'm afraid," said Frank politely, "that it wasn't very nice. We ought to have had knives and forks or at least a tumbler to drink out of. I don't know what you must think of us."

"Think of you!" said Miss Rutherford. "I think you're the two nicest children I ever met."

She stumped off and joined Jimmy Kinsella. Priscilla saw her putting on her shoes and stockings as the boat rowed away. She shouted a farewell. Miss Rutherford waved a stocking in reply.

"There," said Priscilla, turning to Frank, "what do you think of that? The two nicest children! I don't mind of course; but I do call it rather rough on you after talking so grand and having on your best first eleven coat and all."

CHAPTER IX

Frank learned several things while the sails were being hoisted. The word halyard became familiar to him and connected itself definitely with certain ropes. He discovered that a sheet is, oddly enough, not an expanse of canvas, but another rope. He impressed carefully on his mind the part of the boat in which he might, under favourable circumstances, expect to find the centreboard tackle.

The wind, which had dropped completely at low water, sprang up again, this time from the west, with the rising tide. This was pleasant and promised a fair run home, but Priscilla eyed the sky suspiciously. She was weather-wise.

"It'll die clean away," she said, "towards evening. It always does on this kind of day when it has worked round with the sun. Curious things winds are, Cousin Frank, aren't they? Rather like ices in some ways, I always think."

Frank had considerable experience of ices, and had been obliged, while playing various games, to take some notice of the wind from time to time; but he missed the point of Priscilla's comparison. She explained herself.

"If you put in a good spoonful at once," she said, "it gives you a pain in some tooth or other and you don't enjoy it. On the other hand, if you put in a very little bit it gets melted away before you're able to taste it properly. That's just the way the wind behaves when you're out sailing. Either it has you clinging on to the main sheet for all you're worth or else it dies away and leaves you flapping. It's only about once a month that you get just what you want."

It seemed to Frank, when the boat got under way, that they had happened on the one propitious day. The *Tortoise* slipped pleasantly along, her sails well filled, the boom pressed forward against the shroud, the main sheet an attenuated coil at Priscilla's feet.

"I'm feeling a bit bothered," said Priscilla.

"We ought to have been back for luncheon," said Frank. "I know that."

"It's not luncheon that's bothering me; although it's quite likely that we won't be back for dinner either. What I can't quite make up my mind about is what we ought to do next about those spies."

"Go after them again to-morrow."

"That's all well enough; but things are much more mixed up than that. In some ways I rather wish we had Sylvia Courtney with us. She's president of our Browning Society and tremendously good at every kind of complication. What I feel is that we're rather like those boys in the poem who went out to catch a hare and came on a lion unaware. I haven't got the passage quite right but you probably know it."

Frank did. He could not, since English literature is still only fitfully studied in public schools, have named the author. But he quoted the lines with fluent confidence. It was by turning them into Greek Iambics that he had won the head-master's prize.

"That's it," said Priscilla. "And that's more or less what has happened to us. We went out to chase a simple, ordinary German spy and we have come on two other mysteries of the most repulsively fascinating kind. First there's Miss Rutherford, if that's her real name, who says she's fishing for sponges, which is certainly a lie."

"I don't know about it's being a lie," said Frank. "She explained it to me after you'd gone."

"Oh, that about zoophytes. You don't believe that surely?"

"I do," said Frank. "There are lots of queer things in the British Museum. I was there once."

"My own belief is," said Priscilla, "that she simply trotted out those zoophyte things and the British Museum when she found that we weren't inclined to swallow the ordinary sponge. At the same time I can't believe that she's a criminal of any kind. She struck me as being an uncommonly good sort. The wind's dropping. I told you it would. Very soon now we shall have to row. Can you row, Cousin Frank?"

Frank replied with cheerful confidence that he could. He had sat at Priscilla's feet all day and bowed to her superior knowledge of sailing. When it came to rowing he was sure that he could hold his own. He understood the phraseology of the art, had learned to take advantage of sliding seats, could keep his back straight and had been praised by a member of a University eight for his swing.

"The other mystery," said Priscilla, "is Inishbawn. The Kinsellas won't let the spies land on the island. They won't let Miss Rutherford. They won't let you, They tell every kind of ridiculous story to head people off."

The thought of his prowess as an oarsman had restored Frank's self-respect. He recollected the reason given by Jimmy Kinsella for not allowing Miss Rutherford to land on Inishbawn.

"I don't see anything ridiculous about it," he said. "Young Kinsella simply said that it wasn't a suitable place for ladies. There are lots of places we men go to where we wouldn't take————"

His sentence tailed away. Priscilla's eyes expressed an amount of amusement which made him feel singularly uncomfortable.

"That," she said, "is the most utter rot I've ever heard in my life. And in any case, even if it was true, it wouldn't apply to us. Jimmy Kinsella distinctly said that I might land on the island as much as I like, but that he jolly well wouldn't have you. We may just as well row now as later on. The breeze is completely gone."

She got out the oars and dropped the rowlocks into their holes. She pulled stroke oar herself. Frank settled himself on the seat behind her. He found himself in a position of extreme discomfort. The *Tortoise* was designed and built to be a sailing boat. It was not originally contemplated that she should be rowed far or rowed fast. When Frank leaned back at the end of his stroke he bumped against the mast. When he swung forward in the proper way he hit Priscilla between the shoulders with his knuckles. When the boat shot forward the boom swung inboard. If this happened at the end of a stroke Frank was hit on the shoulder. If it happened at the beginning of a stroke the spar struck him on the ear. However he shifted his position he was unable to avoid sitting on some rope. The centreboard case was between his legs and when he tried to get his injured foot against anything firm he found it entangled in ropes which he could not kick away. Priscilla complained.

"Put a little more beef into it, Cousin Frank," she said. "I'm pulling her head round all the time."

Frank put all the energy he could into a series of short jerky strokes, using the muscles of his arms, failing altogether to get the weight of his body on the oar. At the end of twenty minutes Priscilla gave him a rest.

"There's no use our killing ourselves," she said. "The tide's under us. It's a jolly lucky thing it is. If it was the other way we wouldn't get home to-night. I wonder now whether the Kinsellas think you've any connection with the police. You don't look it in the least, but you never can tell what people will think. If they do mistake you for anything of the sort it might account for their not wanting you to land on Inishbawn."

"Why?"

"Oh, I don't know why exactly—not yet. But there often are things knocking about which it wouldn't at all do for the police to see. That might happen anywhere. There's an air of wind coming up behind us. Just get in that oar of yours. We may as well take the good of what's going."

A faint ripple on the surface of the water approached the *Tortoise*. Before it reached her the boom swung forward, lifting the dripping main sheet from the water, and the boat slipped on.

"But of course," said Priscilla, "that idea of your being a policeman in disguise doesn't account for their telling Miss Rutherford that there was something on the island which it wouldn't be nice for a lady to see. And it doesn't account for the swine-fever story that Joseph Antony Kinsella told the spies."

"What was that?"

"Oh, nothing much. Only that his wife and children had come out all over in bright yellow spots."

"But perhaps they have."

"Not they. You might just as well believe in Peter Walsh's rats. That leaves us with three different mysteries on hand." Priscilla hooked her elbow over the tiller and ticked off the three mysteries on the fingers of her right hand. "The sponge lady, whose name may be Miss Rutherford, one. Inishbawn Island, that's two. The original spies, which makes three. I'm afraid we'll have to row again. Do you think you can, Cousin Frank?"

"Of course I can."

"Don't be offended. I only meant that you mightn't be able to on account of your ankle. How is your ankle?"

"It's all right," said Frank, "That is to say it's just the same."

No other favouring breeze rippled the surface of the bay. For rather more than an hour, with occasional intervals for rest, Frank tugged at his oar, bumped his back, and was struck on the side of the head by the boom. He was very much exhausted when the *Tortoise* was at length brought alongside the slip at the end of the quay. Priscilla still seemed fresh and vigorous.

"I wonder," said Frank, "if we could hire a boy."

"Dozens," said Priscilla, "if you want them... What for?"

"To wheel that bath-chair. I can't walk, you know. And I don't like to think of your pushing me up the hill. You must be tired."

"That," said Priscilla, "is what I call real politeness. There are lots of other kinds of politeness which aren't worth tuppence. But that kind is rather nice. It makes me feel quite grown up. All the same I'll wheel you home."

She pushed the bath-chair up the hill from the village without any obvious effort. At the gate of the avenue she stopped. Two small children were playing just inside it. A rather larger child set on the doorstep of the gate lodge with a baby on her knee.

"What time is it, Cousin Frank?" said Priscilla.

"It's ten minutes past seven."

"Susan Ann, where's your mother?"

The girl with the baby on her knee struggled to her feet and answered:

"She's up at the house beyond, Miss."

"I just thought she must be," said Priscilla, "when I saw William Thomas and the other boy playing there, and you nursing the baby. If your mother wasn't up at the house you'd all be in your beds."

She wheeled the bath-chair on until she turned the corner of the avenue and was lost to the sight of the children who peered after her. Then she paused.

"Cousin Frank," she said, "it's just as well for you to be prepared for some kind of fuss when we get home."

"We're awfully late, I know."

"It's not that. It's something far worse. The fuss that's going on up there at the present moment is a thunderstorm compared to what there would be over our being late."

"How do you know there's a fuss?"

"Before she was married," said Priscilla, "Mrs. Geraghty—that's the woman at the gate lodge, the mother of those four children—was our upper housemaid. Aunt Juliet simply loved her. She rubs her into all the other servants day and night. She says she was the only sufficient housemaid. I'm not sure that that's quite the right word. It may be efficient. Any how she says she's the only something-or-other-ficient housemaid she ever had; which of course is a grand thing for Mrs. Geraghty, though not really as nice as it seems, because whenever anything perfectly appalling happens Aunt Juliet sends for her. Then she and Aunt Juliet rag the other servants until things get smoothed out again. The minute I saw those children sporting about when by rights they ought to be in bed I knew that Mrs. Geraghty had been sent for. Now you understand the sort of thing you have to expect when we get home. I thought I'd just warn you, so that you wouldn't be taken by surprise."

Frank felt that he still might be taken by surprise and urged Priscilla to give him some further details about the catastrophe.

"We'll find out soon enough," said Priscilla. "At least we may. If it's the kind of thing that's visible, streams of water running down the front stairs or anything like that, we'll see for ourselves, but if it happens to be a more inward sort of disaster which we can't see—and that's the kind there's always the worst fuss about—then it may take us some time to find out. Aunt Juliet doesn't think it's good for children to know about inward disasters, and so she never talks of them when I'm there except in what she calls French, and not much of that because Father can't understand her. They may, of course, confide in you. It all depends on whether they think you're a child or not."

"I'm not."

"*I* know that, of course. And Aunt Juliet saw you in your evening coat last night at dinner, so she oughtn't to. But you never can tell about things of that kind. Look at the sponge lady for instance. She said you were the nicest child she ever saw. Still they may tell you."

Frank did not like being reminded of Miss Rutherford's remark. Priscilla's repetition of it goaded him to a reply which he immediately afterwards felt to be unworthy.

"If they do tell me," he said, "I won't tell you."

"Then you'll be a mean, low beast," said Priscilla.

Frank pulled himself together with an effort. He realised that it would never do to bandy schoolboy repartee with Priscilla. His loss of dignity would be complete. And besides, he was very likely to get the worst of the encounter. He was out of practise. Prefects do not descend to personalities.

"My dear Priscilla," he said, "I only meant that I wouldn't tell you if it was the sort of thing a girl oughtn't to hear."

"Like what Jimmy Kinsella has on Inishbawn," said Priscilla. "Do you know, Cousin Frank, you're quite too funny for words when you go in for being grand. Now would you like me to wheel you up to the hall-door and ring the bell, or would you rather we sneaked round through the shrubbery into the yard, and got in by the gunroom door and so up the back stairs?"

"I don't care," said Frank.

"The back way would be the wisest," said Priscilla, "but in the state of grandeur you're in now——"

"Oh, do drop it, Priscilla."

"I don't want to keep it up."

"Then go by the back door."

"Do you promise to tell me all about it, supposing they tell you, and they may? You can never be sure what they'll do."

"Yes, I promise."

"A faithful, solemn oath?"

"Yes."

"Whether it's the sort of thing a girl ought to be told or not?"

"Yes. Only do go on. It'll take me hours to dress, and we're awfully late already."

Priscilla trotted briskly through the shrubbery, crossed the yard and helped Frank out of the chair at the gunroom door. She gave him her arm while he hobbled up the back stairs. At the top of the first flight she deserted him suddenly. She darted forward, half opened a baize covered swing door and peeped through.

"I just thought I heard them at it," she said. "Mrs. Geraghty and the two housemaids are rioting in the long gallery, dragging the furniture about and, generally speaking, playing old hokey. That gives us a certain amount of information, Cousin Frank."

CHAPTER X

ROSNACREE HOUSE was built early in the 19th century by the Lentaigne of that day, one Sir Francis. At the beginning of that century the Irish gentry were still an aristocracy. They ruled, and had among their number men who were gentlemen of the grand style, capable of virile passions and striking deeds, incapable, constitutionally and by training, of the prudent foresight of careful tradesmen. Lord Thormanby, who rejoiced in a brand new Union peerage and was a wealthy man, kept race horses. Sir Francis, who, except for the Union peerage, was as big a man as Lord Thormanby, kept race horses too. Lord Thormanby bought a family coach of remarkable proportions. Sir Francis ordered a duplicate of it from the same coach-builder. Lord Thormanby employed an Italian architect to build him a house. Sir Francis sought out the same architect and gave him orders to build another house, identical with Lord Thormanby's in design, but having each room two feet longer, two feet higher and two feet broader than the corresponding room at Thormanby Park. The architect, after talking a good deal about proportions in a way which Sir Francis did not understand, accepted the commission and erected Rosnacree House.

The two additional cubic feet made all the difference. Lord Thormanby's fortune survived the building operations. Lord Francis Lentaigne's estate was crippled.

His successors struggled with a burden of mortgages and a mansion considerably too large for their requirements. Sir Lucius, when his turn came, shut up the great gallery, which ran the whole length of the second storey of the house, and lived with a tolerable amount of elbow room in five downstairs sitting rooms and fourteen bedrooms. Miss Lentaigne made occasional raids on the gallery in order to see that the fine old-fashioned furniture did not rot. Neither she nor her brother thought of using the room.

For Frank Mannix the white tie which is worn in the evening was still something of a novelty and therefore a difficulty. He was struggling with it, convinced of the great importance of having the two sides of its bow symmetrical, when Priscilla tapped at his bedroom door. In response to his invitation to enter she opened the door half way and put her head and shoulders into the room.

"I thought I'd just tell you as I was passing," she said, "that it's all right about your ankle."

Frank, who had just re-bandaged the injured limb, asked her what she meant.

"I've seen Aunt Juliet," she said, "and I find that she's quite dropped Christian Science and is frightfully keen on Woman's Suffrage. That's always the way with her. When she's done with a thing she simply hoofs it without a word of apology to anyone. It was the same with the uric acid. She'd talk of nothing else in the morning and before night it was withered like the flower of the field upon the housetop, 'whereof the mower filleth not his arm.' I expect you know the sort I mean."

She shut the door and Frank heard her running down the passage. A couple of minutes later he heard her running back again. This time she opened the door without tapping.

"I can't think," she said, "what Woman's Suffrage can possibly have to do with the big gallery, but they must be mixed up somehow or Mrs. Geraghty and the housemaids wouldn't be sporting about the way they are. They're at it still. I've just looked in at them."

During dinner the conversation was very largely political. Sir Lucius inveighed with great bitterness against the government's policy in Ireland. Now and then he recollected that Frank's father was a supporter of the government. Then he made such excuses for the Cabinet's blundering as he could. Miss Lentaigne also condemned the government, though less for its incurable habit for truckling to the forces of disorder in Ireland, than for its cowardly and treacherous treatment of women. She made no attempt to spare Frank's feelings. Indeed, she pointed many of her remarks by uncomplimentary references to Lord Torrington, Secretary of State for War, and the immediate chief of Mr. Edward Mannix, M.P. Lord Torrington, so the public understood, was the most dogged and determined opponent of the enfranchisement of women. He absolutely refused to receive deputations of ladies and had more than once said publicly that he was in entire agreement with a statement attributed to the German Emperor, by which the energies of women were confined to babies, baking and bazaars for church purposes. Miss Lentaigne scorched this sentiment with invective, and used language about Lord Torrington which was terrific. Her abandonment of the cause of Christian Science appeared to be as complete as the most enthusiastic general practitioner could desire. Frank was exceedingly uncomfortable. Priscilla was demure and silent.

When Miss Lentaigne, followed by Priscilla, left the room, Sir Lucius became confidential and friendly. He pushed the decanter of port towards Frank.

"Fill up your glass, my boy," he said. "After your long day on the sea—
— By the way I hope your aunt—I keep forgetting that she's not your
aunt—I hope she didn't say anything at dinner to hurt your feelings. You
mustn't mind, you know. We're all rather hot about politics in this country.
Have to be with the way these infernal Leagues and things are going on.
You don't understand, of course, Frank. Nor does your father. If he did he
wouldn't vote with that gang. Your aunt—I mean to say my sister is—well,
you saw for yourself. She usedn't to be, you know. It's only quite lately that
she's taken the subject up. And there's something in it. I can't deny that
there's something in it. She's a clever woman. There's always something in
what she says. Though she pushes things too far sometimes. So does
Torrington, it appears. Only he pushes them the other way. I think he goes
too far, quite too far. Of course, my sister does too, in the opposite
direction."

Sir Lucius sighed.

"It's all right, Uncle Lucius," said Frank. "I don't mind a bit. I'm not well
enough up in these things to answer Miss Lentaigne. If father was here——
"

"What's that? Is your father coming here?"

"Oh, no," said Frank. "He's in Schlangenbad."

"Of course, of course. By the way, your father's pretty intimate with
Torrington, isn't he? The Secretary of State for War."

"My father's under-secretary of the War Office," said Frank.

"Now, what sort of a man is Torrington? He's a distant cousin of mine.
My great aunt was his grandmother or something of that sort. But I only
met him once, years ago. Apart from politics now, I don't profess to admire
his politics—I never did. How men like your father and Torrington can mix
themselves up with that damned socialist crew—But apart from politics,
what sort of a man is Torrington?"

"I never saw him," said Frank. "I've been at school, you know, Uncle
Lucius."

"Quite so, quite so. But your father now. Your father must know him
intimately. I know he's rich, immensely rich. American mother, American
wife, dollars to burn, which makes it all the harder to understand his
politics. But his private life—what does your father think of him?

"Last time father stopped there," said Frank, "he was called in the
morning by a footman who asked him whether he'd have tea, coffee or

chocolate. Father said tea. 'Assam, Oolong, or Sooching, sir,' said the footman, 'or do you prefer your tea with a flavour of Orange Pekoe?'"

"By gad!" said Sir Lucius.

"That's the only story I've ever heard father tell about him," said Frank, "but they say———"

"That he has the devil of a temper." said Sir Lucius, "and rides roughshod over every one? I've been told that."

"Father never said so."

"Quite right. He wouldn't, couldn't in fact. It wouldn't be the thing at all. The fact is, Frank, that Torrington's coming here tomorrow, wired from Dublin to say so. He and Lady Torrington. I can't imagine what he wants here. I'd call it damned insolence in any one else, knowing what I must think of his rascally politics, what every decent man thinks of them. But of course he's a kind of cousin. I suppose he recollected that. And he's a pretty big pot. Those fellows invite themselves, like royalty. But I don't know what the devil to do with him, and your aunt's greatly upset. She says it's against her principles to be decently civil to a man who's treated women the way Torrington has."

"If the women had let him alone———" said Frank, "I know. I know. One of them boxed his ears or something, pretty girl, too, I hear; but that only makes it worse. That sort of thing would get any man's back up. But your aunt—that is to say, my sister—doesn't see that. That's the worst of strong principles. You never can see when your own side is in the wrong. But it makes it infernally awkward Torrington's coming here just now. And Lady Torrington! It upsets us all. I wonder what the devil he's coming here for?"

"I don't know," said Frank. "Could he be studying the Irish question? Isn't there some Home Rule Bill or something? Father said next year would be an Irish year."

"That's it. That must be it. Now I wonder who he expects me to have to dinner to meet him. There's no use my wiring to Thormanby to come over for the night. He wouldn't do it. Simply loathes the name of Torrington. Besides, I don't suppose Thormanby is the kind of man he wants to meet. He'd probably rather hear Brannigan or some one of that sort talking damned Nationalism. But I can't ask Brannigan, really can't, you know, Frank. I might have O'Hara, that's the doctor. I don't suppose my sister would mind now. She quite dropped Christian Science as soon as she heard Torrington was coming. But I don't know. O'Hara drinks a bit."

Sir Lucius sat much longer than usual in the dining-room. Frank found himself yawning with uncontrollable frequency. The long day on the sea had made him very sleepy. He did his best to disguise his condition from his uncle, but he felt that his answers to the later questions about Lord Torrington were vague, and he became more and more confused about Sir Lucius' views of Woman Suffrage. One thing alone became clear to him. Sir Lucius was not anxious to join his sister in the drawingroom. Frank entirely shared his feeling.

But in this twentieth century it is impossible for gentlemen to spend the whole evening in the dining-room. Wine drinking is no longer recognised as a valid excuse for the separation of the sexes and tobacco is so universally tolerated that men carry their cigarettes into the drawingroom on all but the most ceremonial occasions. Sir Lucius rose at last.

"It's very hot," said Frank. "May I sit out for a while on the terrace, Uncle Lucius, before I go into the drawingroom. I'd like a breath of fresh air."

He hobbled out and found a hammock chair not far from the drawingroom window. The voices of Miss Lentaigne and his uncle reached him, the one high-pitched and firm, the other, as he imagined, apologetic and deprecatory. The sound of them, the words being indistinguishable, was somewhat soothing. Frank felt as the poet Lucretius did when from the security of a sheltered nook on the side of a cliff he watched boats tossing on the sea. The sense of neighbouring strain and struggle added to the completeness of his own repose. A bed of mignonette scented the air agreeably. Some white roses glimmered faintly in the twilight. Far off, a grey still shadow, lay the bay. Frank's cigarette dropped, half smoked, from his fingers. He slept deliciously.

A few minutes later he woke with a start. Priscilla stood over him. She was wrapt from her neck to her feet in a pale blue dressing-gown. Her hair hung down her back in a tight plait. On her feet were a pair of well worn bedroom slippers. The big toe of her right foot had pushed its way through the end of one of them.

"I say, Cousin Frank, are you awake? I've been here for hours, dropping small stones on your head, so as to rouse you up. I daren't make any noise, for they're still jawing away inside and I was afraid they'd hear me. Could you struggle along a bit further away from the window? I'll carry your chair."

They found a nook behind the rose-bed which Priscilla held to be perfectly safe. Frank settled down on his chair. Priscilla, with her knees pulled up to her chin, sat on a cushion at his feet.

"Aunt Juliet hunted me off to bed at half-past nine," she said. "Dastardly tyranny! And she sent Mrs. Geraghty to do my hair—not that she cared if my hair was never done, but so as to make sure that I really undressed. Plucky lot of good that was!"

The precaution had evidently been of no use at all; but neither Miss Lentaigne nor Mrs. Geraghty could have calculated on Priscilla's roaming about the grounds in her dressing-gown.

"The reason of the tyranny," said Priscilla, "was plain enough. Aunt Juliet was smoking a cigarette."

"Good gracious!" said Frank. "I should never have thought your aunt smoked."

"She doesn't. She never did before, though she may take to it regularly now for a time. I simply told her that she oughtn't to chew the end. No real smoker does; and I could see that she didn't like the wads of tobacco coming off on her tongue. Besides, it was beastly waste of the cigarette. She chawed off quite as much as she smoked. You'd have thought she'd have been obliged to me for giving her the tip, but quite the contrary. She hoofed me off to bed."

"But what has made her take to smoking?"

"She had to," said Priscilla. "I don't think she really likes it, but with her principles she simply had to. It's part of what's called the economic independence of women and she wants to dare the Prime Minister to put her in gaol. I don't suppose he will, at least not unless she does something worse than that; but that's what she hopes. You know, of course, that the Prime Minister is coming tomorrow."

"It's not the Prime Minister," said Frank, "only Lord Torrington."

"That'll be a frightful disappointment to Aunt Juliet after sending down to Brannigan's for those cigarettes. Rose—she's the under housemaid—told me that. Beastly cigarettes they are, too. Rose said the footman said *he* wouldn't smoke them. Ten a penny or something like that. But if Lord Torrington isn't the Prime Minister what is Aunt Juliet doing out the long gallery?"

"Lord Torrington is rather a boss," said Frank, "though he's not the Prime Minister. He's the head of the War Office."

Priscilla whistled.

"Great Scott," she said, "the head of the War Office! And Aunt Juliet hasn't the least idea what's bringing him down here. She said so twice."

"So did Uncle Lucius. He kept wondering after dinner what on earth Lord Torrington wanted."

"But we know," said Priscilla. "This is what I call real sport. I have her jolly well scored off now for sending me to bed. I shouldn't wonder if they made you a knight. It's pretty well the least they can do."

"What are you talking about? I don't know what's bringing him here unless it's something to do with Home Rule."

"Who cares about Home Rule? What he's coming for is the spies. Didn't you say that this Torrington man is the head of the War Office? What would bring him down here if it isn't German spies? And we're the only two people who know where those spies are. Even we don't quite know; but we will tomorrow. Just fancy Aunt Juliet's face when we march them up here in the afternoon, tied hand and foot with the anchor rope, and hand them over to the War Office. We shall be publicly thanked, of course, besides your knighthood, and our names will be in all the papers. Then if Aunt Juliet dares to tell me ever again to go to bed at half past nine I shall simply grin like a dog and run about through the city. She won't like that. You're quite, sure, Cousin Frank, that it really is the War Office man who's coming?"

"Uncle Lucius told me it was Lord Torrington, and I know he's the head of the War Office because my father's the under-secretary."

"That's all right, then. I was just thinking that it would be perfectly awful if we captured the spies and it turned out that he wasn't the man who was after them."

"He may not be after them," said Frank. "It doesn't seem to me a bit likely that he is. You see, Priscilla, my father has a lot to do with the War Office and I know he rather laughs at this spy business."

"That's probably to disguise his feelings. Spies are always kept dead secrets and if possible not let into the newspapers. Perhaps even your father hasn't been told. He doesn't appear to be head boss, and they mightn't mention it to him. That's what makes it such an absolutely gorgeous scoop for us. We'll get off as early as we can tomorrow. You couldn't start before breakfast, could you? The tide will be all right."

"I could, of course, if you don't mind wheeling me down again in that bath-chair."

"Not a little bit. I'll get hold of Rose before I go to bed, and tell her to call us. Rose is the only one in the house I can really depend on. She hates Aunt Juliet like poison ever since that time she had the bad tooth. We can pick up some biscuits and things at Brannigan's as we pass. There's a good chunk of cold salmon somewhere, for we only ate quite a small bit at dinner tonight. I'll nail it if I can keep awake till the cook's in bed, but I don't know can I. This kind of excitement makes me frightfully sleepy. I suppose it's what's called reaction. Sylvia Courtney had it terribly after the English literature prize exam. It was headaches with her and general snappishness of temper. Sleepiness is worse in some ways, though not so bad for the other people. However, I'll do the best I can, and if we don't get the cold salmon we'll just have to do without."

She rose from her cushion, stretched herself and yawned unrestrainedly. Then she rubbed both eyes with her knuckles.

"Priscilla," said Frank, "before you go I wish you'd tell me——"

"Yes. What?"

"Do you really believe those two people we saw today are German spies?"

"Do you mean, really and truly in the inmost bottom of my heart?"

"Yes."

"Well, I don't, of course. It would be too good to be true if they were. But I mean to go on pretending. Don't you?"

"Oh, yes, I'll pretend. I only wanted to know what you thought."

"All the same," said Priscilla, "they did rather scoot when they saw we were after them. Nobody can deny that. That may be because they're pretending, too. I daresay they find it pretty dull being stuck on an island all day, though, of course, it must be rather jolly cooking your own food and washing up plates in the sea. Still they may be tired of that now, and glad enough to pretend to be German spies with us pursuing them. It must be just as good sport for them trying to escape as it is for us trying to catch them. I daresay it's even better, being stalked unwaveringly by a subtle foe ought to give them a delicious creepy feeling down the back. Anyhow we'll track them down. We're much better out of this house tomorrow. It'll be like the tents of Kedar. You and I might be labouring for peace, but everybody else will be making ready for battle. Aunt Juliet will be out for blood the moment she catches sight of the Prime Minister. Good night, Cousin Frank."

CHAPTER XI

Rose, the under housemaid, with the recollection of the scientifically Christian method of treating her toothache fresh in her mind and therefore stimulated by a strong desire to annoy Miss Lentaigne, woke at five a.m. At half past five she called Priscilla and knocked at Frank's door. Priscilla was fully dressed ten minutes later. Frank appeared in the yard at five minutes to six. They started as the stable clock struck six, Priscilla wheeling the bath-chair. Rose yawning widely, watched them from the scullery window.

Priscilla had failed to seize the cold salmon the night before. Rose, foraging early in the morning, with the fear of the cook before her eyes, had secured nothing but half a loaf of bread and a square section of honey. It was therefore something of a disappointment to find that Brannigan's shop was not open when they reached the quay. No biscuits or tinned meats could be bought. Many adventurers would have been daunted by the prospect of a long day's work with such slender provision. It is recorded, for instance, of Julius Caesar, surely the most eminent adventurer of all history, that he hesitated to attempt an expedition against one of the tribes of Gaul "propter inopiam pecuniae," which may very well be translated "on account of a shortage of provisions." But Julius Caesar, at the period of his greatest conquests, was a middle-aged man. He had lost the first careless rapture of youth. Frank and Priscilla, because their combined ages only amounted to thirty-two years, were more daring than Caesar. With a fine faith in the providence which feeds adventurers, they scorned the wisdom which looks dubiously at bread and honey. They did not hesitate at all.

The tide was still rising when they embarked. At that hour in the morning there was no wind and it was necessary to row the *Tortoise* out. Priscilla took both oars herself, remembering the gyrations of the boat the day before when Frank was helping her to row.

"There'll be a breeze," she said, "when the tide turns, but we can't afford to wait here for that. When we're outside the stone perch we'll drop anchor. But the first thing is to set pursuit at defiance by getting beyond the reach of the human voice. If we can't hear whoever happens to be calling us we can't be expected to turn back and it won't be disobedience if we don't."

The tide, with an hour more of flow behind it, crept along the grey quay wall, and eddied past the buoys. Two hookers lay moored, and faint spirals of smoke rose from the stove chimneys of their forecastles. Thin wreaths of grey mist hung here and there over the still surface of the bay. Patches of purple slime lay unbroken on the unrippled surface. Scraps of shrivelled rack, sucked off the shores of the nearer islands, floated past the *Tortoise*. A cormorant, balanced on the top of one of the perches outside Delginish, sat with wings outstretched and neck craned forward, peering out to sea. A fleet of terns floated motionless on the water beyond the island. Two gulls with lazy flappings of their wings, flew westwards down the bay. Priscilla, rowing with short, decisive strokes, drove the *Tortoise* forward.

"It's going to be blazing hot," she said, "and altogether splendidly glorious. I feel rather like a dove that is covered with silver wings and her feathers like gold. Don't you?"

Frank did. Although he would not have expressed himself in the words of the Psalmist, he recognised them. The most reliable tenor in the choir at Haileybury is necessarily familiar with the Psalms.

They reached the stone perch and cast anchor. It was half past seven o'clock. Priscilla got out the bread and honey.

"The proper thing to do," she said, "would be to go on half rations at once, and serve out the bread by ounces and the honey by teaspoonfuls, but I think we won't. I'm as hungry as any wolf."

"Besides," said Frank, "we haven't got a teaspoon."

"I hope your knife is to the fore. I'm not particular as a rule about the way I eat things, but there's no use beginning the day by making the whole boat sticky. I loathe stickiness, especially when I happen to sit on it, which is one of the reasons which makes me glad I wasn't born a bee. They have to, of course, poor things, even the queen, I believe. It can't be pleasant."

The tug of the boat at her anchor rope slackened as the tide reached its height. A light easterly wind came to them from the land. Priscilla swallowed the last morsel of bread and honey as the *Tortoise* drifted over her anchor and swung round.

"Perhaps," she said, "you'd like to practise steering, Cousin Dick. If so, creep aft and take the tiller. I'll get the sail on her and haul up the anchor."

Frank, humbled by the experience of the day before, was doubtful. Priscilla encouraged him. He took the tiller with nervous joy. Priscilla hoisted the lug and then the foresail.

"Now," she said, "I'll get up the anchor and we'll try to go off on the starboard tack. If we don't we'll have to jibe immediately. With this much wind it won't matter, but you might not like the sensation."

Frank did not want to enjoy any sensation of a sudden kind and jibing, as he understood it, was always unexpected. He asked which way he ought to push the tiller so as to make sure of reaching the starboard tack. Priscilla stood beside the mast and delivered a long, very confusing lecture on the effect of the rudder on the boat and the advantage of hauling down one or other of the foresail sheets when getting under way from anchor. Frank did not understand much of what she said, but was ashamed to ask for more information. Priscilla, on her knees under the foresail, tugged at the anchor rope. The *Tortoise* quivered slightly, but did not move. Priscilla, leaning well back, tugged harder. The *Tortoise*—it is impossible to speak of a boat except as a live thing with a capricious will—shook herself irritably.

"She's slap over the anchor," said Priscilla. "I can't think how she gets there for there's plenty of rope out; but there she is and I can't move the beastly thing. Perhaps you'll try. You may be stronger than I am. I expect it has got stuck somehow behind a rock."

Frank felt confident that he was stronger in the arms than Priscilla. He crept forward and put his whole strength into a pull on the anchor rope. The *Tortoise* twisted herself broadside on to the breeze and then listed over to windward. Priscilla looked round her in amazement. The breeze was certainly very light, but it was contrary to her whole experience that a boat with sails set should heel over towards the wind. She told Frank to stop pulling. The *Tortoise* slowly righted herself and then drifted back to her natural position, head to wind.

"The only thing I can think of," said Priscilla, "is that the anchor rope has got round the centreboard. It might. You never can tell exactly what an anchor rope will do. However, if it has, we've nothing to do but haul up the centreboard and clear it."

She took the centreboard rope and pulled. Frank joined her and they both pulled. The centreboard remained immovable. The *Tortoise* was entirely unaffected by their pulling.

"Jammed," said Priscilla. "I feel a jolly sight less like that dove than I did. It looks rather as if we were going to spend the day here. I don't want to cut the rope and lose the anchor if I can possibly help it, but of course it may come to that in the end, though even then I'm not sure that we'll get clear."

"Can we do nothing?" said Frank.

"This," said Priscilla, "is a case for prolonged and cool-headed reasoning. You reason your best and I'll bring all the resources of my mind to bear on the problem!"

She sat down in the bottom of the boat and gazed thoughtfully at the stone perch. Frank, to whom the nature of the problem was obscure, also gazed at the stone perch, but without much hope of finding inspiration. Priscilla looked round suddenly.

"We might try poking at it with the blade of an oar," she said. "I don't think it will be much use, but there's no harm trying."

The poking was a total failure, and Priscilla, reaching far out to thrust the oar well under the keel of the boat, very nearly fell overboard. Frank caught her by the skirt at the last moment and hauled her back.

"We'll have to sit down and think again," she said. "By the way, what was that word which Euclid said when he suddenly found out how to construct an isosceles triangle? He was in his bath at the time, as well as I recollect."

A man is not in the lower sixth at Haileybury without possessing a good working knowledge of the chief events of classical antiquity. Frank rose to his opportunity.

"Are you thinking of Archimedes?" he asked. "What he said was 'Eureka' and what he found out wasn't anything about triangles but—"

"Thanks," said Priscilla. "It doesn't really matter whether it was Euclid or not and it isn't of the least importance what he found out. It was the word I wanted. Let's agree that whichever of us Eureka's it first stands up and shouts the word far across the sea. You've no objection to that, I suppose. The idea may stimulate our imaginations."

Frank had no objection. He felt tolerably certain that he would not have to shout. Priscilla, frowning heavily, fixed her eyes on the stone perch, A few minutes later she spoke again.

"Once," she said, "I was riding my bicycle in father's mackintosh, which naturally was a little long for me. In process of time the tail of it got wound round and round the back wheel and I was regularly stuck, couldn't move hand or foot and had to lie on my side with the bicycle on top of me. That seems to me very much the way we are now with that anchor rope and the centreboard."

"How did you get out?" said Frank hopefully.

That Priscilla had got out was evident. If her position on the bicycle was really analogous to that of the *Tortoise* the same plan of escape might perhaps be tried.

"I lay there," said Priscilla, "until Peter Walsh happened to come along the road. He kind of unwound me."

A boat, heavily laden, was rowing slowly towards them, making very little way against the gathering strength of the ebb tide and the easterly wind.

"Perhaps," said Frank, "the people in that boat, if it ever gets here, will unwind us."

The boat drew nearer and Priscilla declared that it was Kinsella's.

"It's Joseph Antony himself rowing her," she said. "He'd be getting on faster if he had Jimmy along with him, but I suppose he's off with the sponge lady again."

Kinsella reached the *Tortoise* and stopped rowing.

"You're out for a sail again today, Miss?" he said. "Well, it's fine weather for the likes of you."

"At the present moment," said Priscilla, "we're stuck and can't get out."

"Do you tell me that now? And what's the matter with you?"

"The anchor rope is foul of the centreboard and we can't get either the one or the other of them to move."

"Begor!" said Joseph Antony.

"Do you know any way of getting it clear?"

"I do, of course."

"Well, trot it out."

"If you was to take the oars," said Joseph Antony, "and was to row the boat round the way she wasn't going when she twisted the rope on you it would come untwisted again."

"It would, of course. Thank you very much. Rather stupid of us not to have thought of that. It seems quite simple. But that's always the way. The simplest things are far the hardest to think of. Columbus and the egg, for instance."

She got out the oars as she spoke and began turning the *Tortoise* round.

"Begging your pardon, Miss," said Joseph Antony, "but which way is the rope twisted round the plate? If you row her round the wrong way you'll twist it worse than ever."

But luck favored Priscilla. When the *Tortoise* had made one circle the rope shook itself clear. Joseph Antony, dipping his oars gently in the water, drew close alongside.

"I'd be sorry now," he said, "if it was to Inishbawn you were thinking of going. Herself and the children is away off. I'd have been afraid to leave them there with myself up at the quay with a load of gravel."

Priscilla looked at him with a smile of complete scepticism.

"It's not gravel you have there," she said.

"It's a curious thing," said Joseph Antony in an offended tone, "for you to be saying the like of that and the boat up to the seats with gravel before your eyes."

"I don't deny there's gravel on top," said Priscilla, "but there's something else underneath."

Joseph Antony urged his boat further from the *Tortoise*.

"What do you mean, at all?" he said.

"I don't know what you've got," said Priscilla, "but I saw the rim of some sort of a wooden tub sticking out of the gravel in the fore part of the boat."

Joseph Antony began to row vigorously towards the quay. Priscilla hailed him.

"Tell me this now," she said, "Why did you take Mrs. Kinsella and the children off their island? Was it for fear of the rats?"

Joseph Antony lay on his oars.

"It was not rats," he said. "Why would it?"

"Was it for change of air after the fever?"

"Fever! What fever?"

"Was it because there was something on the island that it wouldn't be nice for Mrs. Kinsella or any other woman to see?"

"It was because of a young heifer," said Joseph Antony, "that I was after buying at the fair of Rosnacree ere yesterday, the wickedest one I ever seen. She had her horn druv through Jimmy's leg and pretty nearly trampled the life out of the baby before she was an hour on the island. If so be that you want to be scattered about, an arm here and a leg there, as soon as you set foot on the shore you can go to Inish-bawn, you and the young gentleman along with you. But if it's pleasure you're looking for it would be better for you to go somewhere else for it, the two of yez."

He spoke truculently. It was evident that Priscilla's questioning had seriously annoyed him. He began to row again while he was speaking and was out of earshot before Priscilla could reply. She waved her hand to him gaily.

The trouble with the anchor rope had delayed the start of the *Tortoise*. It was eleven o'clock before she got under way. Frank had the tiller. Priscilla, seated in the fore part of the boat, gave him instruction in the art of steering. Running before a light breeze makes no high demand upon the helmsman's skill. Frank learned to keep the boat's head steady on her course and realised how small a motion of his hand produced a considerable effect. The time came when the course had to be altered. Priscilla, bent above all on discovering the new camping-ground of the spies, kept in the main channel. There comes a place where this turns northwards. Frank had to push down the tiller in order to bring the boat on her new course. He began to understand the meaning of what he did. The island of Inishrua lay under his lee. Priscilla scanned its slope for the sight of a tent. Frank, now beginning to enjoy his position thoroughly, let the boat away, eased off his sheet and ran down the passage between Inishrua and Knockilaun, the next island to the northward. Cattle browsed peacefully in the fields. A dog rushed from a cottage door and barked. Two children came down to the shore and gazed at the boat curiously. There was no encampment on either island.

Frank pressed down the tiller and hauled in his sheet. Priscilla insisted on his working the main sheet himself. He did it awkwardly and slowly, having only one hand and some fingers of the other, which held the tiller. Then he had his first experience of the joy of beating a small boat against the wind. The passage between the islands is narrow and the tacks were necessarily very short. Frank made all the mistakes common to beginners, sailing at one moment many points off the wind, at the next trying to sail with the luff of his lug and perhaps his foresail flapping piteously. But he learned how to stay the boat and became fascinated in guessing the point on the land which he might hope to reach at the end of each tack. Priscilla kept him from becoming over proud. She showed him, each time the boat went about, the spot which with reasonably good steering he ought to have reached. It was always many yards to windward.

At the end of the passage the boat stood on the starboard tack towards a small round island which lay to the east of Inishrua.

"That's Inishgorm," said Priscilla. "I don't see how they can possibly be there, for there's not a place on it to pitch a tent except the extreme top of the island. But we may as well have a look at it."

Inishgorm ends on the west in a rocky promontory. The *Tortoise* passed it and then Frank stayed her again. The next tack brought them into a little bay with deep, clear water. They stood right on until they were within a few yards of the land. Terns, anxious for the safety of their chicks, rose with shrill cries, circled round the boat, swooping sometimes within a few feet of the sail and then soaring again. Their excitement died away and their cries got fewer when the boat went about and stood away from the island. Priscilla pointed out a long low reef which lay under their lee. Round-backed rocks stood clear of the water at intervals. Elsewhere brown sea wrack was plainly visible just awash. On one of the rocks two seals lay basking in the sun. At the point of the reef a curious patch of sharply rippled water marked where two tides met. A long tack brought the *Tortoise* clear of the windward end of the reef. Frank paid out the main sheet and let the boat away for another run down a passage between the reef and a series of small flat islands.

"This," said Priscilla, "is the likeliest place we've been today. I shouldn't wonder a bit if we came on them here."

The navigation seemed to Frank bewilderingly intricate. Small bays opened among the islands. Rocks obtruded themselves in unexpected places. It was never possible to keep a straight course for more than a couple of minutes at a time. Priscilla gave order in quick succession, "Luff her a little," "Let her away now," "Hold on as you're going," "Steady," "Don't let her away any more." Now and then she threatened him with the possibility of a jibe. Frank, becoming accustomed to everything else, still dreaded that manoeuvre.

A loud hail reached them from the narrow mouth of a bay to windward of them. Priscilla looked round. The hail was repeated. Far up on the northern shore of the bay lay a boat, half in, half out of the water. Beyond her stern, knee deep in the water, with kilted skirts, stood a woman shouting wildly and waving a pocket handkerchief.

"It's the sponge lady," said Priscilla. "Luff, luff her all you can. We'll go in there and see what she wants."

The *Tortoise* slanted up into the wind. Her sails flapped and filled again. Frank pulled manfully on the sheet. There were two short tacks, swift changes of position, slacking and hauling in of sheets. Then Frank found himself, once more on the starboard tack, standing straight for the lady who waved and shouted to them.

"It's a gravelly shore," said Priscilla. "We'll beach her. Sail her easy now, Cousin Frank, and slack away your main sheet if you find there's too much way on her. We don't want to knock a hole in her bottom. Keep her just to windward of Jimmy Kinsella's boat."

The orders were too numerous and too complicated. Frank could keep his head on the football field while hostile forwards charged down on him, could run, kick or pass at such a crisis without setting his nerves a-quiver. He lost all power of reasoning when the *Tortoise* sprang towards Jimmy Kinsella's boat and the gravelly shore. He had judged with absolute accuracy the flight of the ball which the Uppingham captain drove hard and high into the long field. As it left the bat he had started to run, had calculated the curve of its fall, had gauged the pace of his own running, had arrived to receive it in his outstretched hands. He failed altogether in calculating the speed of the *Tortoise*. He suddenly forgot which way to push the tiller in order to attain the result he desired. A wild cry from Priscilla confused him more than ever. He was dimly aware of a sudden check in the motion of the boat. He saw Priscilla start up, and then the lady, who a moment before was standing in the sea, precipitated herself head first over the bow. At the same moment the *Tortoise* grounded on the gravel with a sharp grinding sound. Frank looked about him amazed. Jimmy Kinsella, standing on the shore with his hands in his pockets, spoke slowly.

"Bedamn," he said, "but I never seen the like. With the whole of the wide sea for you to choose out of was there no place that would do you except just the one place where the lady happened to be standing?"

CHAPTER XII

Priscilla's reproaches were sharper and less broadly philosophic in tone.

"Why didn't you luff when I told you?" she said. "Didn't I say you were to keep up to windward of Jimmy Kinsella's boat? If you couldn't do that why hadn't you the sense to let out the main sheet? If we hadn't run into the sponge lady we'd have stripped the copper band off our keel. As it is, I expect she's dead. She hit her head a most frightful crack against the mast."

Miss Rutherford was lying on her stomach across the fore part of the gunwale of the *Tortoise*. Her head was close to the mast. She was groping about with her hands in the bottom of the boat. The lower part of her body, which was temporarily, owing to her position, the upper part, was outside the boat. Her feet beat the air with futile vigour. She wriggled convulsively and after a time her legs followed her head and shoulders into the boat. She rose on her knees, very red in the face, a good deal dishevelled, but laughing heartily.

"I'm not a bit dead," she said, "but I expect my hair's coming down."

"It is," said Priscilla. "I don't believe you have a hairpin left unless one or two have been driven into your skull. Are you much hurt?"

"Not at all," said Miss Rutherford. "Is your mast all right? I hit it rather hard."

Priscilla looked at the mast critically and stroked the part hit by Miss Rutherford's head to find out if it was bruised or cracked.

"I'm most awfully sorry," said Frank. "I don't know how I came to be such a fool. I lost my head completely. I put the tiller the wrong way. I can't imagine how it all happened."

"I don't think," said Miss Rutherford, "that I ever had an invitation to luncheon accepted quite so heartily before. You actually rushed into my arms."

"Were you inviting us to lunch?" said Priscilla.

"I've been inviting you at the top of my voice," said Miss Rutherford, "for nearly a quarter of an hour. I'm so glad you've come in the end."

"We couldn't hear what you were saying," said Priscilla. "All we knew was that you were shouting at us. If we'd known it was an invitation——"

"You couldn't have come any quicker if you'd heard every word," said Miss Rutherford.

"I'm frightfully sorry," said Frank again. "I can't tell you——"

"If I'd known it was luncheon," said Priscilla, "I'd have steered myself and run no risks. We haven't a thing to eat in our boat and I'm getting weak with hunger."

Miss Rutherford stepped overboard again.

"Come on," she said, "we're going to have the grandest picnic ever was, I went down to the village yesterday evening after I got home and bought another tin of Californian peaches."

"How did you know you'd meet us?" said Priscilla.

"I hoped for the best. I felt sure I'd meet you tomorrow if I didn't today. I should have dragged the peaches about with me until I did. Nothing would have induced me to open the tin by myself. I've also got two kinds of dessicated soup and——"

"Penny-packers?" said Priscilla. "I know the look of them, but I never bought one on account of the difficulty of cooking. I don't believe they'd be a bit good dry."

"But I've borrowed Professor Wilder's Primus stove," said Miss Rutherford, "and I've got two cups and an enamelled mug to drink it out of."

"We could have managed with the peach tin," said Priscilla, "after we'd finished the peaches. I hate luxury. But, of course, it's awfully good of you to think of the cups."

"I hesitated about suggesting that we should take turns at the tin," said Miss Rutherford. "I knew you wouldn't mind, but I wasn't quite sure——"

She glanced at Frank.

"Oh, he'd have been all right," said Priscilla. "I'm training him in."

"I've also got a pound and a half of peppermint creams," said Miss Rutherford.

"My favourite sweet," said Priscilla. "You got them at Brannigan's, I hope. He keeps a particularly fine kind, very strong. You have a delicious chilly feeling on your tongue when you draw in your breath after eating them. But Brannigan's is the only place where you get them really good."

"I forget the name of the shop, but I think it must have been Brannigan's. The man advised me to buy them the moment he heard you were to be of the party. He evidently knew your tastes. Then—I'm almost ashamed to confess it after what you said about luxury; but after all you needn't eat it unless you like——

"What is it?" said Priscilla. "Not milk chocolate, surely."

"No. A loaf of bread."

"Oh, bread's all right. It'll go capitally with the soup. Frank was clamouring for bread yesterday, weren't you, Cousin Frank? If there's any over after the soup we can make it into tipsy cake with the juice of the peaches. That's the way tipsy cake is made, except for the sherry, which always rather spoils it, I think, on account of the burny taste it gives. That and the whipped cream, which, of course, is rather good though considered to be unwholesome. But you can't have things like that out boating."

"Come on," said Miss Rutherford, "we'll start the Primus stove, and while the water is boiling we'll eat a few of the peppermint creams as *hors d'oeuvres.*"

Priscilla jumped from the bow of the boat to the shore. "Jimmy Kinsella," she said, "go and help Mr. Mannix out of the boat. He's got a sprained ankle and can't walk. Then you can take our anchor ashore and shove out the boat. She'll lie off all right if you haul down the jib. Miss Rutherford and I will go and light the Primus stove. I've always wanted to see a Primus stove, but I never have except in a Stores List and then, of course, it wasn't working."

"Come on," said Miss Rutherford. "I have it all ready in a sheltered nook under the bank at the top of the beach."

She took Priscilla's hand and began to run across the seaweed towards the grass. Half way up Priscilla stopped abruptly and looked round. Jimmy Kinsella had his arm round Frank and was helping him out of the boat.

"Hullo, Jimmy!" said Priscilla. "I'd better come back and give you a hand. You'll hardly be able to do that job by yourself."

"I will, of course," said Jimmy. "Why not?"

"I thought, perhaps, you wouldn't," said Priscilla, "on account of the hole in your leg."

"What hole?"

"The hole your father's new heifer made when she drove her horn through your leg," said Priscilla. "I suppose there is a hole. There must be if the horn went clean through. It can't have closed up again yet."

"I don't know," said Jimmy. "Did ever I meet a young lady as fond of the funning as yourself, Miss. Many's the time my da did be saying that the like of Miss Priscilla——"

"Your da, as you call him," said Priscilla, "says a deal more than his prayers."

"Do tell me about the hole in Jimmy's leg," said Miss Rutherford. "He never mentioned it to me."

"Nor wouldn't," said Priscilla, "because it's like the rats and the spotted fever and the bad smell, or what ever it was he told you. It's simply not there."

Miss Rutherford lit the methylated spirits in the upper part of the Primus stove. Priscilla pumped up the paraffin with enthusiasm. The water was put on to boil. Then Priscilla asked for the packets of desiccated soup.

"I find," she said, "that it's a capital plan to read the directions for use before you actually do the thing, whatever it is. Last term I spoiled a whole packet of printing paper—photographic, you know—by not doing that. I read them afterwards and found out exactly where I'd gone wrong, which was interesting, of course, but not much real use. Sylvia Courtney rather rubbed it in. That's the sort of girl she is."

"A most disagreeable sort," said Miss Rutherford. "I have met some like her. In fact they're rather common."

"I wouldn't say disagreeable. In fact I rather love Sylvia Courtney at times. But she has her faults. We all have, which in some ways is rather a good thing. If there weren't any faults it would be so dull for people like Aunt Juliet. You're not a Ministering Child, I suppose?"

"No. Are you? I expect you must be."

"I was once. Sylvia Courtney brought me to the meeting. We all had to do some sewing and afterwards there was tea. I joined, of course. The sub. was only sixpence, and there was always tea, with cake, though not good cake. Afterwards I found that I'd sworn a most solemn oath always to do a kind act to some one every day. That's the sort of way you get let in at those meetings."

"You didn't read the directions for use beforehand that time."

"No. But in the end it turned out all right. It was just before the hols when it happened, so, of course, Aunt Juliet had to be my principal victim. I wouldn't do kind acts to Father. He wouldn't understand them, not being educated up to Ministering Children. But Aunt Juliet is different, for I knew that by far the kindest thing I could do to her was to have a few faults. So I did and have ever since, though I stopped being a Ministering Child next term and so wriggled out of the swear."

Frank, leaning on Jimmy Kinsella, came towards them from the boat. He was bent on being particularly polite to Miss Rutherford, feeling that he ought to atone for his unfortunate blunder with the boat He took off his cap and bowed.

"I hope," he said, "that you've been successful in catching sponges."

"I've not got any to-day," said Miss Rutherford. "I haven't begun to fish for them. The tide isn't low enough yet. How are you getting on with the spies? Caught any?"

"Oh," said Frank, "we don't really think they are spies, you know."

"All the same," said Priscilla, "the president of the War Office is out after them. At least we think he must be. We don't see what else he can be after, nor does Father."

"Lord Torrington is to arrive at my uncle's house to-day," said Frank.

"Then they must be spies," said Miss Rutherford. "Not that I ever doubted it."

"That water is pretty near boiling," said Priscilla, "What about dropping in the soup?"

"Which shall we have?" said Miss Rutherford. "There's Mulligatawny and Oxtail?"

"Mulligatawny is the hot sort," said Priscilla, "rather like curry in flavour. I'm not sure that I care much for it. By the way, talking of hot things, didn't you say you had some peppermint creams?"

Miss Rutherford produced the parcel. Priscilla put two into her mouth and made a little pile of six others beside her on the ground. Frank said that he would wait for his share till after he had his soup. Miss Rutherford took one. The desiccated Oxtail soup was emptied into the pot. Priscilla retained the paper in which it had been wrapped.

"'Boil for twenty minutes,'" she read, "'stirring briskly.' That can't be really necessary. I've always noticed that these directions for use are too precautious. They go in frightfully for being on the safe side. I should say myself that we'd be all right in trying it after five minutes. And stirring is rather rot. Things aren't a bit better for being fussed over. In fact Father says most things come out better in the end if they're left alone. 'Add salt to taste, and then serve.' It would have been more sensible to say 'then eat.' But I suppose serve is a politer word. By the way, have you any salt?"

"Not a grain," said Miss Rutherford. "I entirely forgot the salt."

"It's a pity," said Priscilla, "that we didn't think of putting in some sea water. Potatoes are ripping when boiled in sea water and don't need any salt. Peter Walsh told me that once and I expect he knows, I never tried myself."

She glanced at the sea as she spoke, feeling that it was, perhaps, not too late to add the necessary seasoning in its liquid form. A small boat, under a patched lug sail, was crossing the mouth of the bay at the moment. Priscilla sprang to her feet excitedly.

"That's Flanagan's old boat," she said. "I'd know it a mile off. Jimmy! Jimmy Kinsella!"

Jimmy was securing the anchor of the *Tortoise*. He looked round.

"Isn't that Flanagan's old boat?" said Priscilla.

"It is, Miss, surely. There's ne'er another boat in the bay but herself with the bit of an old flour sack sewed on along the leach of the sail. It was only last week my da was saying——"

"We haven't a moment to lose," said Priscilla. "Miss Rutherford, you help Frank down. I'll run on and get up the foresail."

"But the soup?" said Miss Rutherford, "and the peppermint creams, and the rest of the luncheon?"

"If you feel that you can spare the peppermint creams," said Priscilla, "we'll take them. But we can't wait for the soup."

"Take the bread, too," said Miss Rutherford, "and the peaches. It won't delay you a minute to put in the peaches!"

"If you're perfectly certain you don't want them for yourself, we'll be very glad to have them."

"Nothing would induce me to eat a Californian peach in selfish solitude," said Miss Rutherford, "I should choke if I tried."

"Right," said Priscilla. "You carry them down and sling them on board. I'll help Frank. Now, then, Cousin Frank, do stand up. I can't drag you down over the seaweed on your side. You've got to hop more or less."

Miss Rutherford, with the loaf of bread, the peaches and the peppermint creams in her hand, ran down to the boat. Frank and Priscilla followed her. Jimmy had put the anchor on board and was holding the *Tortoise* with her bow against the shingle.

"Take me, too," said Miss Rutherford. "I love chasing spies more than anything else in the world."

"All right," said Priscilla. "Bound in and get down to the stern. Now, Frank, you're next. Oh, do go on. Jimmy, give him a lift from behind. I'll steer this time."

She hauled on the foresail halyard, got the sail up and made the rope fast. Then she sprang to the stern, squeezed past Miss Rutherford and took the tiller.

"Shove her off, Jimmy, wade in a bit and push her head round. I'll go off on the starboard tack and not have to jibe. Oh, Miss Rutherford, don't, please don't sit on the main sheet."

The business of getting a boat, which is lying head to wind to pay off and sail away, is comparatively simple. The fact that the shore lies a few yards to windward does not complicate the matter much. The main sheet must be allowed to run out so that the sail does not draw at first. The foresail, its sheet being hauled down, works the boat's head round. Unfortunately for Priscilla, her main sheet would not run out. Miss Rutherford made frantic efforts not to sit on it, but only succeeded in involving herself in a serious tangle. Jimmy Kinsella pushed the boat's head round. Both sails filled with wind. Priscilla held the tiller across the boat without effect The *Tortoise* heeled over, and with a graceful swerve sailed up to the shore again.

"Oh bother!" said Priscilla, "shove her off again, Jimmy. Wade in with her and push her head right round. Thank goodness I have the main sheet clear now."

This time the *Tortoise* swung round and headed for the entrance of the bay.

"Jimmy," shouted Miss Rutherford, "there's some soup in the pot. Go and eat it. Afterwards you'd better come on in your boat and see what happens to us."

"There's no necessity for any excitement," said Priscilla. "Let everybody keep quite calm. We are bound to catch them."

The *Tortoise* swung round the rocks at the mouth of the bay. Flanagan's old boat was seen a quarter of a mile ahead, running towards a passage which seemed absolutely blocked with rocks. The *Tortoise* began to overhaul her rapidly.

"I almost wish," said Miss Rutherford, "that you'd allowed Frank to steer. When we're out for an adventure we ought to be as adventurous as possible."

"They're trying the passage through Craggeen," said Priscilla, with her eyes on Flanagan's old boat. "That shows they're pretty desperate. Hand me the peppermint creams. There's jolly little water there at this time of the tide. It'll be sheer luck if they get through."

"Take five or six peppermints," said Miss Rutherford, "if you feel that they'll steady your nerves. You'll want something of the sort. I feel thrills down to the tips of my fingers."

Flanagan's old boat ran on. Seen from the *Tortoise* she seemed to pass through an unbroken line of rocks. She twisted and turned now southwards, now west, now northwards. The *Tortoise* sped after her.

"Now, Cousin Frank," said Priscilla, "get hold of the centreboard rope and haul when I tell you. There'll be barely water to float us, if there's that. We'll never get through with the centreboard down."

She headed the boat straight for a gravelly spit of land past which the tide swept in a rapid stream. A narrow passage opened suddenly. Priscilla put the tiller down and the *Tortoise* swept through. A mass of floating seaweed met them. The *Tortoise* fell off from the wind and slipped inside it. A heavy bump followed.

"Up centreboard," said Priscilla. "I knew it was shallow."

Frank pulled vigorously. Another bump followed.

"Bother!" said Priscilla. "We're done now."

The *Tortoise* swept up into the wind. Her sails flapped helplessly.

"What's the matter?" said Miss Rutherford.

"Rudder's gone," said Priscilla. "That last bump unshipped it."

She held the useless tiller in her hand. The rudder, swept forward by the tide, drifted away until it went ashore on a reef at the northern end of the passage. The *Tortoise*, after making one or two ineffective efforts to sail without a rudder, grounded on the beach of Craggeen Island. Priscilla jumped out.

"Just you two sit where you are," said said, "and don't let the boat drift. I'll run on to the point of the island and see where those spies are going to. Then we'll get the rudder again and be after them."

"Frank," said Miss Rutherford, when Priscilla had disappeared, "have you any idea how we are to keep the boat from drifting?"

"There's the anchor," said Frank.

"I don't trust that anchor a bit. It's such a small one, and the boat seems to me to be in a particularly lively mood."

The *Tortoise*, her bow pressed against the gravel, appeared to be making efforts to force her way through the island. Every now and then, as if irritated by failure, she leaned heavily over to one side.

"I think," said Miss Rutherford, "I'll stand in the water and hold her till Priscilla comes back. It's not deep."

Frank's sense of chivalry would not allow him to sit dry in the boat while a lady was standing up to her ankles in water beside him. He struggled overboard and stood on one leg holding on to the gunwale of the *Tortoise*. Priscilla was to be seen on the point of the island watching Flanagan's old boat.

"Let's eat some peppermint creams," said Miss Rutherford. "They'll keep us warm."

"I'm awfully sorry about all this," said Frank. "I don't know what you'll think of us. First I run into you and then Priscilla wrecks you on this island."

"I'm enjoying myself thoroughly," said Miss Rutherford. "I wonder what will happen next. We can't go on without a rudder, can we?"

"She'll get it back. It's quite near us."

"So it is. I see it bobbing up and down against the rocks there. I think I'll go after it myself. It will be a pleasant surprise for Priscilla when she comes back to find that we've got it. Do you think you can hold the boat by yourself? She seems quieter than she was."

Miss Rutherford waded round the stern of the *Tortoise* and set off towards the rudder. The water was not deep in any part of the channel, but there were holes here and there. When Miss Rutherford stepped into them she stood in water up to her knees. There were also slippery stones and once she staggered and very nearly fell. She saved herself by plunging one arm elbow deep in front of her. She hesitated and looked round.

"Thank goodness," she said, "here's Jimmy Kinsella coming in the other boat. He'll get the rudder."

CHAPTER XIII

Beyond the rock-strewn passage of Craggeen lies the wide roadstead of Finilaun. Here the water is deep, and the shelter, from every quarter, almost complete. Across the western end of it stretches like a bent bow, the long island of Finilaun. On the south, reaching almost to the point of Finilaun, is Craggeen, and between the two is a shallow strait. On the east is the mainland, broken and bitten into with long creeks and bays. On the north lies a chain of islands, Ilaunure, Curraunbeg and Curraunmor, separated from each other by narrow channels, through which the tide runs strongly in and out of the roadstead.

Across the open roadstead Flanagan's old boat crept under her patched lug sail. Priscilla, standing on the shore of Craggeen, watched eagerly. At first she could see the occupants of the boat quite plainly, a man at the tiller, a woman sitting forward near the mast. She had no difficulty in recognising them. The man wore the white sweater which had attracted her attention when she first saw him, a garment most unusual among boatmen in Rosnacree Bay. The woman was the same who had mopped her dripping companion with a pocket handkerchief on Inishark. They talked eagerly together. Now and then the man turned and looked back at Craggeen. The woman pointed something out to him. Priscilla understood.

They could see the patch of the *Tortoise*'s sail above the rocks which blocked the entrance of the passage. They were no doubt wondering anxiously whether they were still pursued. Flanagan's old boat, her sail bellied pleasantly by the following wind, drew further and further away. Priscilla could no longer distinguish the figures of the man and woman. She watched the sail. It was evident that the boat was making for one of the three northern islands. Soon it was clear that her destination was the eastern end of Curraunbeg. Either she meant to run through the passage between that island and Curraunmor, or the spies would land on Curraunbeg. The day was clear and bright. Priscilla's eyes were good. She saw on the eastern shore of Curraunbeg a white patch, distinguishable against the green background of the field. It could be nothing else but the tents of the spies' encampment. Flanagan's old boat slipped round the corner of the island and disappeared. Priscilla was satisfied. She knew where the spies had settled down.

She returned to the *Tortoise*. Frank had left the boat and was sitting on the shore. Miss Rutherford, with the recovered rudder on her knees, sat beside him. Jimmy Kinsella was standing in front of them apparently delivering a speech. The two boats lay side by side close to the shore.

"What's Jimmy jawing about?" said Priscilla.

"I'm after telling the lady," said Jimmy, "that you'll sail no more today."

"Will I not? And why?"

"You will not," said Jimmy, "because the rudder iron is broke on you."

"That's the worst of these boats," said Priscilla. "The rudder sticks down six inches below the bottom of them and if there happens to be a rock anywhere in the neighborhood it's the rudder that it's sure to hit."

"You'll excuse me saying so, Miss, but you'd no right to be trying to get through Craggeen at this time of the tide. It couldn't be done."

"It could," said Priscilla, "and, what's more, it would, only for that old rudder."

"Any way," said Jimmy; "you'll sail no more today, and it'll be lucky if you sail tomorrow for you'll have to give that rudder to Patsy, the smith, to put a new iron on it and that same Patsy isn't one that likes doing anything in a hurry."

"I'm going on to Curraunbeg," said Priscilla, "I'll steer with an oar."

"Is it steer with an oar, Miss?"

"Haven't you often done it yourself, Jimmy?"

"Not that one," said Jimmy, pointing to the *Tortoise*.

"Sure my da's said to me many's the time how that one is pretty near as giddy as yourself."

"Your da talks too much," said Priscilla. "Come on, Cousin Frank. What about you, Miss Rutherford? Are you coming?"

"You'll not go," said Jimmy, "or if you do, you'll walk."

Priscilla looked out at the sea. The tide was falling rapidly. Through the opening of the passage which led into Finilaun roadstead there was no more than a trickle of water running like a brook over the stony bottom.

"It'll be as much as you'll do this minute," said Jimmy, "to get back the way you came, and you'll only do that same by taking the sails off of her and poling her along with an oar."

Priscilla surrendered. It is, after all, impossible to sail a boat without water. The *Tortoise* lay afloat in a pool, but the Finilaun end of the passage was hardly better than a lane-way of wet stones. At the other end there was still high water, but very little of it. Priscilla acted promptly in the emergency. She had no desire to lie imprisoned for hours on Craggeen, she had lain the day before on the bank off Inishark. She took the sails off the *Tortoise* and, standing on the thwart amidships, began poling the boat back into the open water at the south-eastern end of the passage. Jimmy, also poling, followed in his boat.

Miss Rutherford, the broken rudder still on her knees, and Frank, were left on shore.

"Do you think," she said, "that Priscilla intends to maroon us here? She's gone without us."

"I'm awfully sorry," said Franks "It's not my fault. I couldn't stop her."

"She's got all the food there is, even the peppermint creams. I wish I'd thought of snatching that parcel from the boat before she started. She'd have come back when she found out they were gone. I wonder whether Jimmy finished the soup? I wonder what he's done with the Primus stove. It wasn't mine, and I know Professor Wilder sets a value on it. Perhaps they'll pick it up on their way and return it. If they do I shan't so much mind what happens to us."

"I don't think they'll really leave us here," said Frank. "Even Priscilla wouldn't do that. I wish I could walk down to the corner of the island and see where they've gone."

Jimmy Kinsella appeared, strolling quietly along the shore.

"The young lady says, Miss," he said "that if you wouldn't mind walking down to the far side of the gravel spit, which is where she has the boats, she'd be glad, for she wouldn't like to be eating what's in the boat without you'd be there to have some yourself."

"Priscilla is perfectly splendid," said Miss Rutherford, "and we're not going to be marooned after all. Come along, Frank."

"The young lady says, Miss," said Jimmy, "that if you'd go to her the best way you can by yourself that I'd give my arm to the gentleman and get him along over the stones so as not to hurt his leg and that same won't be easy for the shore's mortal rough."

Miss Rutherford refused to desert Frank. She recognised that the shore was all that Jimmy said it was. Large slippery boulders were strewed about it for fifty yards or so between the place where she stood and the gravel spit. She insisted on helping Jimmy to transport Frank. In the end they descended upon Priscilla, all three abreast. Frank, with one arm round Jimmy's neck and one round Miss Rutherford's, hobbled bravely.

"I don't know," said Priscilla, "that this is exactly an ideal place for luncheon, but we can have it here if you like, and in some ways I'm rather inclined to. You never know what may happen if you put things off. Last time the but was snatched out of our mouths by a callous destiny just as it was beginning to smell really good. By the way, Jimmy, what did you do with the soup?"

"It's there beyond, Miss, where you left it."

"I expect it's all boiled away by this time," said Priscilla, "but of course the Primus stove may have gone out. You never know beforehand how those patent machines will act. If it has gone out the soup will be all right, though coldish. Perhaps we'd better go back there."

"Which would you like to do yourself, Priscilla," said Miss Rutherford.

"Now that those spies have escaped us again," said Priscilla, "it doesn't matter to me in the least where we go. But this place is a bit stony for sitting in for long. I'm beginning to feel already rather as if a plougher had ploughed upon my back and made large furrows; but of course I'm thinking principally of Frank on account of his sprained ankle. A grassy couch would be much pleasanter for him, and there is grass where we left the Primus stove. We can row back. It isn't a very long pull."

"The wind's dropped, Miss, with the fall of the tide," said Jimmy, "and what's left of it has gone round to the southward."

"That settles it," said Priscilla. "Frank, you and Miss Rutherford, go in the *Tortoise*. Jimmy and I will row the other boat and tow you."

"I can row all right," said Frank.

To be treated as incapable by Priscilla when they were alone together was unpleasant but tolerable. To be held up as an object of scorn to Miss Rutherford was not tolerable. He had already exposed himself to her contempt by running her down. He was anxious to show her that he was not altogether a fool in a boat.

"You can't, much," said Priscilla. "At least you didn't seem as if you could yesterday; but if you like you can try. We'll take the oars out of the *Tortoise* into your boat, Jimmy, and pull four."

"I don't see how that could be, Miss, for there's only three seats in my boat along with the one in the stern and you couldn't row from that."

"Don't be a fool, Jimmy. I'll pull two oars in the middle. Frank will take one in the bow, and you'll pull stroke. Miss Rutherford will have the *Tortoise* all to herself."

Frank found it comparatively easy to row in Jimmy Kinsella's boat. The oar was short and stumpy with a very narrow blade. It was worked between two thole pins of which one was cracked and required tender treatment. It was impossible to pull comfortably while sitting in the middle of the seat; he still hit Priscilla in the back when he swung forward; but there was no boom to hit him and there was no mast behind him to bump his own back against. Priscilla was too fully occupied managing her own two oars to pay much attention to him. Jimmy Kinsella pulled away with dogged indifference to what any one else was doing. Miss Rutherford sat in the stern of the *Tortoise* and shouted encouraging remarks from time to time. She had, apparently, boated on the Thames at some time in her life, for she was mistress of a good deal of rowing slang which she used with vigour and effect. It cheered Frank greatly to hear the more or less familiar words, for he realised almost at once that neither Priscilla nor Jimmy Kinsella understood them. He felt a warm affection for Miss Rutherford rise in his heart when she told Jimmy, who sat humped up over his oar, to keep his back flat. Jimmy merely smiled in reply. He had known since he was two years old that the flatness or roundness of the rower's back has nothing whatever to do with the progress of a boat in Rosnacree Bay. A few minutes later she accused Priscilla of "bucketing," and Frank loved her for the word. Priscilla replied indignantly with an obvious misapprehension of Miss Rutherford's meaning. Frank, who was rowing in his best style, smiled and was pleased to catch sight of an answering smile on Miss Rutherford's lips. He had established an understanding with her. She and he, as representatives of the rowing of a higher civilisation, could afford to smile together over the barbarous methods of Priscilla and Jimmy Kinsella.

The tide was still against them, though the full strength of the ebb was past. The stream which ran through the narrow water-way had to be reckoned with.

The *Tortoise*, when being towed, behaved after the manner of her kind. She hung heavily on the tow rope for a minute; then rushed forward as if she wished to bump the stern of Jimmy's boat At the last moment she used to change her mind and swoop off to the right or left, only to be brought up short by the rope at which she tugged with angry jerks until, finding that it really could not be broken, she dropped sulkily astern. These manoeuvres, though repeated with every possible variation, left Priscilla and Jimmy Kinsella entirely unmoved. They pulled with the same stolid indifference whatever pranks the *Tortoise* played. They annoyed Frank. Sometimes when the tow rope hung slack in the water, he pulled through his stroke with ease and comfort. Sometimes when the *Tortoise* hung back heavily he seemed to be pulling against an impossible dead weight. But his worst experience came when the *Tortoise* altered her tactics in the middle of one of his strokes. Then, if it happened that she sulked suddenly, he was brought up short with a jerk that jarred his spine. If, on the other; hand, she chose to rush forward when he had his weight well on the end of his oar, he ran a serious risk of falling backwards after the manner of beginners who catch crabs. The side swoops of the *Tortoise* were equally trying. They seemed to Frank to disturb hopelessly the whole rhythm of the rowing. Nothing but the encouragement which came to him from Miss Rutherford's esoteric slang kept him from losing his temper. He could not have been greatly blamed if he had lost it. It was after three o'clock. He had breakfasted, meagrely, on bread and honey, at half past seven. He had spent the intervening seven and a half hours on the sea, eating nothing but the one peppermit cream which Miss Rutherford pressed on him while he held the *Tortoise* at Craggeen. Priscilla had eaten a great many peppermint cream and was besides more inured to starvation on the water of the bay than Frank was. But even Priscilla, when the excitement of getting away from Craggeen had passed, seemed slightly depressed. She scarcely spoke at all, and when she replied to Miss Rutherford's accusation of "bucketing" did so incisively.

The boats turned into the bay from which Miss Rutherford had first hailed the *Tortoise*. They were safely beached. Priscilla ran up to the nook under the hill where the Primus stove was left. Miss Rutherford and Jimmy stayed to help Frank.

"It's all right," shouted Priscilla. "A good deal has boiled away, but the Primus stove evidently went out in time to prevent the bottom being boiled out of the pot. Want of paraffin, I expect."

"Never mind," said Miss Rutherford, "I have some more in a bottle. We can boil it up again."

"It's hardly worth while," said Priscilla. "I expect it would be quite good cold, what's left of it. Thickish of course, but nourishing."

"We'll make a second brew," said Miss Rutherford. "I have another package. Jimmy, do you know if there's any water in this neighbourhood?"

"There's a well beyond," said Jimmy, "at the end of the field across the hill, but I don't would the likes of yez drink the water that does be in it."

"Saltish?" said Priscilla.

"It is not then. But the cattle does be drinking out of it and I wouldn't say it was too clean."

"If we boil it," said Frank, "that won't matter."

He had read, as most of us did at the time, accounts of the precautions taken by the Japanese doctors during the war with Russia to save the soldiers under their care from enteric fever. He believed that boiling removed dirt from water.

"There's worms in it," said Jimmy. "It's hardly ever you take a cupful out of it without you'd feel the worms on your tongue and you drinking it."

Miss Rutherford looked at Priscilla, who appeared undismayed at the prospect of swallowing worms. Then she looked at Frank. He was evidently doubtful. His faith in boiling did not save him from a certain shrinking from wormy soup.

"Once we were out for a picnic," said Priscilla, "and when we'd finished tea we found a frog, dead, of course, in the bottom of the kettle. It hadn't flavoured the tea in the least. In fact we didn't know it was there till afterwards."

She poured out the cold soup into the two cups and the enamelled mug as she spoke. Then she handed the pot to Jimmy.

"Run now," she said, "and fill that up with your dirty water. We'll have the stove lit and the other packet of soup ready by the time you're back."

The soup which had not boiled away was very thick indeed. It turned out to be impossible to drink it, but Priscilla discovered that it could be poured out slowly, like clotted cream, on pieces of bread held ready for it under the rims of the cups. It remained, spreading gradually, on top of the bread long enough to allow a prompt eater to get the whole thing into his mouth without allowing any of the soup to be wasted by dripping on to the ground. The flavour was excellent.

Jimmy returned with the water. Miss Rutherford put the pot on the stove at once. It was better, she said, to boil it without looking at it.

"The directions for use," said Priscilla, "say that the water should be brought to the boil before the soup is put in. But that, of course, is ridiculous. We'll put the dry soup in at once and let it simmer. I expect the flavour will come out all right if we leave it till it does boil."

"In the meanwhile," said Miss Rutherford, "we'll attack the Californian peaches."

They ate them, as they had eaten the others the day before, in their fingers, straight out of the tin with greedy rapture. Five half peaches, nearly all the juice, and a large chunk of bread, were given to Jimmy Kinsella, who carried them off and devoured them in privacy behind his boat.

"Tomorrow," said Priscilla, "we'll have another go at the spies. They're desperately afraid of us. I could see that when they were escaping across Finilaun harbour."

"By the expression of their faces?" said Miss Rutherford.

"Not exactly. It was more the way they were going on. Sylvia Courtney was once learning off a poem called 'The Ancient Mariner.' That was when she was going in for the prize in English literature. She and I sleep in the same room and she used to say a few verses of it every night while we were doing our hairs. I never thought any of it would come in useful to me, but it has; which just shows that one never ought to waste anything. The bit I mean was about a man who walked along a road at night in fear and dread. He used to look round and then turn no more his head, because he knew a frightful fiend did close behind him tread. That's exactly what those two spies did today when they were sailing across Finilaun; so you see poetry is some use after all. I used to think it wasn't; but it is. It's frightfully silly to make up your mind that anything in the world is no use. You never can tell until you've tried and that may not be for years."

"The spies," said Miss Rutherford, "are, I suppose, encamped somewhere on the far side of Finilaun harbour."

"On Curraunbeg," said Priscilla. "I saw the tents."

"I may be going in that direction myself tomorrow," said Miss Rutherford.

Priscilla got up and stepped across to the place where Frank was sitting. She stooped down and whispered to him. Then she returned to her own seat and winked at him, keeping her left eye closed for nearly half a minute, and screwing up the corresponding corner of her mouth.

"We hope," said Frank, "that you'll join us at luncheon tomorrow wherever we may meet. It's our turn to bring the grub."

"With the greatest pleasure," said Miss Rutherford. "Shall I bring the stove?"

"I didn't like to invite you," said Priscilla, "until I found out whether Frank had any money to buy things with. As it turns out he has lots. I haven't. That's the reason I whispered to him, although I know it's rude to whisper when there's any one else there. Of course, I may be able to collar a few things out of the house; but I may not. With that Secretary of War staying in the house there is bound to be a lot of food lying about which nobody would notice much if it was gone. But then it's not easy to get it unless you happen not to be allowed in to dinner, which may be the case. If I'm not—Frank, I'm afraid, is sure to be on account of his having a dress coat—but if I'm not, which is what may happen if Aunt Juliet thinks it would score off me not to, then I can get lots of things without difficulty because the cook can't possibly tell whether they've been finished up in the dining-room or not."

"We'll hope for the best," said Miss Rutherford. "A jelly now or a few meringues would certainly be a pleasant variety after the tinned and dried provisions of the last two days."

The peppermint creams were finished before the second brew of soup came to the boil on the Primus stove. Priscilla poured it out. It was hot, of about the consistency usual in soup, and it smelt savoury. Nevertheless Miss Rutherford, after watching for an opportunity to do so unseen, poured hers out on the ground. Frank fingered his mug irresolutely and once took a sip. Priscilla, after looking at her share intently, carried it off and gave it to Jimmy Kinsella.

"It's curious," she said when she came back, "but I don't feel nearly so keen on soup as I did. I daresay it's the peaches and the peppermint creams. I used to think it was rather rot putting off the sweets at dinner until after the meaty things. Now, I know it isn't. Sometimes there's really a lot of sense in an arrangement which seems silly at first, which is one of the things which always makes me say that grownup people aren't such fools as you might suppose if you didn't really know."

"We'll remember that at lunch tomorrow," said Miss Rutherford.

No one mentioned worms.

For the second time the weather, generally malign and irresponsible, favoured Priscilla. With the rising tide a light westerly breeze sprang up. She hoisted the sails and sat in the stern of the boat with an oar. She tucked the middle of it under her armpit, pressed her side tight against the gunwale, and with the blade trailing in the water steadied the *Tortoise* on her course. There is a short cut back to Rosnacree quay from the bay in which Miss Rutherford was left. It winds among a perfect maze of rocks, half covered or bare at low water, gradually becoming invisible as the tide rises. Priscilla, whose self-confidence was unshaken by her disaster in Craggeen passage, took this short cut in spite of a half-hearted protest from Frank. "I don't exactly know the way," she said, "but now that we've lost the rudder there's nothing very much can happen to us. We can keep the centreboard up as we're running, and if we do go on a rock, the tide will lift us off again. It's rising now. Besides, it saves us miles to go this way, and it really won't do for you to be late for dinner."

CHAPTER XIV

Thomas Antony Kinsella sat with his legs dangling over the edge of the quay. Beneath him lay his boat. The tide was flowing, but it had not yet floated her. She was supported on an even keel by the mooring ropes made fast from her bow and stern to bollards on the quay. Her sails and gear lay in confusion on her thwarts. She was still half full of gravel although some of her cargo had been shovelled out and lay in a heap behind Kinsella. He was apparently disinclined to shovel out the rest, an excusable laziness, for the day was very hot.

With the point of a knife Kinsella scraped the charred ash from the bowl of his pipe. Then he cut several thin slices from a plug of black twist tobacco, rolled them slowly between the palm of one hand and the thumb of the other; spat thoughtfully over the side of the quay into his boat, charged his pipe and put it into his mouth. There he held it for some minutes while he stared glassily at the top of his boat's mast. He spat again and then drew a match from his waistcoat pocket.

Sergeant Rafferty of the Royal Irish Constabulary strolled quietly along the quay. It was his duty to stroll somewhere every day in order to intimidate malefactors. He found the quay on the whole a more interesting place than any of the country roads round the town, so he often chose it for the scene of what his official regulations described as a "patrol." When he reached Kinsella he stopped.

"Good day to you," he said.

Kinsella, without looking round, struck his match on a stone beside him and lit his pipe. He sucked in three draughts of smoke, spat again and then acknowledged the sergeant's greeting.

"It's a fine day," said the sergeant

"It is," said Kinsella, "thanks be to God."

The sergeant stirred the pile of gravel on the quay thoughtfully with his foot. Then, peering over Kinsella's shoulder, he took a look at the gravel which still remained in the boat.

"Tell me this, now, Joseph Antony," he said. "Who might that gravel be for? It's the third day you're after bringing in a load and there's ne'er a cart's been down for it yet?"

"I couldn't say who it might be for."

"Do you tell me that now? And who's to pay you for it?"

"Sweeny 'll pay for it," said Kinsella. "It was him ordered it."

The sergeant stirred the gravel again with his foot Timothy Sweeny was a publican who kept a small shop in one of the back streets of Rosnacree. He was known to the sergeant, but was not regarded with favour. There is a way into Sweeny's house through a back-yard which is reached by climbing a wall. Sweeny's front door was always shut on Sundays and his shutters were put up during those hours when the law regards the consumption of alcohol as undesirable. But the sergeant had good reason to suppose that many thirsty people found their way to the refreshment they craved through the back-yard. Sweeny was an object of suspicion and dislike to the sergeant. Therefore he stirred the gravel on the quay again and again looked at the gravel in the boat. There is no law against buying gravel; but it seemed to the sergeant very difficult to believe that Sweeny had bought four boatloads of it. Joseph Antony Kinsella felt that some explanation was due to the sergeant.

"It's a gentleman up the country," he said, "that Sweeny's buying the gravel for. I did hear that he's to send it by rail when I have the whole of it landed."

He watched the sergeant out of the corners of his eyes to see how he would receive this statement. The sergeant did not seem to be altogether satisfied.

"What are you getting for it?" he asked.

"Five shillings a load."

"You're doing well," said the sergeant.

"It's good gravel, so it is, the best."

"It may be good gravel," said the sergeant, "but the gentleman that's buying it will buy it dear if you take the half of every load you bring in home in the evening and fetch it here again the next morning along with a little more."

The sergeant stared at the gravel in the boat as he spoke. His face had cleared, and the look of suspicion had left his eyes. Sweeny, so his instinct told him, must be engaged in some kind of wrongdoing.

Now he understood what it was. The gentleman up the country was to be defrauded of half the gravel he paid for. Curiously enough, considering that his wrongdoing had been detected, the look of anxiety left Kinsella's face. He sucked at his pipe, found that it had gone out, and slipped it into his waistcoat pocket.

"If neither Sweeny nor the gentleman is making any complaint," he said, "it would suit you to keep your mouth shut."

"I'm not blaming you," said the sergeant "Sure, anybody'd do the same if they got the chance."

"If there's people in the world," said Kinsella, "that hasn't sense enough to see that they get what they pay for, oughtn't we to be thankful for it?"

"You're right there," said the sergeant

Kinsella took out his pipe and lit it again. Sergeant Rafferty after examining the sea with attentive scrutiny for some minutes, strolled back towards his barracks.

Peter Walsh slid off the window sill of Brannigan's shop and took a long look at the sky. Having satisfied himself that its appearance was very much what he expected he walked down the quay to the place where Kinsella was sitting.

"It's a fine evening," he said.

"It is," said Kinsella, "as fine an evening as you'd see, thanks be to God."

Peter Walsh sat down beside his friend and spat into the boat beneath him.

"I seen the sergeant talking to you," he said.

"That same sergeant has mighty little to do," said Kinsella.

"It'll be as well for us if he hasn't more one of these days."

"What do you mean by that, Peter Walsh?"

"What might he have been talking to you about?"

"Gravel, no less."

"Asking who it might be for or the like? Would you say, now, Joseph Antony, that he was anyways uneasy in his mind?"

"He was uneasy," said Kinsella, "but he's easy now."

"Did you tell him who the gravel was for?"

"Is it likely I'd tell him when I didn't know myself? What I told him was that Timothy Sweeny had the gravel bought off me at five shillings a load and that it was likely he'd be sending it by rail to some gentleman up the country that would have it ordered from him."

"And what did he say to that?"

"What he as good as said was that Timothy Sweeny and myself would have the gentleman cheated out of half the gravel he'd paid for by the time he'd got the other half. There was a smile on his face like there might be on a man, and him after a long drink, when he found out the way we were getting the better of the gentleman up the country. Believe you me, Peter Walsh, he wouldn't have rested easy in his bed until he did find out, either that or some other thing."

"That sergeant is as cute as a pet fox," said Peter Walsh. "You'd be hard set to keep anything from him that he wanted to know."

Kinsella sat for some minutes without speaking. Then he took a match from his pocket and lit his pipe for the third time.

"I'd be glad," he said, "if you'd tell me what it was you had in your mind when you said a minute ago that the sergeant might maybe have more to do than he'd care for one of these days."

Peter Walsh looked carefully round him in every direction and satisfied himself that there was no one within earshot.

"Was I telling you," he said, "about the gentleman, and the lady along with him that came in on the train today?"

"You were not."

"Well, he came, and I'm thinking that he's a high-up man."

"What about him?"

"The sergeant was sent for up to the big house," said Peter Walsh, "soon after the strange gentleman came. I don't know rightly what they wanted with him. Sweeny was asking Constable Maloney after; but sure the boy knew no more than I did myself."

"It's a curious thing," said Kinsella, "so it is, damned curious."

"Damned," said Peter Walsh.

"I wouldn't be sorry if the whole lot of them was drownded one of these days."

"I wouldn't like anything would happen to the young lady."

"Is it Priscilla? I wasn't meaning her. But any way, Peter Walsh, you know well the sea wouldn't drown that one."

"It would not, surely. Why would it?"

"What I had in my mind," said Kinsella, "was the rest of them."

He looked sadly at the sky and then out across the sea, which was perfectly calm.

"But there'll be no drowning," he added with a sigh, "while the weather holds the way it is."

"There's a feel in the air," said Peter Walsh hopefully, "like as if there might be thunder."

A small boat, rowed by a boy, stole past them up the harbour. Neither of the two men spoke until she reached the slip at the end of the quay.

"I'd be sorry," said Kinsella, "if anything would happen to them two that does be going about in Flanagan's old boat. There's no harm in them barring the want of sense."

"It would be as well for them to be kept off Inishbawn for all that."

"They never offered to set foot on the island," said Kinsella, "since the day I told them that herself and the childer had the fever. The way it is with them, they wouldn't care where they'd be, one place being the same to them as another, if they'd be let alone."

"That's what they will not be, then."

"On account of Priscilla?"

"Her and the young fellow she has with her. They're out hunting them two that has Flanagan's old boat the same as it might be some of the boys at a coursing match and the hare in front of them. Such chasing you never seen! It was up out of their beds they were this morning at six o'clock, when you'd think the likes of them would be asleep."

"I seen them," said Kinsella.

"And the one of them is as bad as the other. You'd be hard put to it to say whether it was Priscilla has put the comether on the young fellow or him that had her druv' on to be doing what it would be better for her to leave alone."

"Tell me this now, Peter Walsh, that young fellow is by the way of having a sore leg on him, so they tell me. Would you say now but that might be a trick the way it would put us off from suspecting any mischief he might be up to?"

"I was thinking myself," said Peter, "that he might be imposing on us; but it's my opinion now that the leg's genuine. I followed them up last night, unbeknown to them, to see would he get out of the perambulator when he was clear of the town and nobody to notice him. But he kept in it and she wheeled him up to the big house every step of the way."

The evidence was conclusive and carried complete conviction to Kinsella's mind.

"What would be your own opinion," said Peter Walsh, "about that one that does be going about the bay in your own boat along with Jimmy?"

"I wouldn't say there'd be much harm in her. Jimmy says it's hard to tell what she'd be after. He did think at the first go off that it might be cockles; but it's not, for he took her to Carribee strand, where there's plenty of them, and the devil a one she'd pick up. Nor it's not periwinkles. Nor dilishk, though they do say that the dilishk is reckoned to be a cure for consumption, and you'd think it might be that. But Jimmy says it's not, for he offered her a bit yesterday and she wouldn't look at it."

"I don't know what else it could be," said Peter Walsh.

"Nor I don't know. But Jimmy says she doesn't speak like one that would be any ways in with the police."

"She was in Brannigan's last night, buying peppermint drops and every kind of foolishness, the same as she might be a little girleen that was given a penny and her just out of school."

"If she hasn't more sense at her time of life," said Kinsella, "she never will."

"Seeing it's that sort she is, I wouldn't say we'd any need to be caring where she goes so long as it isn't to Inishbawn."

"She'll not go there," said Kinsella, "for if she does I'll flay the skin of Jimmy's back with the handle of a hay-rake, and well he knows it."

"If I was easy in my mind about the strange gentleman that's up at the big house——"

"It's a curious thing, so it is, him sending for the sergeant the minute he came."

"Bedamn," said Peter Walsh, "but it is."

The extreme oddness of the strange gentleman's conduct affected both men profoundly. For fully five minutes they sat staring at the sea, motionless, save when one or the other of them thrust his head forward a little in order to spit. Kinsella at last got out his pipe, probed the tobacco a little with the point of his knife so as to loosen it, pressed it together again with his thumb, and then lit it.

"I wouldn't mind the sergeant," he said, "cute and all as he thinks himself, I wouldn't mind him. It's the strange gentleman I'm thinking of."

The *Tortoise* stole round the end of the quay while he spoke. Kinsella eyed her. He noticed at once that Priscilla was steering with an oar. In his acutely suspicious mood every trifle was a matter for investigation.

"What's wrong with her," he said, "that she wouldn't steer with the rudder when she has one?"

"It might be," said Peter Walsh, "that she's lost it. You couldn't tell what the likes of her would do."

"She was in trouble this morning when I seen her," said Kinsella, "but she had the rudder then."

Priscilla hailed them from the boat

"Hullo, Peter!" she shouted. "Go down to the slip and be ready to take the boat. Have you the bath chair ready?"

"I have, Miss. It's there standing beside the slip where you left it this morning. Who'd touch the like? What's happened the rudder?"

"Iron's broken," said Priscilla, "and it must be mended tonight. I say, Kinsella, Jimmy's leg isn't near as bad as you'd think it would be, after having the horn of a wild bull run through it."

"It wasn't a bull at all, Miss, but a heifer."

"I don't see that it makes much difference which it was," said Priscilla.

"Do you hear that now?" said Kinsella to his friend in a whisper. "Believe you me, Peter Walsh, it's as good for the whole of us that she's not in the police."

"What's that you're saying?" said Priscilla.

The boat, though the wind had almost left her sails, drifted up on the rising tide and was already past the spot where the two men were sitting. Peter Walsh got up and shouted his answer after her.

"Joseph Antony Kinsella," he said, "is just after telling me that it's his belief that you'd make a grand sergeant of police."

"It's a good job for him that I'm not," said Priscilla. "For the first thing I'd do if I was would be to go out and see what it is he has going on on Inishbawn."

Peter Walsh, without unduly hurrying himself, arrived at the slip before the *Tortoise*. Priscilla stepped ashore and handed him the rudder.

"Take that to the smith," she said, "and tell him to put a new iron on it this evening. We'll want it again tomorrow morning."

"I'll tell him, Miss; but I wouldn't say he'd do it for you."

"He'd jolly well better," said Priscilla.

"That same Patsy the smith," said Peter Walsh, "has a terrible strong hate in him for doing anything in a hurry whether it's little or big."

"Just you tell him from me," said Priscilla, "that if I don't get that rudder properly settled when I want it tomorrow morning, I'll go out to Inishbawn, in spite of your rats and your heifers."

Peter Walsh's face remained perfectly impassive. Not even in his eyes was there the smallest expression of surprise or uneasiness.

"What would be the good of saying the like of that to him?" he said. "It's laughing at me he'd be, for he wouldn't understand what I'd mean."

"Don't tell me," said Priscilla. "Whatever villainy there is going on between you and Joseph Antony Kinsella, Patsy the smith will be in it along with you."

Peter Walsh helped Frank into the bath-chair. Priscilla, her face wearing a most determined expression, wheeled him away.

"That rudder will be ready all right," she said.

"But what do you think is going on on the island?" asked Frank.

"I don't know."

"Could they be smuggling?"

"They might be smuggling, only I don't see where they'd get anything to smuggle. Anyway, it's no business of ours so long as we get the rudder. I don't think it's at all a good plan, Cousin Frank, to be always poking our noses into other people's secrets, when we don't absolutely have to."

It occurred to Frank that Priscilla had shown some eagerness in probing the private affairs of the young couple who had hired Flanagan's boat. He did not, however, feel it necessary to make this obvious retort.

Peter Walsh, the rudder under his arm, went back to Joseph Antony Kinsella, who was still sitting on the edge of the quay.

"She says," he said, "that without there's a new iron on that rudder tomorrow morning, she'll go out to Inishbawn and the young fellow along with her."

"Let Patsy the smith put it on for her, then."

"Sure he can't."

"And what's to hinder him?"

"He was drunk an hour ago," said Peter Walsh, "and he'll be drunker now."

"Bedamn then, but you'd better take him down and dip him in the tide, for I'll not have that young fellow with the sore leg on Inishbawn. If it was only herself I wouldn't care."

"I'd be afeard to do it," said Peter Walsh.

"Afeard of what?"

"Afeard of Patsy the smith. Sure it's a madman he is when his temper's riz."

"Let you come along with me," said Kinsella, "and I'll wake him up if it takes the brand of a hot iron to do it. He can be as mad as he likes after, but he'll put an iron on that rudder before ever he gets leave to kill you or any other man."

CHAPTER XV

Priscilla wheeled the bath-chair up the hill from the town, chatting cheerfully as she went.

"It'll be rather exciting," she said, "to see these Torrington people. I don't think I've ever come across a regular, full-blown Marquis before. Lord Thormanby is a peer of course, but he doesn't soar to those giddy heights. I suppose he'll sit on us frightfully if we dare to speak. Not that I mean to try. The thing for me to do is to be 'a simple child which lightly draws its breath, and feels its life in every limb.' That's a quotation, Cousin Frank. Wordsworth, I think. Sylvia Courtney says it's quite too sweet for words. I haven't read the rest of it, so of course, can't say, but I think that bit's rather rot, though I daresay Lord Torrington will like it all right when I do it for him."

Frank felt a certain doubt about the policy. Lord Torrington was indeed pretty sure to prefer a simple child to Priscilla in her ordinary mood; but there was a serious risk of her over-doing the part. He warned Priscilla to be exceedingly careful. She brushed his advice aside with an abrupt change of subject.

"I expect," she said, "that Mrs. Geraghty will be up at the house again. Aunt Juliet wouldn't trust anybody else to hook up Lady Torrington's back. I can do my own, of course; but nobody can who is either fat or dignified. I'm pretty lean, but even I have to wriggle a lot."

Mrs. Geraghty was up at the house. This became plain to Priscilla when she reached the gate-lodge. Mr. Geraghty, who was a gardener by profession, was sitting on his own doorstep with the baby in his arms. The baby, resenting the absence of his mother, was howling. Priscilla stopped.

"If you like," she said, "I'll wheel the baby up to the house and give him to Mrs. Geraghty. Aunt Juliet won't like it if I do. In fact she'll dance about with insatiable fury. But it may be the right thing to do all the same. We ought always to do what's right, Mr. Geraghty, even if other people behave like wild boars; that is to say if we are quite sure that it is right; I think it's nearly sure to be right to give a baby to its mother; though there may be times when it's not. Solomon did, and that's a pretty good example; though I don't suppose that even Solomon always knew for certain when he was doing the rightest thing there was. Anyhow, I'll risk it if you like, Mr. Geraghty. You won't mind having the baby on your knee for a bit, will you, Cousin Frank?"

Frank did mind very much. The ordinary healthy-minded, normal prefect dislikes having anything to do with babies even more than he dislikes being called a child by maiden ladies.

He looked appealingly at Mr. Geraghty. The baby, misunderstanding Priscilla's intentions, yelled louder than before.

Mr. Geraghty, fortunately for Frank, was not a man of the heroic kind. Abstract right was less to him than expediency and he missed the point of the comparison between his position and King Solomon's. He thought it better that his baby should suffer than that Miss Lentaigne's anger should be roused. He declined Priscilla's offer.

Near the upper end of Rosnacree avenue there is a corner from which a view of the lawn is obtained. Sir Lucius and another gentleman were pacing to and fro on the grass when Priscilla and Frank reached the corner and caught sight of them.

"Stop," said Frank, suddenly. "Turn back, Priscilla. Go round some other way."

Priscilla stopped. The eager excitement of Frank's tone surprised her.

"Why?" she asked. "It's only father and that Lord of his. We've got to face them some time or other. We may as well get it over at once."

"That's the beast who shoved me over the steamer's gangway," said Frank, "and sprained my ankle."

Sir Lucius and Lord Torrington turned at the end of the lawn and began to walk towards Priscilla and Frank.

"Now I can see his face," said Priscilla, "I don't wonder at your rather loathing him. I think you were jolly lucky to get off with a sprained ankle. A man with a nose like that would break your arm or stab you in the back."

Lord Torrington's nose was fleshy, pitted in places, and of a purple colour.

"Curious taste the King must have," said Priscilla, "to make a man like that a Marquis. You'd expect he'd choose out fairly good-looking people. But, of course, you can't really tell about kings. I daresay they have to do quite a lot of things they don't really like, on account of being constitutional. Rather poor sport being constitutional, I should say; for the King that is. It's pleasanter, of course, for the other people."

Frank knew that the present King was blameless in the matter of Lord Torrington's marquisate. It was inherited from a great-grandfather, who may have had an ordinary, possibly even a beautiful nose. But he attempted no explanation. His anxiety made him disinclined for a discussion of the advantages of having an hereditary aristocracy.

"Do turn back, Priscilla," he said.

"If he is the man who sprained your ankle," she said, "it's far better for you to have it out with him now when I'm here to back you up. If you put it off till dinner time you'll have to tackle him alone. I'm sure not to be let in. Anyhow, we can't go back now. They've seen us."

Lord Torrington and Sir Lucius approached them. Frank plucked nervously at his tie, unbuttoned and then re-buttoned his coat. He felt that he had been entirely blameless during the scrimmage on the gangway of the steamer, but Lord Torrington did not look like a man who would readily own himself to be in the wrong.

"Your daughter, Lentaigne?" said Lord Torrington. "H'm, fifteen, you said; looks less. Shake hands, little girl."

Priscilla put out her right hand demurely. Her eyes were fixed on the ground. Her lips were slightly parted in a deprecating smile, suggestive of timid modesty.

"What's your name?" said Lord Torrington.

"Priscilla Lentaigne."

Nothing could have been meeker than the tone in which she spoke.

"H'm," said Lord Torrington, "and you're Mannix's boy. Not much like your father. At school?"

"Yes," said Frank. "At Haileybury."

"What are you doing in that bath-chair with the young lady wheeling you? Is that the kind of manners they teach at Haileybury?"

"Please," said Priscilla, speaking very gently. "It's not his fault."

"He has sprained his ankle," said Sir Lucius. "He can't walk."

"Oh," said Lord Torrington. "Sprained ankle, is it?"

He turned and walked back to the lawn. Sir Lucius followed him.

"Rather a bear, I call him," said Priscilla. "But, of course, he may be one of those cases of a heart of gold inside a rough skin. You can't be sure. We did 'As You Like It' last Christmas—dramatic club, you know—and Sylvia Courtney had a bit to say about a toad ugly and venomous which yet wears a precious jewel in his head. I'd say he's just the opposite. If there is a precious jewel—and there may be—it's not in his head. Anyhow one great comfort is that he doesn't remember spraining your ankle."

Frank, who recollected Lord Torrington with disagreeable distinctness, did not find any great comfort in being totally forgotten. He would have liked, though he scarcely expected, some expression of regret that the accident had occurred.

"It'll be all the easier," said Priscilla, "to pay him back if he hasn't any suspicion that we have an undying vendetta against him. I rather like vendettas, don't you? There's something rather noble in the idea of pursuing a man with implacable vengeance from generation to generation."

"I don't quite see," said Frank, "what good a vendetta is. We can't do anything while he's in your father's house. It wouldn't be right."

"All the same," said Priscilla, "we'll score off him. For the immediate present we've got to wait and watch his every movement with glittering eyes and cynical smiles concealed behind our ingenuous brows. You needn't say 'ingenuous' isn't a real word, because it is. I put it in an English comp. last term and got full marks, which shows that it must be a good word."

Priscilla was right in supposing that she would not be allowed to dine in the dining-room. Frank faced the banquet without her support. It was not a very pleasant meal for him. Lady Torrington shook hands with him and asked him whether he were the boy whom she had heard reciting a prize poem on the last Speech Day at Winchester. Frank told her that he was at Haileybury.

"I thought it might have been you," said Lady Torrington, "because I seem to remember your face. I must have seen you somewhere, I suppose."

She took no further notice of him during dinner. Lord Torrington took no notice of him at all. The dinner was long and, in spite of the fact that he had a good appetite, Frank did not enjoy himself. He was extremely glad when Lady Torrington and Miss Lentaigne left the dining-room. He was casting about for a convenient excuse for escape when Sir Lucius spoke to him.

"You and Priscilla were out on the bay all day, I suppose?"

"Yes," said Frank, "we started early and sailed about."

"I daresay you'll be able to give us some information then," said Sir Lucius. "Shall I ask him a few questions, Torrington? The police sergeant said——"

"The police sergeant is a damned fool," said Lord Torrington. "She can't be going about in a boat. She doesn't know how to row."

"Frank," said Sir Lucius, "did you and Priscilla happen to see anything of a young lady——"

"You may just as well tell him the story," said Lord Torrington. "It'll be in the papers in a day or two if we can't find her."

"Very well, Torrington. Just as you like. The fact is, Frank, that Lord Torrington is here looking for his daughter, who has——well, a week ago she disappeared."

"Disappeared!" said Lord Torrington. "Why not say bolted?"

"Ran away from home," said Sir Lucius.

"According to your aunt——" said Lord Torrington.

"She's not my aunt," said Frank.

"Oh, isn't she?" Lord Torrington's tone suggested that this was a distinct advantage to Frank. "According to Miss Lentaigne then, the girl has asserted her right to live her own life untrammelled by the fetters of conventionality. That's the way she put it, isn't it, Lentaigne?"

"Lady Isabel," said Sir Lucius, "came over to Ireland. We know that."

"Booked her luggage in advance from Euston," said Lord Torrington, "under another name. I had a detective on the job, and he worried that out. Women are all going mad nowadays; though I had no notion Isabel went in for—well, the kind of thing your sister talks, Lentaigne. I thought she was religious. She used to be perpetually going to church, evensong on the Vigil of St. Euphrosyne, and that kind of thing, but I am told lots of parsons now have taken up these advanced ideas about women. It may have been in church she heard them."

"From Dublin," said Sir Lucius, "she came on here. The police sergeant——"

"Who's a dunderheaded fool," said Lord Torrington.

"He says there's a young lady going about the bay for the last two days in a boat."

"That's the wrong tack altogether," said Lord Torrington. "Isabel would never think of going in a boat. I tell you she can't row."

"Now, Frank," said Sir Lucius, "did you see or hear anything of her?"

Frank would have liked very much to deny that he had seen any lady. His dislike of Lord Torrington was strong in him. He had been snubbed in the train, injured while leaving the steamer, and actually insulted that very afternoon. He felt, besides, the strongest sympathy with any daughter who ran away from a home ruled by Lord and Lady Torrington. But he had been asked a straight question and it was not in him to tell a lie deliberately.

"We did meet a lady," he said, "in fact we lunched with her today, but her name was Rutherford."

"Was she rowing about alone in a boat?" said Lord Torrington.

"She had a boy to row her," said Frank. "She'd hired the boat. She said she came from the British Museum and was collecting sponges."

"Sponges!" said Sir Lucius. "How could she collect sponges here, and what does the British Museum want sponges for?"

"They weren't exactly sponges," said Frank, "they were zoophytes."

"It's just possible," said Lord Torrington, "that she might—Sponges, you say? I don't know what would put sponges into her head. But, of course, she had to say something. What was she like to look at?"

"She had a dark blue dress," said Frank, "and was tallish."

"Fuzzy fair hair?" said Lord Torrington.

"I don't remember her hair."

"Slim?"

"I'd call Miss Rutherford fat," said Frank. "At least, she's decidedly stout."

"Not her," said Lord Torrington. "Nobody could call Isabel fat. That police sergeant of yours is a fool, Lentaigne. I always said he was. If Isabel is in this neighbourhood at all she's living in some country inn."

"The sergeant said he'd make inquiries about the lady he mentioned," said Sir Lucius. "We shall hear more about her tomorrow."

"She had a Primus stove with her," said Frank.

"That's no help," said Lord Torrington. "Anybody might have a Primus stove."

"She said she'd borrowed it from Professor Wilder," said Frank.

"Who the devil is Professor Wilder?"

"He's doing the rotifers," said Frank. "At least Miss Rutherford said he was. I don't know who he is."

"That's not Isabel," said Lord Torrington. "She wouldn't have the intelligence to invent a professor who collected rotifers. I don't suppose she ever heard of rotifers. I never did. What are they?"

"Insects, I fancy," said Sir Lucius. "I daresay Priscilla would know. Shall I send for her?"

"No," said Lord Torrington. "I don't care what rotifers are. Let's finish our cigars outside, Lentaigne. It's infernally hot."

Frank had finished his cigarette. He had no wish to spend any time beyond what was absolutely necessary in Lord Torrington's company. He felt sure that Lord Torrington would insist on walking briskly up and down when he got outside. Frank could not walk briskly, even with the aid of two sticks. He made up his mind to hobble off in search of Priscilla. He found her, after some painful journeyings, in a most unlikely place. She was sitting in the long gallery with Lady Torrington and Miss Lentaigne. The two ladies reclined in easy chairs in front of an open window. There were several partially smoked cigarettes in a china saucer on the floor beside Miss Lentaigne. Lady Torrington was fanning herself with a slow motion which reminded Frank of the way in which a tiger, caged in a zoological garden, switches its tail after being fed. Priscilla sat in the background under a lamp. She had chosen a straight-backed chair which stood opposite a writing table. She sat bolt upright in it with her hands folded on her lap and her left foot crossed over her right. Her face wore a look of slightly puzzled, but on the whole intelligent interest; such as a humble dependent might feel while submitting to instruction kindly imparted by some very eminent person. She wore a white frock, trimmed with embroidery, of a perfectly simple kind. She had a light blue sash round her waist. Her hair, which was very sleek, was tied with a light blue ribbon. Round her neck, on a third light blue ribbon, much narrower than either of the other two, hung a tiny gold locket shaped like a heart. She turned as Frank entered the room and met his gaze of astonishment with a look of extreme innocence. Her eyes made him think for a moment of those of a lamb, a puppy or other young animal which is half-frightened, half-curious at the happening of something altogether outside of its previous experience.

Neither of the ladies at the window took any notice of Frank's entrance. He hobbled across the room and sat down beside Priscilla. She got up at once and, without looking at him, walked demurely to the chair on which Miss Lentaigne was sitting.

"Please, Aunt Juliet," she said, "may I go to bed? I think it's time."

Miss Lentaigne looked at her a little doubtfully. She had known Priscilla for many years and had learned to be particularly suspicious of meekness.

"I heard the stable clock strike," said Priscilla. "It's half-past nine."

"Very well," said Miss Lentaigne. "Good-night."

Priscilla kissed her aunt lightly on her left cheek bone. Then she held out her hand to Lady Torrington.

"You may kiss me," said the lady. "You seem to be a very quiet well behaved little girl."

Priscilla kissed Lady Torrington and then passed on to Frank.

"Good-night, Cousin Frank," she said. "I hope you're not tired after being out in the boat, and I hope your ankle will be better tomorrow."

Her eyes still had an expression of cherubic innocence; but just as she let go Frank's hand she winked abruptly. He found as she turned away, that she had left something in his hand. He unfolded a small, much crumpled piece of blotting paper, taken, he supposed, by stealth from the writing table beside Priscilla's chair. A note was scratched with a point of a pin on the blotting paper.

"Come to the shrubbery, ten sharp. Most important. Excuse scratching. No pencil."

"Priscilla," said Lady Torrington, "is a sweet child, very subdued and modest."

Frank's attention was arrested by the silvery sweetness of the tone in which she spoke. He had a feeling that she meant to convey to Miss Lentaigne something more than her words implied. Miss Lentaigne struck a match noisily and lit another cigarette.

"She may be a little wanting in animation," said Lady Torrington, "but that is a fault which one can forgive nowadays when so many girls run into the opposite extreme and become self-assertive."

"Priscilla," said Miss Lentaigne, "is not always quite so good as she was this evening."

"You must be quite pleased that she isn't," said Lady Torrington, with a deliberate, soft smile. "With your ideas about the independence of our sex I can quite understand that Priscilla, if she were always as quiet and gentle as she was this evening, would be trying, very trying."

Frank became acutely uncomfortable. He had entered the room noisily enough, hobbling on his two sticks; but neither lady seemed to be aware of his presence. He began to feel as if he were eavesdropping, listening to a conversation which he was not intended to hear. He hesitated for a moment, wondering whether he ought to say a formal good-night, or get out of the room as quietly as he could without calling attention to his presence. Miss Lentaigne's next remark decided him.

"Your own daughter," she said, "seems to have imbibed some of our more modern ideas. That must be a trial to you, Lady Torrington."

Frank got up and made his way out of the room without speaking.

CHAPTER XVI

To reach the corner of the shrubbery it was necessary to cross the lawn. Lord Torrington and Sir Lucius, having lit fresh cigars, were pacing up and down in earnest conversation. Frank hobbled across their path and received a kindly greeting from his uncle.

"Well, Frank, out for a breath of fresh air before turning in? Sorry you can't join our march. Lord Torrington is just talking about your father."

"Thanks, Uncle Lucius," said Frank, "but I can't walk. There's a hammock chair in the corner. I'll sit there for a while and smoke another cigarette."

Sir Lucius and Lord Torrington walked briskly, turning each time they reached the edge of the grass and walking briskly back again. Frank realised that Priscilla, if she was to keep her appointment, must cross their track. He watched anxiously for her appearance. The stable clock struck ten. In the shadow of the verandah in front of the dining-room window Frank fancied he saw a moving figure. Sir Lucius and Lord Torrington crossed the lawn again. Half-way across they were exactly opposite the dining-room window, A few steps further on and the direct line between the window and a corner of the shrubbery lay behind them. Priscilla seized the most favourable moment for her passage. Just as the two men reached the point at which their backs were turned to the line of her crossing she darted forward. Half-way across she seemed to trip, hesitated for a moment and then ran on. Before the walkers reached their place of turning she was safe in a laurel bush beside Frank's chair.

"My shoe," she whispered. "It came off slap in the middle of the lawn. I always knew those were perfectly beastly shoes. It was Sylvia Courtney made me buy them, though I told her at the time they'd never stick on, and what good are shoes if they don't. Now they are sure to see it; though perhaps they won't. If they don't I can make another dart and get it."

To avoid all risk of the loss of the second shoe Priscilla took it off before she started. Lord Torrington and Sir Lucius crossed the lawn again. It seemed as if one or other of them must tread on the shoe which lay on their path; but they passed it by. Priscilla seized her chance, rushed to the middle of the lawn and returned again successfully. Then she and Frank retreated, for the sake of greater security, into the middle of the shrubbery.

"Everything's all right," said Priscilla. "I've got lots and lots of food stored away. I simply looted the dishes as they were brought out of the dining-room. Fried fish, a whole roast duck, three herrings' roes on toast, half a caramel pudding—I squeezed it into an old jam pot—and several other things. We can start at any hour we like tomorrow and it won't in the least matter whether Brannigan's is open or not. What do you say to 6 a.m.?"

"I'm not going on the bay tomorrow."

"You must. Why not?"

"Because I want to score off that old beast who sprained my ankle."

The prefect in Frank had entirely disappeared. Two days of close companionship with Priscilla erased the marks made on his character by four long years of training at Haileybury. His respect for constituted authorities had vanished. The fact that Lord Torrington was Secretary of State for War did not weigh on him for an instant. He was, as indeed boys ought to be at seventeen years of age, a primitive barbarian. He was filled with a desire for revenge on the man who had insulted and injured him.

"You don't know," he said, "what Lord Torrington is here for."

"Oh, yes, I do," said Priscilla. "I'm not quite an ass. I was listening to Aunt Juliet and Lady Torrington shooting barbed arrows at each other after dinner. Aunt Juliet got rather the worst of it, I must say. Lady Torrington is one of those people whose garments smell of myrrh, aloes and cassia, and yet whose words are very swords; you know the sort I mean."

"Lord Torrington is chasing his daughter," said Frank, "who has run away from home. I vote we find her first and then help her to hide."

"Of course. That's what we're going to do. That's why we're going off in the boat tomorrow."

"But she's not on the bay," said Frank. "Miss Rutherford is too fat to be her. He said so."

"Who's talking about Miss Rutherford? She's simply sponge-hunting. Nobody but a fool would think she was Miss Torrington."

"Lady Isabel," said Frank. "He's a marquis."

"Anyhow she's not the escaped daughter."

"Then who is?"

"The lady spy, of course. Any one could see that at a glance."

"But she has a man with her. Lord Torrington said—"

"If you can call that thing a man," said Priscilla, "she has. That's her husband. She's run away with him and got married surreptitiously, like young Lochinvar. People do that sort of thing, you know. I can't imagine where the fun comes in; but it's quite common, so I suppose it must be considered pleasant. Anyhow Sylvia Courtney says that English literature is simply stock full of most beautiful poems about people who do it; all more or less true, so there must be some attraction."

Frank made no reply. Priscilla's theory was new to him. It seemed to have a certain plausibility. He wanted to think it over before committing himself to accepting it.

"It's not a thing I'd care to do myself," said Priscilla. "But then people are so different. What strikes me as rather idiotic may be sweeter than butter in the mouth to somebody else. You never can tell beforehand. Anyhow we can count on Aunt Juliet as a firm ally. She can't go back on us on account of her principles."

This was another new idea to Frank. He began to feel slightly bewildered.

"The one thing she's really keen on just at present," said Priscilla, "is that women should assert their independence and not be mere tame parasites in gilded cages. That's what she said to Lady Torrington anyhow. So of course she's bound to help us all she can, so long as she doesn't know that they're married, and nobody does know that yet except you and me. Not that I'd be inclined to trust Aunt Juliet unless we have to; but it's a comfort to know she's there if the worst comes to the worst."

"What do you intend to do?" said Frank.

"Find them first. If we start off early tomorrow well probably get to Curraunbeg before they're up. My idea would be to hand over the young man to Miss Rutherford for a day or two. She's sure to be somewhere about and when she understands the circumstances she won't mind pretending that he, the original spy, I mean, is her husband, just for a while, until the first rancour of the pursuit has died away. She strikes me as an awfully good sort who won't mind. She may even like it. Some people love being married. I can't imagine why; but they do. Anyhow I don't expect there'll be any difficulty about that part of the programme. We'll simply tranship him, tent and all, into Jimmy Kinsella's boat."

"I don't see the good of doing all that," said Frank.

"Why not——?"

"The good of it is this. We must keep Aunt Juliet on our side in case of accidents. She's got a most acute mind and will throw all kinds of obstacles in the way of the pursuers. As long as she thinks that Miss Torrington—Lady Isabel, I mean—is really going in for leading a beautiful scarlet kind of life of her own; but if she once finds out that she's gone and got married to a man, any man, even one who can't manage a boat, she'll be keener than any one else to have her dragged back."

"What do you mean to do with her?" said Frank.

"We'll plant her down on Inishbawn. That's the safest place in the whole bay for her to be. Of course Joseph Antony Kinsella will object; but we'll make him see that it's his duty to succor the oppressed, and anyhow we'll land her there and leave her. I don't exactly know what it is that they're doing on that island, though I can guess. But whatever it is you may bet your hat they won't let Lord Torrington or the police or any one of that kind within a mile of it. If once we get her there she's safe from her enemies. Every man, woman and child in the neighbourhood will combine to keep that sanctuary—bother! there's a word which exactly expresses what a sanctuary is kept; but I've forgotten what it is. I came across it once in a book and looked it out in the dict. to see what it meant. It's used about sanctuaries and secrets. Do you remember what it is?"

Frank did not give his mind to the question. He was thinking, with some pleasure, of the baffled rage of Lord Torrington when he was not allowed to land on Inishbawn. Lady Isabel would be plainly visible sitting at the door of her tent on the green slope of the island. Lord Torrington, with violent language bursting from him, would approach the island in a boat, anticipating a triumphant capture. But Joseph Antony Kinsella would sally like a rover from his anchorage and tow Lord Torrington's boat off to some distant place. With invincible determination the War Lord would return again. From every inhabited island in the bay would issue boats, Flanagan's old one among them. They would surround Lord Torrington, hustle and push him away. Children from cottage doors would jeer at him. Peter Walsh and Patsy, the drunken smith, would add their taunts to the chorus when at last, baffled and despairing, he landed at the quay. The vision was singularly attractive. Frank ran his hand over his bandaged ankle and smiled with joy.

"I know it's used of secrets as well as sanctuaries," said Priscilla, "because Aunt Juliet used to say it about the Confessional when she was thinking of being a Roman Catholic. I told you about that, didn't I?"

"No," said Frank. "But will they be able to stop him landing, really?"

"Of course they will. That was one of the worst times we ever had with Aunt Juliet. Father simply hated it, expecting the blow to fall every day, especially after she took to fasting frightfully hard with finnan haddocks.

That was just after the time she was tremendously down on all religion and wouldn't let him have prayers in the morning, which he didn't mind as much; though, of course, he pretended. Fortunately she found out about uric acid just before she actually did the deed, so that was all right. It always is in the end, you know. That's one of the really good points about Aunt Juliet. All the same I wish I could remember that word."

"I don't quite see," said Frank, "how they'll stop him landing on Inishbawn if he wants to."

"Nor do I; but they will. If Peter Walsh and Joseph Antony Kinsella and Flanagan and Patsy the smith—they're all in the game, whatever it is—if they determine not to let him land on Inishbawn he won't land there."

"But even if they keep him off for a day or two they can't for ever."

"Well," said Priscilla, "he can't stay here for ever either. There's sure to be a war soon and then he'll jolly well have to go back to London and see after it. You told me it was his business to look after wars, so of course he must. Now that we've got everything settled I'll sneak off again and get to bed. If I recollect that word during the night I'll write it down."

Priscilla, leaving Frank to make his own way back to the house as best he could, crept through the laurel bushes to the edge of the lawn. Lord Torrington and Sir Lucius had gone indoors. She could see them through the open window of the long gallery. She stole carefully across the lawn and entered the house by way of the dining-room window. She went very quietly to her bedroom. Before undressing she opened her wardrobe, lifted out two dresses which lay folded on a shelf and took out the store of provisions which she had secured at dinner time. She wrapped up the duck and the fish in paper, nice white paper taken from the bottoms of the drawers in her dressing table. The herrings' roes on toast, originally a savoury, she put in the bottom of the soap dish and tied a piece of paper over the top of it. The caramel pudding rather overflowed the jam pot. It was impossible to press it down below the level of the rim. Priscilla sliced off the bulging excess of it with the handle of her tooth brush and dropped it into her mouth. Then she tied some paper over the top of the jam pot, and wrote, "pudding" across it with a blue pencil. The remainder of her spoil—some rolls, two artichokes and a sweetbread—she wrapped up together.

Then she undressed and got into bed. Half an hour later she woke suddenly. Without a moment's hesitation she got out of bed and lit a candle. The blue pencil was still lying on top of the jam pot which stood on the dressing table. Priscilla took it, and to avoid all possibility of mistake in the morning, wrote word "inviolable" on every one of her parcels.

CHAPTER XVII

It was ten o'clock in the forenoon. Peter Walsh, having breakfasted, strolled down the street towards the quay. When he reached it he surveyed the boats which lay there with a long, deliberate stare. The *Blue Wanderer* was at her moorings. The *Tortoise*, with a new iron on her rudder, had gone out at seven o'clock. There were three boats from the islands and one large hooker lying at the quay. Peter Walsh made quite sure that there was nothing which called for comment or investigation in the appearance of any of these. Then he lit his pipe and took his seat on one of the windows of Brannigan's shop. Four out of the six habitués of this meeting place were already seated. Peter Walsh made the fifth. The sixth man had not yet arrived.

At half past ten Timothy Sweeny left his shop and walked down to the quay. Timothy Sweeny, though not the richest, was the most important man in Rosnacree. His public house was in a back street and the amount of business which he did was insignificant compared to that done by Brannigan. But he was a politician of great influence and had been made a Justice of the Peace by a government anxious to popularise the administration of the law in Ireland. The law itself, as was recognised on all sides, could not possibly be made to command the respect of any one; but it was hoped that it might excite less active hostility if it were modified to suit the public convenience by men like Sweeny who had some personal experience of the unpleasantness of the penalties which it ordained.

It was seldom that Timothy Sweeny left his shop. He was a man of corpulent figure and flabby muscles. He disliked the smell of fresh air and walking was a trouble to him. The five loafers on Brannigan's window sills looked at him with some amazement when he approached them.

"Is Peter Walsh here?" said Sweeny.

"I am here," said Peter Walsh. "Where else would I be?"

"I'd be glad," said Sweeny, "if you'd step up to my house with me for two minutes the way I could speak to you without the whole town listening to what we're saying."

Peter Walsh rose from his seat with quiet dignity and followed Sweeny up the street.

"You'll take a sup of porter," said Sweeny, when they reached the bar of the public house.

Peter finished the half pint which was offered to him at a draught.

"They tell me," said Sweeny, "that the police sergeant was up at the big house again this morning. I don't know if it's true but it's what they're after telling me."

"It is true," said Peter. "I'll say that much for whoever it was that told you. It's true enough. The sergeant was off last night after dark. He thinks he's damned smart that sergeant, and it was after dark he went the way nobody would see him; but he was seen, for Patsy the smith was on the side of the road, mortal sick after the way that Joseph Antony Kinsella made him turn to making a rudder iron and him as drunk at the time as any man ever you seen. It was him told me about the sergeant and where he went last night."

"Well," said Sweeny, "and what did he tell you?"

"He told me that the sergeant went along the road till he met with the gentleman that does be going about the country and has the two ladies with him, the one of them that might be his wife and the other has Jimmy Kinsella engaged to row her round the bay while she'd be bathing."

"There's too many going round the country and the bay and that's a fact. We could do with less."

"We could, surely. But there's no harm in them ones. What the sergeant said to the gentleman Patsy the smith couldn't hear but it was maybe half an hour after when the sergeant went home again and he had a look on him like a man that was middling well satisfied. Patsy the smith saw him for he was in the ditch when he passed, terrible sick, retching the way he thought the whole of his liver would be out on the road before he'd done. Well, there was no more happened last night; but it wasn't more than nine o'clock this morning before that same sergeant was off up to the big house and I wouldn't wonder but it was to tell the strange gentleman that's there whatever it was he heard him last night. He had that kind of a look about him anyway."

"I don't like the way things is going on," said Sweeny. "What is it that's up at the big house at all?"

"They tell me," said Walsh, "that he's a mighty high up gentleman whoever he is."

"He may be, but I'd be glad if I knew what he's doing here, for I don't like the looks of him."

Patsy the smith, pallid after the experience of the night before, walked into the shop.

"If Peter Walsh is there," he said, "the sergeant is down about the quay looking for him."

"You better go to him," said Sweeny, "and mind now what you say to him."

"You'll not say much," said Patsy the smith, "for he'll have you whipped off into one of the cells in the barrack before you've time to speak. He's terrible determined."

Patsy's face was yellow—a witness to the fact that his liver was still in him—and he was inclined to take a pessimistic view of life. Peter Walsh paid no attention to his prophecy. Sweeny looked anxious.

The sergeant was standing outside the door of Brannigan's shop. He accosted Peter Walsh as soon as he caught sight of him.

"Sir Lucius bid me tell you," he said, "that you're to have the *Tortoise* ready for him at twelve o'clock, and that his lordship will be going with him, so he won't be needing you in the boat."

"It would fail me to do that," said Peter, "for she's out, Miss Priscilla and the young gentleman with the sore leg has her."

"Sir Lucius was partly in doubt," said the sergeant, "but it might be the way you say, for I told him myself that the boat was gone. But his lordship wouldn't be put off, and you're to hire another boat."

"What boat?"

"It was Joseph Antony Kinsella's he mentioned," said the sergeant, "when I told him it was likely he'd be in with another load of gravel. But sure one boat's as good as another so long as it is a boat. His lordship wouldn't be turned aside from going."

"Them ones," said Peter Walsh, "must have their own way whatever happens. It's pleasure sailing they're for, I'm thinking, among the islands?"

"It might be," said the sergeant "I didn't ask."

"You could guess though."

"And if I could, do you think I'd tell you? It's too fond of asking questions you are, Peter Walsh, about what doesn't concern you."

The sergeant turned his back and walked away. Peter Walsh watched him enter the barrack. Then he himself went back to Sweeny's shop.

"They're wanting a boat," he said. "Joseph Antony Kinsella's or another."

"And what for?"

"Unless it's to go out to Inishbawn," said Peter, "I don't know what for."

"Bedamn then," said Sweeny, "there's no boat for them."

"I was thinking that myself."

"I wouldn't wonder," said Sweeney, "but something might stop Joseph Antony Kinsella from coming in today after all, thought he's due with another load of gravel."

"He mightn't come," said Patsy the smith. "There's many a thing could happen to prevent him."

"What time were they thinking of starting?" said Sweeny.

"Twelve o'clock," said Peter Walsh.

"Patsy," said Sweeny, "let you take Brannigan's old punt and go down as far as the stone perch to try can you see Joseph Antony Kinsella coming in."

Patsy the smith was in a condition of great physical misery; but the occasion demanded energy and self-sacrifice. He staggered down to the slip, loosed the mooring rope of Brannigan's dilapidated punt and drove her slowly down the harbour, waggling one oar over her stern.

"Let you go round the town," said Sweeny to Peter Walsh, "and find out where the fellows is that came in with the boats that's at the quay this minute. It's time they were off out of this."

Peter Walsh left the shop. In a minute or two he came back again.

"There's Miss Priscilla's boat," he said, "the *Blue Wanderer*. You're forgetting her."

"They'd never venture as far as Inishbawn in her," said Sweeny.

"They might then. The wind's east and she'd run out easy enough under the little lug."

"They'd have to row back."

"The likes of them ones," said Peter Walsh, "wouldn't think about how they'd get back till the time came. I'm uneasy about that boat, so I am."

"Tell me this now," said Sweeny, after a moment's consideration. "Did the young lady say e'er a word to you about giving the boat a fresh lick of paint?"

"She did not. Why would she? Amn't I just after painting the boat?"

"Are you sure now she didn't say she'd be the better of another coat?"

"She might then, some time that I wouldn't be paying much attention to what she said. I'm a terrible one to disremember things anyway."

"You'd better do it then," said Sweeny. "There's plenty of the same paint you had before in Brannigan's, and it will do the boat no harm to get a lick with it."

Peter Walsh left the shop again and walked in a careless way down the street. Sweeny followed him at a little distance and spoke to the men who were sitting on Brannigan's window sills. They rose at once and walked down to the slip. In a few minutes the *Blue Wanderer* was dragged from her moorings and carried up to a glassy patch of waste land at the end of the quay. Her floor boards were taken out of her, her oars, rudder and mast were laid on the grass. The boat herself was turned bottom upwards.

In the course of the next half hour the owners of the boats which lay alongside the quay sauntered down one by one. Brown lugsails were run up on the smaller boats. The mainsail of the hooker was slowly hoisted. At half past eleven there was not a single boat of any kind left afloat in the harbour. Peter Walsh, his coat off and his sleeves rolled up, was laying long stripes of green paint on the already shining bottom of the Blue Wanderer. He worked with the greatest zeal and earnestness. Timothy Sweeny looked at the empty harbour with satisfaction. Then he went back to the shop and dosed comfortably behind his bar.

Patsy the smith stood in the stern of the punt and waggled his oar with force and skill. He disliked taking this kind of exercise very much indeed. His nature craved for copious, cooling drafts of porter, drawn straight from the cask and served in large thick tumblers. He had intended to spend the morning in taking this kind of refreshment. The day was exceedingly hot. When he reached the end of the quay his mouth was quite dry inside and his legs were shaking under him. He looked round with eyes which were strikingly bloodshot. There was no sign of Joseph Antony Kinsella's boat on the long stretch of water between him and the stone perch. If he could have articulated at all he would have sworn. Being unable to swear he groaned deeply and took his oar again. The punt wobbled forward very much as a fat duck walks.

When he reached Delgipish he looked round again. A mile out beyond the stone perch he saw a boat moving slowly towards him. His eyes served him badly and although he could see the splash of the oars in the water he could not make out who the rower was. A man of weaker character, suffering the same physical torture, would have allowed himself to drift on the shore of Delginish and there would have awaited the coming of the boat he had seen. But Patsy the smith was brave. He was also nerved by the extreme importance of his mission. It was absolutely necessary that something should happen to prevent Joseph Antony bringing his boat to Rosnacree harbour. The sight of one brown sail and then another stealing round the end of the quay gave him fresh courage. Timothy Sweeny and Peter Walsh had done their work on shore. He was determined not to fail in carrying through his part of a masterly scheme.

For twenty minutes Patsy the smith sculled on. It seemed to him sometimes as if each sway of his body, each tug of his tired arms must be the last possible. Yet he succeeded in going on. He dared not look round lest the boat he had seen should prove after all not to be the one he sought. Such a disappointment would, he knew, be more than he could bear. At last the splash of oars reached his ears and he heard himself hailed by name. The voice was Kinsella's. The relief was too much for Patsy. He sat down on the thwart behind him and was violently sick. Kinsella laid his boat alongside the punt and looked calmly at his friend. Not until the worst spasms were over did he speak.

"Faith, Patsy," he said, "it must have been a terrible drenching you gave yourself last night, and the stuff was good too, as good as ever I seen. What has you in the state you're in at all?"

The sickness had to some extent revived Patsy the smith. He was able to speak, though with difficulty.

"Go back out of that," he said.

"And why would I go back?"

"Timothy Sweeny says you're to go back, for if you come in to the quay today there'll be the devil and all if not worse."

"If that's the way of it I will go back; but I'd be glad, so I would, if I knew what Sweeny means by it. It's a poor thing to be breaking my back rowing a boatload of gravel all the way from Inishbawn and then to be told to turn round and go back; and just now too, when the wind has dropped and it's beginning to look mighty black over to the eastward."

"You're to go back," said Patsy, "because the strange gentleman that's up at the big house is wanting your boat."

"Let him want!"

"He'll get it, if so be that you go in to the quay, and when he has it the first thing he'll do is to go out to Inishbawn. It's there he wants to be and it's yourself knows best what he'd find if he got there. Go back, I tell you."

"If you'll take my advice," said Kinsella, "you will go back yourself. There's thunder beyond there coming up, and there'll be a breeze setting towards it from the west before another ten minutes is over our heads. I don't know will you care for that in the state you're in this minute, with that old punt and only one oar. The tide'll be running strong against the breeze and there'll be a kick-up at the stone perch."

Patsy the smith saw the wisdom of this advice. Tired as he was he seized his one oar and began sculling home. Kinsella watched him go and then did a peculiar thing. He took the shovel which lay amidships in his boat and began to heave his cargo of gravel into the sea. As he worked a faint breeze from the west rose, fanned him and died away. Another succeeded it and then another. Kinsella looked round him. The four boats which had drifted out from the quay before the easterly breeze of the morning, had hauled in their sheets. They were awaiting a wind from the west. The heavy purple thunder cloud was rapidly climbing the sky. Kinsella shovelled hard at his gravel. His boat, lightened of her load, rose in the water, showing inch by inch more free board. A steady breeze from the west succeeded the light occasional puffs. It increased in strength. The four boats inside him stooped to it. They sped across and across the channel towards the stone perch in short tacks. Kinsella hoisted his sail and took the tiller. The boat swung up into the wind and coursed away to the south west, close hauled to a stiff west wind. The thunder cloud burst over Rosnacree.

Sir Lucius and Lord Torrington drove into the town and pulled up in front of Brannigan's shop at a quarter to twelve. They looked round the empty harbour in some surprise. Sir Lucius went at once into the shop. Lord Torrington, being an Englishman with a proper belief in the forces of law and order, walked a few yards back and entered the police barracks.

"Brannigan," said Sir Lucius, "where's my boat? and where's that ruffian Peter Walsh?"

"Your boat, is it?" said Brannigan.

"I sent down word to Peter Walsh to have her ready for me at twelve, or, if my daughter had taken her out——"

"It would be better," said Brannigan, "if you were to see Peter Walsh yourself. Sure I don't know what's happened to your boat."

"Where's Peter Walsh?"

"He's down at the end of the quay putting an extra coat of paint on Miss Priscilla's boat. I don't know what sense there is in doing the like, but of course he wouldn't care to go contrary to what the young lady might say."

Sir Lucius left the shop abruptly. At the door he ran into Lord Torrington and the police sergeant.

"Damn it all, Lentaigne," said Lord Torrington, "how are we going to get out?"

"There was boats in it," said the police sergeant, "plenty of them, when I gave your lordship's message to Peter Walsh."

"Where are they now?" said Lord Torrington. "What's the good of telling me they were here when they're not?"

The police sergeant looked cautiously round.

"I wouldn't say," he said at last, "but they're gone out of it, every one of the whole lot of them."

Peter Walsh, his paint brush in his hand, and an expression of respectful regret, on his face, came up to Sir Lucius and touched his hat.

"What's the meaning of this?" said Sir Lucius. "Didn't I send you word to have a boat, either my own or some other, ready for me at twelve?"

"The message the sergeant gave me," said Peter Walsh, "was to engage Joseph Antony Kinsella's boat for your honour if so be that Miss Priscilla had your own took out."

"And why the devil didn't you?" said Lord Torrington.

"Because she's not in it, your honour; nor hasn't been this day. I was waiting for her and the minute she came to the quay I'd have been in her, helping Joseph Antony to shovel out the gravel the way she'd be fit for two gentlemen like yourselves to go in her."

"Is there no other boat to be got?" said Lord Torrington.

"Launch Miss Priscilla's at once," said Sir Lucius.

"Sure the paint's wet on the bottom of her."

"Launch her," said Sir Lucius, "paint or not paint."

"I'll launch her if your honour bids me," said Peter Walsh. "But what use will she be to you when she's in the water? She'll not work to windward for you under the little lug that's in her, and it's from the west the wind's coming now."

He looked round the sky as he spoke.

"Glory be to God!" he said. "Will you look at what's coming. There's thunder in it and maybe worse."

Sir Lucius took Lord Torrington by the arm and led him out of earshot of the police sergeant and Peter Walsh.

"We'd better not go today, Torrington. There's a thunder storm coming. We'd simply get drenched."

"I don't care if I am drenched."

"And besides we can't go. There isn't a boat. We couldn't get anywhere in that little thing of Priscilla's. After all if she's on an island today she'll be there tomorrow."

"If that fool of a sergeant told us the truth this morning," said Lord Torrington, "and there's some man with her I want to break every bone in his body as soon as I can."

"He'll be there tomorrow," said Sir Lucius, "and I'll see that there's a boat here to take us out."

CHAPTER XVIII

Priscilla and Frank left the quay at half past seven against a tide which was still rising, but with a pleasant easterly breeze behind them. Once past the stone perch Priscilla set the boat on her course for Craggeen and gave the tiller to Frank. She herself pulled a spinnaker from beneath the stern sheets and explained to Frank that when she had hoisted it the boat's speed would be considerably increased. Then she made him uncomfortable by hitting him several times in different parts of the body with a long spar which she called the spinnaker boom.

The setting of this sail struck Frank as an immensely complicated business. He watched Priscilla working with a whole series of ropes and admired her skill greatly, until it occurred to him that she was not very sure of what she was doing. A rope, which she had made fast with some care close beside him, had to be cast loose, carried forward, passed outside a stay, and then made fast again. There appeared to be three corners to the spinnaker, and all three were hooked turn about on the end of the boom. Even when the third was unhooked again and the one which had been tried first restored to its place Priscilla seemed a little dissatisfied with the result. Another of the three corners was caught and held by the clip-hooks on the end of the halliard. Priscilla moused these carefully, explaining why she did so, and then found that she had to cut the mousing and catch the remaining corner of the sail with the hooks. When at last she triumphantly hoisted it the thing went up in a kind of bundle. Its own sheet was wrapped round it twice, and a jib sheet which had somehow wandered away from its proper place got twined round and round the boom which remained immovable near the mast. Priscilla surveyed the result of her work with a puzzled frown. Then she lowered the sail and turned to Frank.

"I thoroughly understand spinnakers," she said, "in theory. I don't suppose that there's a single thing known about them that I don't know. But they're beastly confusing things when you come to deal with them in practical life. Lots of other things are like that. It's exactly the same with algebra. I expect I've told you that I simply loathe algebra. Well, that's the reason. I understand it all right, but when it comes to doing it, it comes out just like that spinnaker. However it doesn't really matter. That's the great comfort about most things. You get on quite well enough without them, though of course you would get on better with, if you could do them."

The *Tortoise* did in fact slip along at a very satisfactory pace in spite of the lightness of the wind. It was just half past eight when they reached the mouth of the bay in which they had lunched the day before with Miss Rutherford.

"I feel rather," said Priscilla, "as if I could do with a little breakfast There's no use going on shore. Let's anchor and eat what we want in the boat."

Frank who was very hungry agreed at once. He rounded the boat up into the wind and Priscilla flung the anchor overboard. Then she picked her parcels one by one from the folds of the spinnaker in which they had wrapped themselves.

"It won't do," she said, "to eat everything today at the first go off the way we did yesterday. Specially as we've promised to give Miss Rutherford luncheon. The duck, for instance, had better be kept."

She laid the duck down again and covered it, a little regretfully, with the spinnaker. She took up the jampot which contained the caramel pudding. Her face brightened as she looked at it.

"By the way, Cousin Frank," she said. "That word is inviolable."

"That word?"

"The sanctuary and secret word," said Priscilla. "Don't you remember I couldn't get it last night. But I did after I went to sleep which was jolly lucky. I hopped up at once and wrote it down. Now we know what Inishbawn will be for Lady Torrington's poor daughter when we get her there. All the same I don't think we'd better eat the caramel pudding at breakfast. It mightn't be wholesome for you at this hour—on account of your sprained ankle, I mean, and not being accustomed to puddings at breakfast. Besides I expect Miss Rutherford would rather like it. What do you say to starting with an artichoke each?"

Frank was ready to start with anything that was given him. He ate the artichoke greedily and felt hardly less hungry when he had finished it. Priscilla too seemed unsatisfied. She said that they had perhaps made a mistake in beginning with the artichokes. But her sense of duty and her instinct for hospitality triumphed over her appetite. Feeling that temptation might prove overpowering, she put the slices of cold fish out of sight under the spinnaker with the remark that they ought to be kept for Miss Rutherford. She and Frank ate the herrings' roes on toast, the sweetbread and one of the four rolls. Then though Frank still looked hungry, Priscilla hoisted the foresail and hauled up the anchor.

They reached the passage past Craggeen when the tide was at the full and threaded their way among the rocks successfully. They passed into the wide water of Finilaun roads. A long reach lay before them and the wind had begun to die down as the tide turned. Priscilla, leaving Frank to steer, settled herself comfortably on the weather side of the boat between the centreboard case and the gunwale. Far down to leeward another boat was slipping across the roads towards the south. She had an old stained jib and an obtrusively new mainsail which shone dazzlingly white in the sun. Priscilla watched her with idle interest for some time. Then she announced that she was Flanagan's new boat.

"He bought the calico for the sail at Brannigan's," she said, "and made it himself. Peter Walsh told me that. I'm bound to say it doesn't sit badly; but of course you can't really tell about the sit of a sail when the boat's off the wind. I'd like to see it when she's close-hauled. That's the way with lots of other things besides sails. I dare say now that Lord Torrington is quite an agreeable sort of man when his daughter isn't running away."

"I'm sure he's not," said Frank.

"You can't be sure," said Priscilla. "Nobody could, except of course Lady Torrington and she doesn't seem to me the sort of person who's much cowed in her own house. I wish you'd heard her going for Aunt Juliet last night, most politely, but every word she said had what's called in French a 'double entendre' wrapped up in it. That means——"

"I know what it means," said Frank.

"That's all right then. I thought perhaps you wouldn't. I always heard they rather despised French at boys' schools, which is idiotic of course and may not be true."

Frank recollected a form master with whom, at one stage of his career at school he used to study the adventures of the innocent Telemaque. This gentleman refused to read aloud or allow his class to read aloud the text of the book, alleging that no one who did not suffer from a malformation of the mouth could pronounce French properly. Still even this master must have attached some meaning to the phrase "double entendre," though he might not have used it in precisely Priscilla's sense.

"Flanagan has probably been over to Curraunbeg," said Priscilla, "to see how his old boat is looking. After what Jimmy Kinsella is sure to have told him about the way they're treating her he's naturally a bit anxious. I wonder will he have the nerve to charge them anything extra at the end for dilapidations. It's curious now that we don't see the tents on Curraunbeg. I saw them yesterday from Craggeen. Perhaps they've moved round to the other side of the island."

"There's a boat coming out from behind the point now," said Frank. "Perhaps they're moving again."

Priscilla leaned over the gunwale and stared long at the boat which Frank pointed out.

"There's a man and a woman in her," he said.

"It's not Flanagan's old boat though," said Priscilla. "I rather think it's Jimmy Kinsella. I hope Miss Rutherford hasn't been hunting them on her own, under the impression that they're German spies. We oughtn't to have told her that. She's so frightfully impulsive you can't tell what she'd do."

Jimmy Kinsella had recognised the *Tortoise* shortly after he rounded the point of Curraunbeg. He dropped his lug sail and began to row up to windward evidently meaning to get within speaking distance of Priscilla. The boats approached each other at an angle. Miss Rutherford stood up in the stern of hers, waved a pocket handkerchief and shouted. Priscilla shouted in reply. Frank threw the *Tortoise* up into the wind and Jimmy Kinsella pulled alongside.

"They've gone," said Miss Rutherford. "They've escaped you again."

"You've frightened them away," said Priscilla. "I wish you wouldn't."

"No," said Miss Rutherford, "I didn't Honour bright! They'd gone before I got there. The people on the island said they packed up early this morning and when they saw Flanagan passing in his new boat they hailed him and got him to take them off."

"Wasn't that the boat we saw just now?" said Frank.

"Yes," said Priscilla. "Frightfully annoying, isn't it?"

"Never mind," said Miss Rutherford. "I know where they're gone. The people on the island told me. To Inishminna. Wasn't Inishminna the name, Jimmy?"

"It was, Miss."

"Climb on board," said Priscilla. "That is to say if you want to come. We must be after them at once. We'll follow Flanagan. Jimmy can row through Craggeen passage and pick you up afterwards."

Miss Rutherford tumbled from her own boat into the *Tortoise*.

"Thanks awfully," she said. "I want to see you arrest those spies more than anything."

"They're not spies," said Priscilla.

"We never really thought they were," said Frank.

"The truth is———" said Priscilla.

She stopped abruptly and looked round. Jimmy Kinsella was some distance astern heading for Craggeen. He appeared to be quite out of earshot. Nevertheless Priscilla lowered her voice to a whisper.

"We're on an errand of mercy," she said.

"Oh," said Miss Rutherford, "not vengeance. I'm disappointed."

"Mercy is a much nicer thing," said Priscilla, "besides being more Christian."

"All the same," said Miss Rutherford, "I'm disappointed. Vengeance is far more exciting."

"To a certain extent," said Priscilla, "we're taking vengeance too. At least Frank is, on account of his ankle you know. So you needn't be disappointed."

"That cheers me up a little," said Miss Rutherford, "but do explain."

"It's quite simple really," said Priscilla. "Though it may seem a little complicated. You explain, Cousin Frank, and be sure to begin at the beginning or she won't understand."

"Lord Torrington," said Frank, "is Secretary of State for War, and his daughter, Lady Isabel—but perhaps I'd better tell you first that as I was coming over to Ireland I met———"

"'Now who be ye would cross Lochgyle,'" said Priscilla, waving her hands towards the sea, "'this dark and stormy water?'"

"'Oh I'm the chief of Ulva's Isle, and this Lord Ullin's daughter.' You know that poem, I suppose."

"I've known it for years," said Miss Rutherford.

"Well, thats it," said Priscilla. "You have the whole thing now."

"I see," said Miss Rutherford, "I see it all now, or almost all. This is far better than spies. How did you ever think of it?"

"It's true," said Priscilla.

"Lord Torrington," said Frank, "is over here stopping with my uncle, and he came specially to find his daughter who's run away."

"'One lovely hand stretched out for aid,'" said Priscilla, "'and one was round her lover.' That's what we want to avoid if we can. I call that an errand of mercy. Don't you?"

"It's far and away the most merciful errand I ever heard of," said Miss Rutherford. "But why don't you hurry? At any moment now her father's men may reach the shore."

"We can't," said Priscilla, "hurry any more than we are. The wind's dropping every minute. Luff her a little bit, Frank, or she won't clear the point. The tide's taking us down, and that point runs out a terrific distance."

"The only thing I don't quite see yet," said Miss Rutherford, "is where the vengeance comes in."

"That's to be taken on her father," said Priscilla.

"Quite right," said Miss Rutherford, "as a matter of abstract justice; but I rather gathered from the way you spoke, Priscilla, that Frank had some kind of private feud with the old gentleman."

"He shoved me off the end of the steamer's gangway," said Frank, "and sprained my ankle. He has never so much as said he was sorry."

"Good," said Miss Rutherford. "Now our consciences are absolutely clear. What we are going to do is to carry off the blushing bride to some distant island."

"Inishbawn," said Priscilla.

The *Tortoise* had slipped through the passage at the south end of Finislaun. She was moving very slowly across another stretch of open water. On her lee bow lay Inishbawn. The island differs from most others in the bay in being twin. Instead of one there are two green mounds linked together by a long ridge of grey boulders. Tides sweep furiously round the two horns of it, but the water inside is calm and sheltered from any wind except one from the south east. On the slope of the northern hill stands the Kinsellas' cottage, with certain patches of cultivated land around it. The southern hill is bare pasture land roamed over by bullocks and a few sheep which in stormy weather or night cross the stony isthmus to seek companionship and shelter near the cottage.

"Isn't that Inishbawn?" said Miss Rutherford. "Jimmy Kinsella told me it was the day I first met you."

"That's it," said Priscilla, "that's where we mean to put her."

"It's not half far enough away," said Miss Rutherford. "Lord Ullin or Torrington or whatever lord it is will quite easily follow her there. We must go much further, right out into the west to High Brasail, where lovers are ever young and angry fathers do not come."

"Inishbawn will do all right," said Priscilla.

"Priscilla says," said Frank, "that the people won't let Lord Torrington land on Inishbawn."

"They certainly seemed to have some objection to letting any one land," said Miss Rutherford. "Every time I suggested going there Jimmy has headed me off with one excuse or another."

"They have very good reasons," said Priscilla. "I have more or less idea what they are; but of course I can't tell you. It's never right to tell other people's secrets unless you're perfectly sure that you know them yourself, and I'm not sure. You hardly ever can be unless you happen to be one of the people that has the secret and in this case I'm not."

"I don't want to ask embarrassing questions," said Miss Rutherford, "though I'm almost consumed with curiosity about the secret. But are you quite sure that it's of a kind that will really prevent Lord Torrington landing there?"

"Quite absolutely, dead, cock sure," said Priscilla. "If I'm right about the secret and I think I am, though of course it's quite possible that I may not be, but if I am there isn't a man about the bay who wouldn't die a thousand miserable deaths rather than let Lord Torrington and the police sergeant land on that island."

"Then all we've got to do," said Miss Rutherford, "is to get her there and she's safe."

Priscilla hurriedly turned over the corner of the spinnaker and got out the jam pot. She glanced at its paper cover.

"Inishbawn is an inviolable sanctuary," she said. "What a mercy it is that I wrote down that word last night. I had forgotten it again. It's a desperately hard word to remember."

"It's a very good word," said Miss Rutherford.

"It's useful anyhow," said Priscilla. "In fact, considering what we're going to do I don't see how we could very well get on without it. I suppose it's rather too early to have luncheon."

"It's only half past eleven," said Frank, "but——"

"I breakfasted early," said Miss Rutherford.

"We scarcely breakfasted at all," said Frank.

"All right," said Priscilla, "the wind's gone hopelessly. It's much too hot to row, so I suppose we may as well have luncheon though it's not the proper time."

"Let us shake ourselves free of the wretched conventions of ordinary civilisation," said Miss Rutherford. "Let us eat when we are hungry without regard to the clock. Let us gorge ourselves with California peach juice. Let us suck the burning peppermint—"

"We haven't any today," said Priscilla. "Brannigan's wasn't open when we started."

"The principle is just the same," said Miss Rutherford. "Whatever food you have is sure to be refreshingly unusual."

CHAPTER XIX

The *Tortoise* lay absolutely becalmed. The ebbing tide carried her slowly past Inishbawn towards the deep passage between the end of the breakwater of boulders and the point on which the lighthouse stands. The air was extraordinarily close and oppressive. Even Priscilla seemed affected by it. She lay against the side of the boat with her hands trailing idly in the water. Frank sat with the useless tiller in his hand and watched the boom swing slowly across as the boat swayed this way or that with the current. Miss Rutherford, her face glistening with heat, had gone to sleep in a most uncomfortable attitude soon after luncheon. Her head nodded backwards from time to time and whenever it did so she opened her eyes, smiled at Frank, rearranged herself a little and then went to sleep again.

The cattle on Inishbawn had forsaken their scanty pasture and stood knee-deep in the sea. Not even the wild new heifer, which had gored Jimmy Kinsella, if such a creature existed at all, would have had energy to do much. A dog, which ought perhaps to have been barking at the cattle, lay prostrate under the shadow afforded by a grassy bank. A flock of white terns floated motionless a few yards from the *Tortoise*, looking like a miniature fleet of graceful, white-sailed pleasure boats. They had no heart to go circling and swooping for fish.

Perhaps it would have been useless if they had. The fish themselves may well have been lying, in search of coolness among the weedy stones at the bottom of the sea. Of all living creatures the jelly fish alone seemed to retain any spirit. Immense crowds of them drifted past the *Tortoise*, swelling out and closing again their concave bodies, revolving slowly round, dragging long purple tendrils deliriously through the warm water. They swept past Priscilla's drooping hands, touching them with their yielding bodies and brushing them softly with their tendrils. Now and then she lifted one from the water, watched it lie flaccid on the palm of her hand and then dropped it into the sea again.

A faint air of wind stole across from Inishbawn. The *Tortoise*, utterly without steerage way, felt it and turned slowly towards it. It was as if she stretched her head out for another such gentle kiss as the wind gave her. Priscilla felt it, and with returning animation made a plunge for an unusually large jelly fish, captured it and held it up triumphantly.

"It's a pity you're not out after jelly fish, Miss Rutherford," she said, "instead of sponges. There are thousands and thousands of them. We could fill the boat with them in half an hour."

Miss Rutherford made no reply. She had succeeded in wriggling herself into such a position that her head rested on the thwart of the boat. Her face was extremely red, and, owing perhaps to the twisted position of her neck, she was snoring. Priscilla looked at Frank and smiled.

"I wonder," she said, "if we ought to wake her up. She won't like it, of course, but it may be the kindest thing to do. It wouldn't be at all nice for her if she smothered in her sleep."

Frank blinked lazily. He was very nearly asleep.

"You're a nice pair," said Priscilla. "What on earth is the point of dropping off like that in the middle of the day? Ghastly laziness I call it."

Another puff of wind and then another came from the west. The *Tortoise* began to move through the water. Frank woke up and paid serious attention to his steering. Priscilla looked round the sea and then the sky. The thunder storm was breaking over Rosnacree, five miles to the east, and a heavy bank of dark clouds was piled up across the sky.

"It looks uncommonly queer," said Priscilla, "rather magnificent in some ways, but I wish I knew exactly what it's going to do. I don't understand this breeze coming in from the west. It's freshening too."

A long deep growl reached them from the east.

"Thunder," said Frank.

"Must be," said Priscilla. "The clouds are coming up against the wind. Only thunder does that—and liberty. At least Wordsworth says liberty does. I never saw it myself. I told you we were doing 'The Excursion' last term. It's in that somewhere. I say, this breeze is freshening. Keep her just as she's going, Cousin Frank. We'll be able to let her go in a minute. Oh, do look at the water!"

The sea had turned a deep purple colour. In spite of the ripples which the westerly breeze raised on its surface it had a curious look of sulky menace.

"Miss Rutherford," said Priscilla, "wake up, we're going to have a thunder storm."

Miss Rutherford sat up with a start

"A storm!" she said. "How splendid! Any chance of being wrecked?"

"Not at present," said Priscilla, "but you never know what may happen. If you feel at all nervous I'll steer myself."

"Nervous!" said Miss Rutherford. "I'm delighted. There's nothing I should like more than to be wrecked on a desert island with you two. It would just complete the most glorious series of adventures I've ever had. Do try and get wrecked."

"Hadn't we better go in to Inishbawn and wait till it's over?" said Frank.

"Nonsense," said Priscilla. "Wetting won't hurt us, and anyway we'll be at Inishminna in half an hour with this breeze."

The *Tortoise* was racing through the dark water. She was listed over so that her lee gunwale seemed likely to dip under. Miss Rutherford, in spite of her wish for shipwreck, scrambled up to windward. They reached the point of Ardilaun and fled, bending and staggering, down the narrow passage between it and Inishlean. Priscilla took the mainsheet in her hand and ordered Frank to luff a little. There was another period of rushing, heavily listed, with the wind fair abeam. Now and then, as a squall struck the sails, Priscilla let the mainsheet run out and allowed the *Tortoise* to right herself. The sea was flecked with the white tops of short, steep waves, raised hurriedly, as it were irritably by the wind. A few heavy drops of rain fell. The whole sky became very dark. A bright zig-zag of light flashed down, the thunder crashed over head. The rain came down like a solid sheet of water.

"Let her away again now," said Priscilla. "We can run right down on Inishark. Be ready to round her up into the wind when I tell you. I daren't jibe her."

"Don't," said Frank. "I say, you'd better steer."

"Can't now. We couldn't possibly change places. Are you all right, Miss Rutherford?"

"Splendid. Couldn't be better. I'm soaked to the skin. Can't possibly be any wetter even if we swim for it."

Inishark loomed, a low dark mass under their bow, dimly seen through a veil of blinding rain which fell so heavily that the floor boards under their feet were already awash.

"We'll have to bail in a minute or two if this goes on," said Priscilla. "I wonder where the tin is?"

A roar of thunder drowned her voice. Miss Rutherford and Frank saw her gesticulate wildly and point towards the island. Two small patches of white were to be seen near the shore.

"Their tents," yelled Priscilla. "We have them now if we don't sink. Luff her up, Cousin Frank, luff her up for all you're worth. We must get her off on the other tack or we'll be past them."

She hauled on the mainsheet as she spoke. The *Tortoise* rounded up into the wind, lay over till the water began to pour over her side, righted herself again and stood suddenly on an even keel, her sails flapping wildly, the boat herself trembling like a creature desperately frightened. Then she fell off on her new tack. Priscilla dragged Miss Rutherford up to windward. Frank, guided by instinct rather than by any knowledge of what was happening, scrambled up past the end of the long tiller. Priscilla let the main sheet run out again. The *Tortoise* raced straight for the shore.

"Keep her as she's going, Cousin Frank. I'll get the sail off her."

For a minute or two there was wild confusion. Priscilla treading on Miss Rutherford without remorse or apology, struggled with the halyard. The sail bellied hugely, dipped into the sea to leeward and was hauled desperately on board. The rain streamed down on them, each drop starting up again like a miniature fountain when it splashed upon the wood of the boat. The *Tortoise*, nearly half full of water, still staggered towards the shore under her foresail. Priscilla hauled at the rope of the centreboard.

"Run her up on the beach," she shouted. "If we do knock a hole in her it can't be helped. Oh glory, glory! look at that!"

One of the tents tore itself from its fastenings, flapped wildly in the air and then collapsed on the ground, a writhing heaving mass of soaked canvas. The *Tortoise* struck heavily on the shore. Priscilla leaped over her bows and ran up the beach with the anchor in her hand. She rammed one of its flukes deep into the gravel. Then she turned towards the boat and shouted:

"You help Frank out, Miss Rutherford. I must run on and see what's happening to those tents."

A young woman, rain soaked and dishevelled, knelt beside the fallen tent. She was working with fierce energy at the guy ropes, such of them as still clung to their pegs. They were hopelessly entangled with the others which had broken free and all of them were knotted and twisted round corners of the flapping canvas.

"If I were you," said Priscilla, "I'd leave those things alone till the storm blows over. You're only making them worse."

The young woman looked round at Priscilla and smoothed her blown wet hair from her face.

"Come and help me," she said, "please."

"What's the good of hurrying?" said Priscilla.

"My husband's underneath."

"Well, I suppose he's all right. In fact, I daresay he's a good deal drier there than we are outside. We'd far better go into your tent and wait."

"He'll smother."

"Not he. If he's suffering from anything this minute I should say it is draughts."

The canvas heaved convulsively. It was evident that some one underneath was making desperate efforts to get out.

"He's smothering. I know he is."

"Very well," said Priscilla. "I'll give you a help if you like; I don't know much about tents and I may simply make things worse. However, I'll try."

She attacked a complex tangle of ropes vigorously. Miss Rutherford, with Frank leaning on her shoulder, staggered up the beach. Just as they reached the tents the head of a young man appeared under the flapping canvas. Then his arms struggled out. Priscilla seized him by the hands and pulled hard.

"Oh, Barnabas!" said the young lady, "are you safe?"

"He's wet," said Priscilla, "and rather muddy, but he's evidently alive and he doesn't look as if he was injured in any way."

The young man looked round him wildly at first. He was evidently bewildered after his struggle with the tent and surprised at the manner of his rescue. He gradually realised that there were strangers present. His eyes rested on Miss Rutherford. She seemed the most responsible member of the party. He pulled himself together with an effort and addressed her in a tone of suave politeness which, under the circumstances, was very surprising.

"Perhaps," he said, "I ought to introduce myself. My name is Pennefather, Barnabas Pennefather. The Rev. Barnabas Pennefather. This is my wife, Lady Isabel Pennefather. I have a card somewhere."

He began to fumble in various packets.

"Never mind the card," said Priscilla. "We'll take your word for it."

"We," said Miss Rutherford, "are a rescue party. We've been in search of you for days. This is Priscilla. This is Frank. My own name is Martha Rutherford."

"A rescue party!" said Mr. Pennefather.

"Did mother send you after us?" said Lady Isabel. "If she did you may go away again. I won't go back."

"Quite the contrary," said Priscilla, "we're on your side."

"In fact," said Miss Rutherford, "we're here to save you from——"

"At first," said Priscilla, "we fancied you might be spies, German spies. Afterwards we found out you weren't. That often happens you know. Just as you think you're perfectly certain you're right, it turns out that you're quite wrong."

"Then you really were pursuing us," said Lady Isabel. "I always said you were, didn't I, Barnabas?"

"Is Lord Torrington here?" said Mr. Pennefather.

"Not exactly here," said Priscilla, "at least not yet. But he will be soon. When we left home this morning he was fully bent on hunting you down and I rather think the police sergeant must have given him the tip about where you are."

"The police!" said Mr. Pennefather.

"I don't so much mind if it's only father," said Lady Isabel.

"You may not," said Priscilla. "But I expect Mr. Pennefather will. Lord Torrington is very fierce. In his rage and fury he sprained Frank's ankle. He might have broken it. In fact, the railway guard thought he had. I don't know what he'll do to you when he catches you."

"Does he know we're married," said Mr. Pennefather.

"Is mother with him?" said Lady Isabel.

"She is," said Priscilla. "But it's all right. Aunt Juliet will keep her in play. You can count on Aunt Juliet until she finds out that you're married—after that——— But it will be all right. We have come to conduct you to a place of safety."

"An inviolable sanctuary," said Miss Rutherford. "But we shall all have colds in the head before we get there if we don't do something to dry ourselves."

"Barnabas," said Lady Isabel, "do go and change your clothes. He fell into the sea the other day, and he is so liable to take cold."

"We saw him," said Priscilla. "Go and change your clothes, Mr. Pennefather. By the time you've done that Jimmy Kinsella will have arrived and you can be off at once with Miss Rutherford. The sooner we're all out of this the better. Though Lord Torrington doesn't look like a man who would come out in a thunder storm even to catch his daughter."

"Your black suit is in the hold-all in my tent," said Lady Isabel.

The Reverend Barnabas Pennefather disappeared into the tent which was still standing. Priscilla looked around her cheerfully.

"It's clearing up," she said. "There's quite a lot of blue sky to be seen over Rosnacree. We'll all dry soon."

She gathered the bottom of her skirt tight into her hands and wrung the water out of it.

"Where are you going to take him to?" she said to Miss Rutherford.

"Am I to take him?" said Miss Rutherford. "I didn't know that was part of the plan. I thought we were all going together to Inishbawn, the sanctuary."

"Didn't I tell you," said Priscilla. "We decided that you were to have charge of Barnabas for a few days until the trouble blows over a bit. You're to pretend that he's your husband. You don't mind, do you?"

"I'd much rather have Frank," said Miss Rutherford.

"What on earth would be the use of that?" said Priscilla.

"But, of course, I'll marry Barnabas with pleasure," said Miss Rutherford, "if it's really necessary and Lady Isabel doesn't object."

"I won't be separated from Barnabas," said Lady Isabel, "and I'm sure he'll never agree to leave me."

"All the same you'll have to," said Priscilla, "both of you. We can't pretend you're not married if you're going about together on Inishbawn."

"But I don't want to pretend I'm not married. I'm proud of what we've done."

"You'll sacrifice the respect and affection of Aunt Juliet," said Priscilla, "the moment it comes out that you're married. As long as she thinks you're out on your own defying the absurd conventions by which women are made into what she calls 'bedizened dolls for the amusement of the brutalised male sex,' she'll be all on your side. But once she thinks you've given up your economic independence she'll simply turn round and help Lady Torrington to hunt you down."

Mr. Pennefather emerged from the tent. He wore a black suit of clothes of strictly clerical cut and a collar which buttoned at the back of his neck. Except that he was barefooted and had not brushed his hair he would have been fit to attend a Church Conference. His self-respect was restored by his attire. He walked over to Frank, who was dripping on a stone, and handed him a visiting card. Frank read it.

"Reverend Barnabas Pennefather—St. Agatha's Clergy House—Grosvenor Street, W."

"I am the senior curate," he said. "The staff consists of five priests besides the vicar."

"They want to take you away from me," said Lady Isabel. "But you won't go, say you won't, Barnabas."

Mr. Pennefather took his place at his wife's side. He held her hand in his.

"Nothing on earth," he said, "can separate us now."

"Very well," said Priscilla. "You're rather ungrateful, both of you, considering all we're doing for you, and I don't think you're exactly polite to Miss Rutherford, however——"

"Don't mind about me," said Miss Rutherford. "I feel snubbed, of course, but I wasn't really keen on having him for a husband, even temporarily."

Mr. Pennefather looked at her with shocked surprise. A deep flush spread slowly over his face. His eyes blazed with righteous indignation.

"Woman——" he began.

"If you don't mind," said Priscilla, "I think we'll call you Barnabas. It's rather long, of course, and solemn. The natural thing would be to shorten it down to Barny, but that wouldn't suit you a bit. The rain's over now. I think I'll go down and bail out the *Tortoise*. Then we'll all start. You people can be taking down the tent that's standing, and folding up the other one."

"Where are we going to?" said Mr. Pennefather.

"To a sanctuary," said Miss Rutherford, "an inviolable sanctuary. Priscilla has that written down on the cover of a jam pot, so there's no use arguing about it."

"She says we'll be safe," said Lady Isabel.

"I refuse to move," said Mr. Pennefather, "until I know where I'm going and why."

"You talk to him, Cousin Frank," said Priscilla. "I see Jimmy Kinsella coming round the corner in his boat and I really must bail out the *Tortoise*."

"If you don't move out of this pretty quick," said Frank to Mr. Pennefather, "Lord Torrington will have you to a dead cert."

"'And fast before her father's men,' said Miss Rutherford, "'three days we fled together. And should they find us in this glen——'"

"Oh, Barnabas," said Lady Isabel, who knew Campbell's poem and anticipated the end of the quotation, "Oh, Barnabas, let's go, anywhere, anywhere."

"I never saw any man," said Frank, "in such a wax as Lord Torrington."

"I haven't met him myself," said Miss Rutherford, "but I expect that when he begins to speak he'll shock you even worse than I did."

"We don't mind Father," said Lady Isabel. "It's Mother."

"They're both on your track," said Frank.

Mr. Pennefather looked from one to another of the group around him. Then he turned slowly on his heel and began to roll up his tent. Lady Isabel and Miss Rutherford set to work to pack the camp equipage. Frank took off his coat and wrung the water out of it. Then he spread it on the ground and looked at it. It was the coat worn by members of the First Eleven. He had won his right to it when he caught out the Uppingham captain in the long field. Now such triumphs and glories seemed incredibly remote. The voices of Priscilla and Jimmy Kinsella reached him from the shore. They were arguing hotly.

Frank looked at them and saw that they were both on their knees in the *Tortoise* scooping up water in tin dishes.

The bailing was finished at last. The packing was nearly done. Priscilla walked up to the camp dragging Jimmy Kinsella with her by the collar of the coat.

"Barnabas," she said, "have you got a revolver?"

Mr. Pennefather looked up from a roll of blankets which he was strapping together.

"No," he said. "I don't carry revolvers."

"I think you ought to," said Priscilla. "I mean whenever you happen to be running away with the daughter of the First Lord of the War Office or any one like that. But, of course, being a clergyman may make a difference. It's awfully hard to know exactly what a clergyman ought to do when he's eloping. At the same time it's jolly awkward you're not having a revolver, for Jimmy Kinsella says he won't go to Inishbawn and we can't all fit in the *Tortoise*."

"Leave him to me," said Frank. "Just bring him over here, Priscilla, and I'll deal with him."

"I'll not take you to Inishbawn," said Jimmy.

Priscilla handed him over to Frank. It was a long time, more than two years, since Frank had acquired some reputation as a master of men in the form Room of Remove A.; but he retained a clear recollection of the methods he had employed. He seized Jimmy Kinsella's wrist and with a deft, rapid movement, twisted it round. Jimmy had not enjoyed the advantages of an English public school education. Torture of a refined kind was new to him. He uttered a shrill squeal.

"Will you go where you're told," said Frank, "or do you want more?"

"I dursn't take yez to Inishbawn," said Jimmy whimpering. "My da would beat me if I did."

Frank twisted his arm again.

"My da will cut the liver out of me," said Jimmy.

"Stop that," said Mr. Pennefather. "I cannot allow bullying."

"It's for your sake entirely that it's being done," said Priscilla. "You're the most ungrateful beast I ever met. It would serve you jolly well right if we left you here to have your own arm twisted by Lord Torrington."

Miss Rutherford was kneeling in front of a beautiful canteen, fitting aluminium plates and various articles of cutlery into the places prepared for them. She stood up and brandished a large carving fork.

"This," she said, "will be just as effective as a revolver. You take it, Frank, and sit close to him in the boat. The moment he stops rowing or tries to go in any direction except Inishbawn you——"

She made a vicious stab in the air and then handed the fork to Frank.

A quarter of an hour later the party started. Mr. Pennefather and Lady Isabel refused to be separated. Priscilla took them in the *Tortoise*. They sat side by side near the mast and held each other's hands. Priscilla, after one glance in their direction, looked resolutely past them for the rest of the voyage. Miss Rutherford sat in the bow of Jimmy Kinsella's boat. Jimmy sat amidships and rowed. Frank, with the carving fork poised for a thrust, sat in the stern. The wind, following the departed thunderstorm, blew from the east. Priscilla set sail on the *Tortoise*. Jimmy hoisted his lug, but was obliged to row as well as sail in order to keep in touch with his consort. The boats grounded almost together on the shingly beach of Inishbawn.

Joseph Antony, who had made his way home through the thunderstorm, put his hand on the bow of the *Tortoise*.

"It'll be better for you not to land," he said.

"I know all about that," said Priscilla. "You needn't bother to invent anything fresh."

"You can't land here," said Joseph Antony. "Aren't there islands enough in the bay? Jimmy, will you push that boat off from the shore and take the lady and gentleman that's in her away out of this."

The carving fork descended an inch towards Jimmy's leg. His father menaced him with a threatening scowl. Jimmy sat quite still. Like the leader of the House of Lords during the last stage of a recent political crisis, he had ceased to be a free agent.

"I don't want to land on your beastly island," said Priscilla. "If there wasn't as much as a half-tide rock in the whole bay that I could put my foot on I wouldn't land here, and you can tell your wife from me that if that baby of hers was to die for the want of a bit of flannel, I won't steal another scrap from Aunt Juliet's box to give it to her."

"Sure you know well enough, Miss," said Joseph Antony, "that there's ne'er a one would be more welcome to the island than yourself. But the way things is at present——"

"I've a pretty good guess at the way things are," said Priscilla, "and the minute I get back tonight I'm going to tell Sergeant Rafferty."

Joseph Antony smiled uneasily.

"You wouldn't do the like of that," he said.

"I will," said Priscilla, "unless you allow me to land these two at once."

Joseph Antony looked long and carefully at Mr. Pennefather.

"What about the other young gentleman?" he said, "the one that has the sore leg?"

"He doesn't want to set foot on Inishbawn," said Priscilla.

"And the young lady," said Joseph Antony, "that does be taking the water in the little boat along with Jimmy?"

"She'll let Jimmy row her off to any corner of the bay you like," said Priscilla, "if you'll allow the other two to land."

Joseph Antony looked at Mr. Pennefather again.

"I wouldn't say there was much harm in him," he said.

"There's none," said Priscilla, "absolutely none. Isn't he paying £4 a week for that old boat of Flanagan's. Doesn't that show you the kind of man he is?"

"Unless," said Joseph Antony, "it could be that he's signed the pledge for life."

"Have you signed the pledge for life, Barnabas?" said Priscilla. "Let go of her hand for one minute and answer the question that's asked you."

"Does he mean a temperance pledge?" said Mr. Pennefather.

"I do," said Joseph Antony. "Are you a member of the Total Abstinence Sodality?"

"I take a little whisky after my work on Sunday evenings," said Mr. Pennefather, "and, of course, when I'm dining out I——"

"That'll do," said Joseph Antony. "A man that takes it one time will take it another. I suppose now you're not any ways connected with the police?"

"He is not," said Priscilla. "Can't you see he's a clergyman?"

"It's beyond me," said Joseph Antony, "what brings you to Inishbawn at all."

"The way things are with you at present," said Priscilla, "it wouldn't be a bad thing to have a clergyman staying with you on the island. It would look respectable."

"It would, of course," said Joseph Antony.

"If any question ever came to be asked," said Priscilla, "about what's going on here, it would be a grand thing for you to be able to say that you had the Rev. Barnabas Pennefather stopping along with you."

"It would surely," said Joseph Antony.

Priscilla jumped out of the boat and drew Kinsella a little way up the beach.

"If anything was to come out," she whispered, "you could say that it was the strange clergyman and that you didn't know what was going on."

"I might," said Joseph Antony.

Priscilla turned to the boat joyfully.

"Hop out, Barnabas," she shouted, "and take the tents and things with you. It's all settled. Joseph Antony will give you the run of his island and you'll be perfectly safe."

Mr. Pennefather climbed over the bows of the *Tortoise*.

Lady Isabel tugged at the hold-all, which was tucked away under a thwart and heaved it with a great effort into her husband's arms. He staggered under the weight of it. Joseph Antony Kinsella's instinctive politeness asserted itself.

"Will you let me take that from you?" he said. "The like of them parcels isn't fit for your reverence to carry."

Lady Isabel got the rest of her luggage out of the *Tortoise*. Then she and Mr. Pennefather went to Jimmy Kinsella's boat and unloaded it. They had a good deal of luggage altogether. When everything was stacked on the beach Mrs. Kinsella, with her baby in her arms, came down and looked at the pile with amazement. Three small, bare-legged Kinsellas, young brothers of Jimmy's, followed her. She turned to Priscilla.

"Maybe now," she said, "them ones is after being evicted? Tell me this, was it out of shops or off the land that they did be getting their living before the trouble came on them?"

"Arrah, whist, woman," said Joseph Antony, "have you no eyes in your head. Can't you see that the gentleman's a clergyman?"

"Glory be to God!" said Mrs. Kinsella, "and to think now that they'd evict the like of him!"

Lady Isabel held out her hand to Priscilla.

"Goodbye," she said, "and thank you so much for all you've done. If you see my mother——"

"We'll see her tonight," said Priscilla. "I shan't be let in to dinner, but I'll see her afterwards when Aunt Juliet is smoking in the hope of shocking your father."

"Don't tell her we're here," said Lady Isabel.

"Come along, Frank," said Priscilla. "I'll help you out of that boat and into the *Tortoise*. We must be getting home. Goodbye, Miss Rutherford."

"It really is goodbye this time," said Miss Rutherford. "I'm off tomorrow morning."

"Back to London?" said Frank. "Hard luck."

"To that frowsy old Museum," said Priscilla, "full of skeletons of whales and stuffed antelopes and things."

"I feel it all acutely," said Miss Rutherford. "Don't make it worse for me by enumerating my miseries."

"And I don't believe you've caught a single sponge," said Priscilla. "Will they be frightfully angry with you?"

"I've got a few," said Miss Rutherford, "fresh water ones that I caught before I met you. I'll make the most of them."

"Anyhow," said Priscilla, "it'll be a great comfort to you to feel that you've taken part in a noble deed of mercy before you left."

"That's something, of course," said Miss Rutherford, "but you can't think how annoying it is to have to go away just at this crisis of the adventure. I shall be longing day and night to hear how it ends."

"I'll write and tell you, if you like," said Priscilla.

"Do," said Miss Rutherford. "Just let me know whether the sanctuary remains inviolable and I shall be satisfied."

"Right," said Priscilla. "Goodbye. We needn't actually kiss each other, need we? Of course, if you want to frightfully you can; but I think kissing's rather piffle."

Miss Rutherford contented herself with wringing Priscilla's hand. Then she and Priscilla helped Frank out of Jimmy Kinsella's boat and into the *Tortoise*.

The wind was due east and was blowing a good deal harder than it was when they ran down to Inish-bawn. The *Tortoise* had a long beat before her, the kind of beat which means that a small boat will take in a good deal of water. Priscilla passed an oilskin coat to Frank. Having been wet through by the thunderstorm and having got dry, Frank had no wish to get wet again. He struggled into the coat, pushing his arms through sleeves which stuck together and buttoned it round him. The *Tortoise* settled down to her work in earnest She listed over until the foaming dark water rushed along her gunwale. She pounded into the short seas, lifted her bow clear of them, pounded down again, breasted them, took them fair on the curve of her bow, deluged herself, Frank's oilskin and even the greater part of her sails with showers of spray. The breeze freshened and at the end of each tack the boat swung round so fast that Frank, with his maimed ankle, had hard work to scramble over the centreboard case to the weather side. He slipped and slithered on the wet floor boards. There was a wash of water on the lee side which caught and soaked whichever leg he left behind him. He discovered that an oilskin coat is a miserably inefficient protection in a small boat. Not that the seas came through it. That does not happen. But while he made a grab at the flying foresail sheet a green blob of a wave would rush up his sleeve and soak him elbow high. Or, when he had turned his back to the wind and settled down comfortably, an insidious shower of spray found means to get between his coat and his neck, and trickled swiftly down, saturating his innermost garments to his very waist. Also it is necessary sometimes to squat with knees bent chinward, and then there are bulging spaces between the buttons of the coat. Seas, leaping joyfully clear of the weather bow, came plump into his lap. It became a subject of interesting speculation whether there was a square inch of his body left dry anywhere.

Priscilla, who had no oilskin, got wet quicker but was no wetter in the end. Her cotton frock clung to her. Water oozed out of the tops of her shoes as she pressed her feet against the lee side of the boat to maintain her position on the slippery floor boards. She had crammed her hat under the stern thwart. Her hair, glistening with salt water, blew in tangles round her head. Her face glowed with excitement. She was enjoying herself to the utmost.

Tack after tack brought them further up the bay. The wind was still freshening, but the sea, as they got nearer the eastern shore, became calmer. The *Tortoise* raced through it. Sharp squalls struck her occasionally. She dipped her lee gunwale and took a lump of solid water on board. Priscilla luffed her and let the main sheet run through her fingers. The *Tortoise* bounced up on even keel and shook her sails in an ill-tempered way. Priscilla, with a pull at the tiller, set her on her course again. A few minutes later the sea whitened and frothed to windward and the same process was gone through again. The stone perch was passed. The tacks became shorter, and the squalls, as the wind descended from the hills, were more frequent.

But the sail ended triumphantly. Never before had Priscilla rounded up the *Tortoise* to her mooring buoy with such absolute precision. Never before had she so large an audience to witness her skill. Peter Walsh was waiting for her at the buoy in Brannigan's punt. Patsy the smith, quite sober but still yellow in the face, was standing on the slip. On the edge of the quay, having torn themselves from their favourite seat, were all the loafers who usually occupied Brannigan's window sills. Timothy Sweeny had come down from his shop and stood in the background, a paunchy, flabby figure of a man, with keen beady eyes.

"The weather's broke, Miss," said Peter Walsh, as he rowed them ashore. "The wind will work round to the southeast and your sailing's done for this turn."

"It may not," said Priscilla, stepping from the punt to the slip, "you can't be sure about the wind."

"But it will, Miss," said one of the loafers, leaning over to speak to her.

Another and then another of them took up the words. With absolute unanimity they assured her that sailing next day would be totally impossible.

"Unless you're wanting to drown yourselves," said Patsy the smith sullenly.

"The glass has gone down," said Timothy Sweeny, coming forward.

"Help the gentleman ashore," said Priscilla, "and don't croak about the weather."

"The master was saying today," said Peter Walsh, "that he'd take the *Tortoise* out tomorrow, and the gentleman that's up at the house along with him. I'd be glad now, Miss, if you'd tell him it'll be no use him wasting his time coming down to the quay on account of the weather being broke and the wind going round to the southeast."

"And the glass going down," said Sweeny.

"It'll be better for him to amuse himself some other way tomorrow," said Patsy the smith.

"I'll tell him," said Priscilla.

"And if the young gentleman that's with you," said Peter Walsh, "would say the same I'd be glad. We wouldn't like anything would happen to the master, for he's well liked."

"It would be a disgrace to the whole of us," said Patsy the smith, "if the strange gentleman was to be drownded."

"They'd have it on the papers if anything happened him," said Sweeny, "and the place would be getting a bad name, which is what I wouldn't like on account of being a magistrate."

Priscilla began to wheel the bath-chair away from the quay. Having gone a few steps she turned and winked impressively at Peter Walsh. Then she went on. The party on the quay watched her out of sight.

"Now what," said Sweeny, "might she mean by that kind of behaviour?"

"It's as much as to say," said Peter Walsh, "that she knows damn well where it is the master and the other gentleman will be wanting to go."

"She's mighty cute," said Sweeny.

"And what's more," said Peter Walsh, "she'll stop him if she's able. For she doesn't want them out on Inishbawn, no more than we do."

"Are you sure now that she meant that?" said Sweeny.

"I'm as sure as if she said it, and surer."

"She's a fine girl, so she is," said Patsy the smith.

"Devil the finer you'd see," said one of the loafers, "if you was to search from this to America."

This, though a spacious, was a thin compliment.

There are never, even at the height of the transatlantic tourist season, very many girls between Rosnacree and America.

"Anyway," said Sweeny hopefully, "it could be that the wind will go round to the southeast before morning. The glass didn't rise any since the thunder."

"It might," said Peter Walsh.

A southeast wind is dreaded, with good reason, in Rosnacree Bay. It descends from the mountains in vicious squalls. It catches rushing tides at baffling angles and lashes them into white-lipped fury. Sturdy island boats of the larger size, boats with bluff bows and bulging sides, brave it under their smallest lugs. But lesser boats, and especially light pleasure crafts like the *Tortoise* do well to lie snug at their moorings till the southeasterly wind has spent its strength.

CHAPTER XX

Timothy Sweeny, J. P., as suited a man of portly figure and civic dignity, was accustomed to lie long in his bed of a morning. On weekdays he rose, in a bad temper, at nine o'clock. On Sundays, when he washed and shaved, he was half an hour later and his temper was worse. An apprentice took down the shutters of the shop on weekdays at half past nine. By that time Sweeny, having breakfasted, sworn at his wife and abused his children, was ready to enter upon the duties of his calling.

On the morning after the thunderstorm he was wakened at the outrageous hour of half past seven by the rattle of a shower of pebbles against his window. The room he slept in looked out on the back-yard through which his Sunday customers were accustomed to make their way to the bar. Sweeny turned over in his bed and cursed. The window panes rattled again under another shower of gravel. Sweeny shook his wife into consciousness. He bade her get up and see who was in the back-yard. Mrs. Sweeny, a lean harassed woman with grey hair, fastened a dingy pink nightdress round her throat with a pin and obeyed her master.

"It's Peter Walsh," she said, after peering out of the window.

"Tell him to go to hell out of that," said Sweeny.

Mrs. Sweeny wrapped a shawl round her shoulders, opened the bottom of the window and translated her husband's message.

"Himself's asleep in his bed," she said, "but if you'll step into the shop at ten o'clock he'll be glad to see you."

"I'll be obliged to you, ma'am," said Peter Walsh, "if you'll wake him, for what I'm wanting to say to him is particular and he'll be sorry after if there's any delay about hearing it."

"Will you shut that window and have done talking," said Sweeny from the bed. "There's a draught coming in this minute that would lift the feathers from a goose."

Mrs. Sweeny, though an oppressed woman, was not wanting in spirit. She gave Peter Walsh's message in a way calculated to rouse and irritate her husband.

"He says that if you don't get up out of that mighty quick there'll be them here that will make you."

"Hell to your soul!" said Sweeny, "what way's that of talking? Ask him now is the wind in the southeast or is it not?"

"I can tell you that myself," said Mrs. Sweeny. "It is not; for if it was it would be in on this window and my hair would be blew off my head."

"Ask him," said Sweeny, "what boats is in the harbor, and then shut down the window."

Mrs. Sweeny put her head and shoulders out of the window.

"Himself wants to know," she said, "what boats is at the quay. You needn't be looking at me like that, Peter Walsh. He's sober enough. Hard for him to be anything else for he's been in his bed the whole of the night."

"Will you tell him, ma'am," said Peter Walsh, "that there's no boats in it only the *Tortoise*, and that one itself won't be there for long for the wind's easterly and it's a fair run out to Inishbawn."

Mrs. Sweeny repeated this message. Sweeny, roused to activity at last, flung off the bedclothes.

"Get out of the room with you," he said to his wife, "and shut the door. It's down to the kitchen you'll go and let me hear you doing it."

Mrs. Sweeny was too wise to disobey or argue. She snatched a petticoat from a chair near the door and left the room hurriedly. Sweeny went to the window.

"What the hell work's this, Peter Walsh?" he said. "Can't you let me sleep quiet in my bed without raising the devil's own delight in my back-yard. If I did right I'd set the police at you."

"I'll not be the only one the police will be at," said Peter, "if that's the way of it. So there you have it plain and straight."

"What do you mean?"

"What I mean is this. The young lady is off in her own boat. She and the young fellow with the sore leg along with her, and she says the master and the strange gentleman will be down for the *Tortoise* as soon, as ever they have their breakfast ate. That's what I mean and I hope it's to your liking."

"Can you not go out and knock a hole in the bottom of the damned boat?" said Sweeny, "or run the blade of a knife through the halyards, or smash the rudder iron with the wipe of a stone? What good are you if you can't do the like of that? Sure there's fifty ways of stopping a man from going out in a boat when there's only one boat for him to go in?"

"There may be fifty ways and there may be more; but I'd be glad if you'd tell me which of them is any use when there's a young police constable sitting on the side of the quay that hasn't lifted his eye off the boat since five o'clock this morning?"

"Is there that?"

"There is. The sergeant was up at the big house late last night. I saw him go myself. What they said to him I don't know, but he had the constable out sitting opposite the boat since five this morning the way nobody'd go near her."

"Peter Walsh," said Sweeny, and this time he spoke in a subdued and serious tone, "let you go in through the kitchen and ask herself to give you the bottle of whisky that's standing on the shelf under the bar. When you have it, come up here for I want to speak to you."

"Peter Walsh did as he was told. When he reached the bedroom he found Sweeny sitting on a chair with a deep frown on his face. He was thinking profoundly. Without speaking he held out his hand. Peter gave him the whisky. He swallowed two large gulps, drinking from the bottle. Then he set it down on the floor beside him. Peter waited. Sweeny's eyes, narrowed to mere slits, were fixed on a portrait of a plump ecclesiastic which hung in a handsome gold frame over the chimney piece. His hands strayed towards the whisky bottle again. He took another gulp. Then, looking round at his visitor, he spoke.

"Listen to me now, Peter Walsh. Is there any wind?"

"There is surely, a nice breeze from the east and there's a look about it that I wouldn't be surprised if it went to the southeast before full tide."

"Is there what would upset a boat?"

"There's no wind to upset any boat that's handled right. And you know well, Mr. Sweeny, that the master can steer a boat as well as any man about the bay."

"Is there wind so that a boat might be upset if so be there happened to be some kind of mistake and her jibing?"

"There will be that much wind," said Peter Walsh, "at the top of the tide. But what's the use? Don't I tell you, and don't you know yourself that the master isn't one to be making mistakes in a boat?"

"How would it be now if you was in her, you and the strange gentleman, and the master on shore, and you steering? Would she upset then, do you think?"

"It could be done, of course, but——"

"Nigh hand to one of the islands," said Sweeny, "in about four foot of water or maybe less. I'd be sorry if anything would happen the gentleman."

"I'd be sorry anything would happen myself. But it's easy talking. How am I to go in the boat when the master has sent down word that he's going himself?"

Sweeny took another gulp of whisky and again thought deeply. At the end of five minutes he handed the bottle to Peter Walsh.

"Take a sup yourself," he said.

Peter Walsh took a "sup," a very large "sup," with a sigh of appreciation. It had been very trying for him to watch Sweeny drinking whisky while he remained dry-lipped.

"Let you go down to the kitchen," said Sweeny, "and borrow the loan of my shot gun. There's cartridges in the drawer of the table beyond in the room. You can take two of them."

"If it's to shoot the master," said Peter Walsh, "I'll not do it. I've a respect for him ever since——"

"Talk sense. Do you think I want to have you hanged?"

"Hanged or drowned. The way you're talking it'll be both before I'm through with this work."

"When you have the gun," said Sweeny, "and the cartridges in it, you'll go round to the back yard where you were this minute and you'll fire two shots through this window, and mind what you're at, Peter Walsh, for I won't have every pane of glass in the back of the house broke, and I won't have the missus' hens killed. Do you think now you can hit this window from where you were standing in the yard?"

"Hit it! Barring the shot scatters terrible I'll put every grain of it into some part of you if you stay where you are this minute."

"I'll not be in this chair at the time," said Sweeny. "I'll be in the bed, and what shots come into the room will go over me with the way you'll be shooting. But any way I'll have the mattress and the blankets rolled up between me and harm. It'll be all the better if there's a few grains in the mattress."

"I don't know," said Peter Walsh, "that I'll be much nearer drowning the strange gentleman after I've shot you. But sure I'll do it if you like."

"When you have that done," said Sweeny, "and you'd better be quick about it—you'll go down to the barrack and tell Sergeant Rafferty that he's to come round here as quick as he can. The missus'll meet him at the door of the shop and she'll tell him what's happened."

"I suppose then you'll offer bail for me," said Peter Walsh, "for if you don't, no other one will, and it'll be hard for me to go out upsetting boats if they have me in gaol for murdering you."

"It's not that she'll tell him, but a kind of a distracted story. She'll have very little on her at the time. She has no more than an old night dress and a petticoat this minute. I'm sorry now she has the petticoat itself. If I'd known what would have to be I'd have kept it from her. It doesn't be natural for a woman to be dressed up grand when a lot of murdering ruffians from behind the bog has been shooting her husband half the night."

"Bedam," said Peter Walsh, "is that the way it is?"

"It is that way. And I wouldn't wonder but there'll be questions asked about it in Parliament after."

"You'll be wanting the doctor," said Peter Walsh, "to be picking the shot out of you."

"As soon as ever you've got the sergeant," said Sweeny, "you'll go round for the doctor."

"And what'll he say when there's no shot in you?"

"Say! He'll say what I bid him? Ain't I Chairman of the Board of Guardians, and doesn't he owe me ten pounds and more this minute, shop debts. What would he say?"

"He's a gentleman that likes a drop of whisky," said Peter Walsh.

"I'll waste no whisky on him. Where's the use when I can get what I want without?"

Peter Walsh meditated on the situation for a minute or two. Then the full splendour of the plan began to dawn on him.

"The master," he said, "will be taking down the depositions that you'll be making in the presence of the sergeant."

"He will," said Sweeny, "for there's no other magistrate in the place only myself and him, and its against the law for a magistrate to take down his own depositions and him maybe dying at the time."

"There'll be only myself then to take the strange gentleman to Inishbawn in the boat."

"And who's better fit to do it? Haven't you known the bay since you were a small slip of a boy?"

"I have surely."

"Is there a rock or a tide in it that isn't familiar to you?"

"There is not."

"And is there a man in Rosnacree that's your equal in the handling of a small boat?"

"Sorra the one."

"Then be off with you and get the gun the way I told you."

At half-past ten Sir Lucius and Lord Torrington drove into the town and pulled up opposite Brannigan's shop. The *Tortoise* lay at her moorings, a sight which gratified Sir Lucius. After his experience the day before he was afraid that Peter Walsh might have beached the boat in order to execute some absolutely necessary repairs. He congratulated himself on having suggested to Sergeant Rafferty that one of the constables should keep an eye on her.

"There's the boat, Torrington," he said. "She's small, and there's a fresh breeze. But if you don't mind getting a bit wet she'll take us round the islands in the course of the day. If your daughter is anywhere about we'll see her."

Lord Torrington eyed the *Tortoise*. He would have preferred a larger boat, but he was a man of determination and courage.

"I don't care how wet I get," he said, "so long as I have the chance of speaking my mind to the scoundrel who has abducted my daughter."

"We'll take oilskins with us," said Sir Lucius, getting out of the trap as he spoke.

The police sergeant approached him.

"Well, Rafferty," said Sir Lucius, "what's the matter with you?"

"Have you any fresh news of my daughter?" said Lord Torrington.

"I have not, my Lord. Barring what Professor Wilder told me I know no more. There was a lady belonging to his party out on the bay looking out for sponges and she came across———"

"You told us all that yesterday," said Sir Lucius. "What's the matter with you now?"

"What they say," said the sergeant cautiously, "is that it's murder."

"Murder! Good heavens! Who's dead?"

"Timothy Sweeny," said the sergeant

"It might be worse," said Sir Lucius. "If the people of this district have had the sense to kill Sweeny I'll have a higher opinion of them in the future than I used to have. Who did it?"

"It's not known yet who did it," said the sergeant, "but there was two shots fired into the house last night. There's eleven panes of glass broken and the wall at the far side of the room is peppered with shot, and I picked ten grains of it out of the mattress myself and four out of the pillow, without counting what might be in Timothy Sweeny, which the doctor is attending to. Number 5 shot it was and Sweeny is moaning terrible. You'd hear him now if you was to step up a bit in the direction of the house."

It would, of course, have been highly gratifying to Sir Lucius to hear Timothy Sweeny groan, but, remembering that Lord Torrington was anxious about his daughter, he denied himself the pleasure.

"If he's groaning as loud as you say," he said, "he can't be quite dead. I don't believe half a charge of No. 5 shot would kill a man like Sweeny anyway."

"If he's not dead," said the sergeant, "he's mighty near it, according to what the doctor is just after telling me. It's likely enough that shot would prey on a man that's as stout as Sweeny more than it might on a spare man like you honour or me. The way the shot must have been fired to get Sweeny after the fashion they did is from the top of the wall in the back yard opposite the bedroom window. By the grace of God there's footmarks on the far side of it and a stone loosened like as if some one had climbed up it."

"Well," said Sir Lucius, "I'm sorry for Sweeny, but I don't see that I can do anything to help you now. If you make out a case against any one come up to me in the evening and I'll sign a warrant for his arrest."

"I was thinking," said the sergeant, "that if it was pleasing to your honour, you might take Sweeny's depositions before you go out in the boat; just for fear he might take it into his head to die on us before evening; which would be a pity."

"Is he able to make a deposition?" said Sir Lucius.

"He's willing to try," said the sergeant, "but it's badly able to talk he is this minute."

Sir Lucius turned to Lord Torrington.

"This is a confounded nuisance, Torrington," he said. "I'm afraid I'll have to ask you to wait till I've taken down whatever lies this fellow Sweeny chooses to swear to. I won't be long."

But Lord Torrington had a proper respect for the forms of law.

"You can't hurry over a job of that sort," he said.

"If the man's been shot at—— Can't I go by myself? I know something about boats. You'll be here for hours."

"You may know boats," said Sir Lucius, "but you don't know this bay."

"Couldn't I work it with a chart? You have a chart, I suppose?"

"No man living could work it with a chart. The rocks in the bay are as thick as currants in a pudding and half of them aren't charted. Besides the tides are——"

"Isn't there some man about the place I could take with me?" said Lord Torrington.

Peter Walsh was hovering in the background with his eyes fixed anxiously on Sir Lucius and the police sergeant. Sir Lucius looking around caught sight of him.

"I'll tell you what I'll do if you like," said Sir Lucius. "I'll send Peter Walsh with you. He's an unmitigated blackguard, but he knows the bay like the palm of his hand and he can sail the boat. Come here, Peter."

Peter Walsh stepped forward, touching his hat and smiling respectfully.

"Peter," said Sir Lucius, "Lord Torrington wants to take a sail round the islands in the bay. I can't go with him myself, so you must. Have you taken any drink this morning?"

"I have not," said Peter. "Is it likely I would with Sweeny's shop shut on account of the accident that's after happening to him?"

"Don't you give him a drop, Torrington, while you're on the sea with him. You can fill him up with whisky when you get home if you like."

"I wouldn't be for going very far today," said Peter Walsh. "It looks to me as if it might come on to blow from the southeast."

"You'll go out to Inishbawn first of all," said Sir Lucius. "After that you can work home in and out, visiting every island that's big enough to have people on it. The weather won't hurt you."

"Sure if his lordship's contented," said Peter, "it isn't for me to be making objections."

"Very well," said Sir Lucius. "Get the sails on the boat. You can tie down a reef if you like."

"There's no need," said Peter. "She'll go better under the whole sail."

"Now, sergeant," said Sir Lucius, "I'll just see them start, and then I'll go back and listen to whatever story Sweeny wants to tell."

Peter Walsh huddled himself into an ancient oilskin coat, ferried out to the *Tortoise* and hoisted the sails. He laid her long side the slip with a neatness and precision which proved his ability to sail a small boat. Lord Torrington stepped carefully on board and settled himself crouched into a position undignified for a member of the Cabinet, on the side of the centreboard case recommended by Peter Walsh.

"Got your sandwiches all right?" said Sir Lucius, "and the flask? Good. Then off you go. Now, Peter, Inishbawn first and after that wherever you're told to go. If you get wet, Torrington, don't blame me. Now, sergeant, I'm ready."

The *Tortoise*, a stiff breeze filling her sails, darted out to mid-channel. Peter Walsh paid out his main sheet and set her running dead before the wind.

"It'll come round to the southeast," he said, "before we're half an hour out."

Sir Lucius waved his hand. Then he turned and followed the sergeant into Sweeny's house.

CHAPTER XXI

The *Blue Wanderer*, with her little lug, sailed slowly even when there was a fresh wind right behind her. It was half-past ten when Priscilla and Frank ran her aground on Inishbawn. Joseph Antony Kinsella had seen them coming and was standing on the shore ready to greet them.

"You're too venturesome, Miss, to be coming out all this way in that little boat," he said.

"We came safe enough," said Priscilla, "didn't ship a drop the whole way out."

"You came safe," said Kinsella, "but will you tell me how you're going to get home again? The wind's freshening and what's more it's drawing round to the southeast."

"Let it. If we can't get home, we can't, that's all. I suppose Mrs. Kinsella will bake us a loaf of bread for breakfast tomorrow. Cousin Frank, you'll have to make Barnabas take you into his tent. He can't very well refuse on account of being a clergyman and so more or less pledged to deeds of charity. I'll curl up in a corner of Lady Isabel's pavilion. By the way, Joseph Antony, how are the young people getting on?"

"I had my own trouble with them after you left," said Kinsella.

"I'm sorry to hear that and I wouldn't have thought it. Barnabas seemed to me a nice peaceable kind of curate. Why didn't you hit him on the head with an oar? That would have quieted him."

"I might, of course; and I would; but it was the lady that was giving me the trouble more than him. Nothing would do her right or wrong but she'd have her tent set up on the south end of the island; and that's what wouldn't suit me at all."

Priscilla glanced at the smaller of the two hills which make up the island of Inishbawn. It stood remote from the Kinsellas' homestead and the patches of cultivated land, separated from them by a rough causeway of grey boulders. From a hollow in it a thin column of smoke arose, and was blown in torn wreaths along the slope.

"It would not suit you a bit," said Priscilla.

"What made her want to go there?" said Frank.

The bare southern hill of Inishbawn seemed to him a singularly unattractive camping ground. It was a windswept, desolate spot.

"She took a notion into her head," said Kinsella, "that his Reverence might catch the fever if he stopped on this end of the island."

"Good gracious!" said Frank, "how can any one catch fever here?"

"On account of Mrs. Kinsella and the children having come out all over large yellow spots," said Priscilla. "I hope that will be a lesson to you, Joseph Antony."

"What I said was for the best," said Kinsella.

"How was I to know she'd be here at the latter end?"

"You couldn't know, of course. Nobody ever can; which is one of the reasons why it's just as well to tell the truth at the start whenever possible. If you make things up you generally forget afterwards what they are, and then there's trouble. Besides the things you make up very often turn against you in ways you'd never expect. It was just the same with a mouse-trap that Sylvia Courtney once bought, when she thought there was a mouse in our room, though there wasn't really and it wouldn't have done her any harm if there had been. No matter how careful she was about tying the string down it used to bound up again and nip her fingers. But Sylvia Courtney never was any good at things like mouse-traps. What she likes is English Literature."

"How did you stop her going to the far end of the island?" said Frank, "if she thought there was an infectious fever for Mr. Pennefather to catch——"

"I dare say you mentioned the wild heifer," said Priscilla.

"I did not then. What I said was rats."

"Rather mean of you that," said Priscilla. "The rats were Peter Walsh's originally. You shouldn't have taken them. That's what's called—What is it called, Cousin Frank? Something to do with plagues, I know. Is there such a word as plague-ism? Anyhow it's what poets do when they lift other poets' rhymes and it's considered mean."

"It was me told Peter Walsh about the rats," said Kinsella, repelling an unjust accusation. "The way they came swimming in on the tide would surprise you, and the gulls picking the eyes out of the biggest of them as they came swimming along. But that wouldn't stop them."

"I'll just run up and have a word with Barnabas," said Priscilla. "It'll be as well for him to know that father and Lord Torrington are out after him today in the *Tortoise.*"

"Do you tell me that?" said Kinsella.

"It'll be all right," said Priscilla. "They'll never get here. But of course Barnabas may want to make his will in case of accidents. Just you help the young gentleman ashore, Kinsella. He can't get along very well by himself on account of the way Lord Torrington treated him. Then you'd better haul the boat up a bit. It's rather beginning to blow and I see the wind really has got round to the southeast. I hardly thought it would, but it has. Winds so seldom do what everybody says they're going to. I'm sure you've noticed that."

She walked up the rough stony beach. A fierce gust, spray-laden and eloquent with promise of rain, swept past her.

"If I'd known," said Kinsella sulkily, "that half the country would be out after them ones, I'd have drownded them in the sea and their tents along with them before I let them set foot on Inishbawn."

"Lord Torrington won't do you any harm," said Frank. "He's only trying to get back his daughter."

"I don't know," said Kinsella, still in a very bad temper, "what anybody'd want with the likes of that girl. You'd think a man would be glad to get rid of her and thankful to anybody that was fool enough to take her off his hands. She's no sense. Miss Priscilla has little enough, but she's young and it'll maybe come to her later. But that other one—The Lord saves us."

He helped Frank on shore as he talked. Then he called Jimmy from the cottage. Between them they hauled the *Blue Wanderer* above high-tide mark.

"There she'll stay," said Kinsella vindictively, "for the next twenty-four hours anyway. Do you feel that now?"

Frank felt a sudden gust of wind and a heavy splash of rain. The sky looked singularly dark and heavy over the southeastern shore of the bay. Ragged scuds of clouds, low flying, were tearing across overhead. The sea was almost black and very angry; short waves were getting up, curling rapidly over and breaking in yellow foam. With the aid of Jimmy Kinsella's arm Frank climbed the beach, passed the Kinsella's cottage and made his way to the place where the two tents were pitched. Priscilla was sitting on a camp stool at the entrance of Lady Isabel's tent. The Reverend Barnabas Pennefather, looking cold and miserable, was crouching at her feet in a waterproof coat. Lady Isabel was going round the tents with a hammer in her hand driving the pegs deeper into the ground.

"I'm just explaining to Barnabas," said Priscilla, "that he's pretty safe here so far as Lord Torrington is concerned. He doesn't seem as pleased as I should have expected."

"It's blowing very hard," said Mr. Pennefather, "and it's beginning to rain. I'm sure our tents will come down and we shall get very wet Won't you sit down, Mr.—Mr———?"

"Mannix," said Priscilla. "I thought you were introduced yesterday. Hullo! What's that?"

She was gazing across the sea when she spoke. She rose from her camp stool and pointed eastwards with her finger. A small triangular patch of white was visible far off between Inishrua and Knockilaun. Frank and Mr. Pennefather stared at it eagerly.

"It looks to me," said Priscilla, "very like the *Tortoise*. There isn't another boat in the bay with a sail that peaks up like that. If I'm right, Barnabas— But I can't believe that Peter Walsh and Patsy the smith and all the rest of them would have been such fools as to let them start."

A rain squall blotted the sail from view.

"Perhaps they couldn't help it," said Frank. "Perhaps Uncle Lucius———"

"Lady Isabel," shouted Priscilla, "come here at once. She won't come," she said to Frank, "if she can possibly help it, because she's furiously angry with me for asking her why on earth she married Barnabas. Rather a natural question, I thought. Barnabas, go and get her."

Mr. Pennefather, who seemed cowed into a state of profound submissiveness, huddled his waterproof round him and went to Lady Isabel. She was hammering an extra peg through the loop of one of the guy lines of the further tent.

"Why do you suppose she did it?" said Priscilla. "I couldn't find that out. It's very hard to imagine why anybody marries anybody else. I often sit and wonder for hours. But it's totally impossible in this case———"

"Perhaps he preaches very well," said Frank. "That might have attracted her."

"Couldn't possibly," said Priscilla. "No girl—at the same time, of course, she has, which shows there must have been some reason. I say, Cousin Frank, she must be absolutely mad with me. She's dragged Barnabas into the other tent. Rather a poor lookout for me, considering that I shall have to sleep with her. There's the *Tortoise* again. It is the *Tortoise*. There's no mistake about it this time."

The rain squall had blown over. The *Tortoise*, now plainly visible, was tearing across the foam-flecked stretch of water between Inishrua and Knockilaun. Priscilla ran to the other tent.

"Lady Isabel," she said, "if you want to see your father drowned you'd better come out."

Lady Isabel scrambled to the door of her tent and stood, her hair and clothes blown violently, gazing wildly round her. Mr. Pennefather, looking abjectly miserable, crawled after her and remained on his hands and knees at her side.

"Where's father?" she said.

"In that boat," said Priscilla, "but he won't be drowned. I only said he would so as to get you out of your tent."

The *Tortoise* stooped forwards and swept along, the water foaming at her bow and leaping angrily at her weather quarter. A fiercer squall than usual rushed at her from the western corner of Inishrua as she cleared the island. She swerved to windward, her boom stretched far out to the starboard side dipped suddenly and dragged through the water. She paid off again before the wind in obedience to a strong pull on the tiller. Priscilla grew excited in watching the progress of the boat.

"Barnabas," she said, "give me your glasses, quick. I know you have a pair, for I saw you watching us through them that day on Inishark."

Mr. Pennefather had the glasses slung across his shoulder in the leather case. He handed them to Priscilla. The squall increased in violence. The whole sea grew white with foam. A sudden drift of fine spray, blown off the face of the water, swept over Inishbawn, stinging and soaking the watchers at the tents.

"Lord Torrington is on board all right," said Priscilla, "but it's not father who's steering. It's Peter Walsh."

The *Tortoise* flew forward, dipping her bow so that once or twice the water lipped over it. She looked pitiful, like a frightened creature from whose swift flight all joy had departed. She reached the narrow passage between Ardilaun and Inishlean. Before her lay the broad water of Inishbawn Roads, lashed into white fury. But the worst of the squall was over. The showers of spray ceased for a moment. It was still blowing strongly, but the fierceness had gone out of the wind.

"She's all right now," said Priscilla, "and anyway there are two life buoys on board."

Then Peter Walsh did an unexpected thing. He put the tiller down and began to haul in his main-sheet. The boat rounded up into the wind, headed straight northwards for the shore of Inishlean. She listed heavily, lay over till it seemed as if the sail would touch the water. For an instant she paused, half righted, moved sluggishly towards the shore. Then, very slowly as it seemed, she leaned down again till her sail lay flat in the water.

At the moment when she righted, before the final heel over, a man flung himself across the gunwale into the sea. In his hands he grasped one of the life buoys.

"It's father," shouted Lady Isabel. "Oh, save him!"

"If he'd stuck to the boat," said Priscilla, "he'd have been all right. She's ashore this minute on the point of Inishlean. Unless Peter Walsh has gone suddenly mad I can't imagine why he tried to round up the boat there and why he hauled in the main-sheet. He was absolutely bound to go over."

"Perhaps he wanted to land there," said Frank.

"Well," said Priscilla, "he has landed, but he's upset the boat. I never thought before that Peter Walsh could be such an absolute idiot."

The condemnation was entirely unjust. Peter Walsh had, in fact, performed the neatest feat of seamanship of his whole life. Never in the course of forty years and more spent in or about small boats had he handled one with such supreme skill and accuracy. Driven desperately by a squally and uncertain southeast wind, with a welter of short waves knocking his boat's head about in the most incalculable way, he had succeeded in upsetting her about six yards from the shore of an island on to the point of which she was certain to drift, with no more than four feet of water under her at the critical moment. The *Tortoise*, having no ballast in her and depending entirely for stability on her fin-like centreboard was not, as Peter Walsh knew very well, in the smallest danger of sinking. He climbed quietly on her gunwale as she finally lay down and sat there, stride-legs, not even wet below the waist, until she grounded on the curved point of the island. The performance was a triumphant demonstration of Peter Walsh's unmatched skill.

In one matter only did he miscalculate. Lord Torrington knew something about boats, possessed that little knowledge which is in all great arts, theology, medicine and boat-sailing, a dangerous thing. He knew, after the first immersion of the gunwale, when the water flowed in, that the boat was sure to upset. He knew that the greatest risk on such occasions lies in being entangled in some rope and perhaps pinned under the sail. He seized the moment when the *Tortoise* righted after her first plunge, grasped a life buoy and flung himself overboard. He was just too soon. A moment later and he would have drifted ashore as the boat did on the point of Inishlean. If he had let go his life buoy and struck out at once he might have reached it. But the sudden immersion in cold water bewildered him. He clung to the life buoy and was drifted past the point.

Then he regained his self-possession and looked round him. As a young man he had been a fine swimmer and even at the age of fifty-five, with the cares of an imperial War Office weighing heavily on him, he had enough presence of mind to realise his situation. A few desperate strokes convinced him of the impossibility of swimming back to Inishlean against the wind and tide. In front of him lay a quarter of a mile of broken water. Beyond that was Inishbawn. It was a long swim, too long for a fully dressed man with no support. But Lord Torrington had a life buoy, guaranteed by its maker to keep two men safely afloat. He had a strong wind behind him and a tide drifting him down towards the island. The water was not cold. He realised that all that was absolutely necessary was to cling to the life buoy, but that he might, if he liked, slightly accelerate his progress by kicking. He kicked hard.

Joseph Antony Kinsella wanted no more visitors on Inishbawn. Least of all did he want one whom he knew to be a "high-up gentleman" and suspected of being a government official of the most dangerous and venomous kind, but Joseph Antony Kinsella was not the man to see a fellow creature drift across Inishbawn Roads without making an effort to help him ashore. With the aid of Jimmy he launched the stout, broad-beamed boat from which Miss Rutherford had fished for sponges. Priscilla raced down from the tents and sprang on board just as Jimmy, knee deep in foaming water, was pushing off. She shipped the rudder. Joseph Antony and Jimmy pulled hard. They forced their way to windward through clouds of spray and before Lord Torrington was half way across the bay Joseph Antony hauled him dripping into the boat.

Peter Walsh, standing in the water beside the stranded *Tortoise*, saw with blank amazement that Kinsella turned the boat's head and rowed back again to Inishbawn.

"Bedamn," he said, "but if I'd known that was to be the way it was to be I might as well have put him ashore there myself and not have wetted him."

On the beach at Inishbawn when the boat grounded, were Lady Isabel, Mrs. Kinsella with her baby, the three small Kinsella boys, Frank Mannix, who, to the further injury of his ankle, had hobbled down the hill, and in the far background, the Reverend Barnabas Pennefather.

Lady Isabel rushed upon her father, flung her arms round his neck and kissed him passionately with tears in her eyes. Lord Torrington did not seem particularly pleased to see her.

"Hang it all, Isabel," he said, "I'm surely wet enough. Don't make me worse by slobbering over me. There's nothing to cry about and no necessity for kissing."

"Mrs. Kinsella," said Priscilla, "go you straight up to the house and get out your husband's Sunday clothes. If he hasn't any Sunday clothes, get blankets and throw a couple of sods of turf on the fire."

"Glory be to God!" said Mrs. Kinsella.

Priscilla took Joseph Antony by the arm and led him a little apart from the group on the beach.

"Get some whisky," she said, "as quick as you can."

"Whisky!" said Kinsella blankly.

"Yes, whisky. Bring it in a tin can or anything else that comes handy."

"Is it a tin can full of whisky? Sure, where could I get the like? Or for the matter of that where would I get a thimble full? Is it likely now that there'd be a tin can full of whisky on Inishbawn?"

Priscilla stamped her foot.

"You've got quarts," she said, "and gallons."

"Arrah, talk sense," said Kinsella.

"Very well," said Priscilla. "I don't want to give you away, but rather than see Lord Torrington sink into his grave with rheumatic fever for want of a drop of whisky I'll expose you publicly. Cousin Frank, come here."

"Whist, Miss, whist! Sure if I had the whisky I'd give it to you."

Lord Torrington, with Lady Isabel weeping beside him, was on his way up to the Kinsellas' cottage. Frank was speaking earnestly to Mr. Pennefather, who seemed disinclined to follow his father-in-law. When he heard Priscilla calling to him he hobbled towards her.

"Cousin Frank," she said, "here's a man who grudges poor Lord Torrington a drop of whisky to save his life, although for weeks past he has been—what is it you do when you make whisky? I forget the word. It isn't brew."

Frank, vaguely recollecting the advertisements which appear in our papers, suggested that the word was required "pot".

Priscilla pointed an accusing finger at Kinsella.

"Here's a man," she said, "who for the last fortnight has been potting whisky—what a fool you are, Cousin Frank! Distil is the word. Joseph Antony Kinsella has been distilling whisky on this island for the last month as hard as ever he could. He's been shipping barrels full of it underneath loads of gravel into Rosnacree, and now he's trying to pretend he hasn't got any. Did you ever hear such utter rot in your life? I'm not telling Lord Torrington yet, Joseph Antony; but in a minute or two I will unless you go and get a good can full."

"For the love of God, Miss," said Kinsella, "say no more. I'll try if I can find a sup somewhere for the gentleman. But as for what you're after saying about distilling——"

"Hurry up," said Priscilla threateningly.

Kinsella went off at a sharp trot towards the south end of the island.

"Of course," said Priscilla in a calmer tone, "he really may not have any more. That might have been the last barrel which I saw under the gravel the day before yesterday when our anchor rope got foul of the centreboard. I don't expect it was quite the last, but it may have been. It's very hard to be sure about things like that. However, if it was the last he'll just have to turn to and distil some more. I don't suppose it takes very long, and there was a fire burning on the south end of the island this morning. I saw it."

Half an hour later Lord Torrington, wrapped in two blankets and a patchwork quilt, clothing which he had chosen in preference to Joseph Antony's Sunday suit, was sitting in front of a blazing fire in the Kinsellas' kitchen. He held in his hand a mug full of raw spirit and hot water, mixed in equal proportions. Each time he sipped at it he coughed. Priscilla sat beside him with a bottle from which she offered to replenish the mug after each sip. Lady Isabel, looking frightened but obstinate, stood opposite him, holding the Reverend Barnabas Pennefather by the hand.

CHAPTER XXII

"To Miss Martha Rutherford, Sponge Department, British Museum, London.

"My dear Miss Rutherford—Having promised to write you the dénouement, I do, of course; though the delay is longer than I expected when promising. It was most exciting. Peter Walsh upset the *Tortoise*—on purpose I now think—but no one else has said so *yet*—and Lord Torrington swam for his life while his lovely daughter wrung her lily hands in shrill despair, this being the exact opposite of what was the case with Lord Ullin's daughter. Joseph Antony Kinsella and Jimmy and I rescued the drowning mariner in your boat. Frank would have done so too, for he says he never rescued any one from a watery grave—though he won a prize for life-saving in his swimming bath at school and I think he wanted to get a medal—but none of us have as yet, nor won't—but he couldn't get down the hill quick enough on account of his sprained ankle, so we were off without him. I jolly well ballyragged Joseph Antony Kinsella until he opened his last cask of illicit whisky. 'Illicit' is what both father and Lord Torrington called it and at first I didn't know what that meant, but I looked it out in the dict. and now do know, also how to spell it, which I shouldn't otherwise. Then we had a most frightful scene in Joseph Antony Kinsella's cottage. Lady Isabel was splendid. I never knew any one could be in love so much, especially with Barnabas. The salt sea was frozen on her cheeks (it had been raining hard), and the salt tears in her eyes. Sylvia Courtney told me that that poem was most affecting, so I read it. Have you? Lord Torrington was frightfully stony-hearted at first and finished two mugs of illicit whisky (with hot water), coughing and swearing the whole time. Barnabas crawled. Then Mrs. Kinsella made tea and hot pancakes in spite of the baby, which screamed; and all was gay, though there was no butter. Peter Walsh came in while we were at tea, having righted the *Tortoise* and bailed her out, but he and Joseph Antony Kinsella went off together, which was just as well, for there weren't too many pancakes, and Lord Torrington, when he began to soften down a bit, turned out to be hungry. In the end we all went home together in Joseph Antony Kinsella's big boat, Lord Torrington having put on his clothes again and father's oilskins, which were providentially saved from the wreck. Lady Isabel and Barnabas held each other's hands the whole time in a way that I thought rather disgusting, though Cousin Frank says it is common enough among those in that state. I hope I never shall be; but of course I may. One can't be really sure beforehand. Anyhow I shan't like it if I am. Lady Isabel did, which made it worse. Father met us at the quay and said he didn't believe there was a single grain of shot in the whole of Timothy Sweeny's fat body and that the entire thing was a plant. I didn't understand this at the time, though now I do; but it's too long to write; though it would interest you if written.

"For days and days Lady Torrington was more obdurate than the winter wind and the serpent's tooth. She said those two things often and often, and the one about the winter wind shows that she has read 'As You Like It.' I don't know the one about the serpent's tooth. It may be in Shakespeare, but is *not* in Wordsworth's 'Excursion.' I think she meant Lady Isabel, not herself. Barnabas slept in the Geraghtys' gate lodge, a bed being made up for him and food sent down, though he was let in to lunch with us after a time. There were terrific consultations which I did not hear, being of course regarded as a child. Nor did Cousin Frank, which was rather insulting to him, considering that he can behave quite like a grown up when he tries. But all came right in the end. We think that Lord Torrington has promised to make Barnabas a bishop in the army, which Cousin Frank says he can do quite easily if he likes, being the head of the War Office. Father kept harping on, especially at luncheon, when Barnabas was there, to find out why they fled to Rosnacree. Rose, the under housemaid, told me that it came out in the end that Lady Isabel simply went to the man at Euston station and asked for a ticket to the furthest off place he sold tickets to. This, may be true. Rose heard it from Mrs. Geraghty, who came up every day to hook Lady Torrington's back. But I doubt it myself. There must be further off places than Rosnacree, though, of course, not many. At one time there threatened to be rather a row about our not giving up the fugitives to justice, and Aunt Juliet tried to say nasty things about aiding and abetting (whatever they mean). But I said that wouldn't have happened because we didn't particularly care for Lady Isabel and simply loathed Barnabas, if it hadn't been for the dastardly way Lord Torrington sprained Frank's ankle, so that they had no one to blame but themselves. Lord Torrington, who isn't really a bad sort at times, quite saw this and said he wouldn't have sprained Frank's ankle if he hadn't been upset at the time on account of Lady Isabel's having eluded his vigilance and escaped. This just shows how careful we ought to be about our lightest and most innocent actions. No one would expect any dire results to come of simply spraining a young man's ankle on a steamer; but they did; which is the way many disasters occur and often we don't find out why even afterwards, though in this case Lord Torrington did, thanks to me.

"Joseph Antony Kinsella and Peter Walsh and Timothy Sweeny and Patsy the smith came up one day on a deputation with a donkey load of turf for father and Lord Torrington, which seemed curious, but wasn't, really because there were bottles and bottles of illicit whisky under the turf. Lord

Torrington made a speech to them and said that all would be forgiven and forgotten and that he would leave the whisky in his will to his grandson, who might drink it perhaps; which shows, we think, that he is taking Barnabas to his heart, or else he would hardly be saving up the whisky in the way he said he would. So, as Shakespeare says, 'All's well that ends well.'

"Your affect, friend,

"Priscilla Lentaigne."

"P. S.—I couldn't write while they were here on account of the thunderous condition of the atmosphere and not knowing exactly how things would turn out, which is the cause of your not getting this letter sooner. Since they left, Barnabas and all, Aunt Juliet has dropped being a suffragette in disgust (you can't wonder after the way Lady Isabel turned out to have deceived her) and has taken up appendicitis warmly. She says it's far more important really than uric acid or fresh air, and is thinking of going up to Dublin next week for an operation. Father says it was bound to be either that or spiritualism because they are the only two things left which she hadn't tried. It's rather unlucky, I think, for Aunt Juliet, being so very intellectual. I'm glad I'm not."

THE END